# Cascade Effect

I0565825

## Leah Petersen

Dragon Moon Press

Copyright © 2013 by Leah Petersen
Cover Art Copyright © 2013 by Charles Bernard

ISBN 978-1-897492-64-2

Dragon Moon Press
www.dragonmoonpress.com

Printed and bound in the United States of America

# Cascade Effect

# Dedication

Dedicated always and forever to Shane, Bren, and Aria, who I dragged along on this crazy ride with me, without even asking them first.

# Acknowledgments

One of the best things to come out of the experience of publishing *Fighting Gravity* was the network of talented writers and readers I met and who have helped me along the way.

There are a lot more of you than I have space to acknowledge here. Don't think that means I don't appreciate all you do, from the bottom of my heart. You know who you are and, rest assured, I do too.

Thank you to all the people who read *Fighting Gravity* and rated, reviewed, or even just enjoyed it. Extra thanks to those who then begged and pestered me into getting the sequel finished.

Special thanks goes to the talented J.M. Frey who is tireless in her support, practical help, and friendship.

Thank you also to Jaimie, who bravely faced the horrid experience of being the only beta reader for my first, really rough draft. And to Jessica Olin and R.B. Wood who took up the mantle after that. Also to Gwen at Dragon Moon Press for pulling all this together in a ridiculous timeframe.

And last, because she's not least, thank you to my fabulous editor and friend, Gabrielle. She deserves all the recognition she gets and more.

I didn't have to lie, cheat, or kidnap anyone to get the emperor of half the galaxy into the infamous slum of Abenez.

"You're welcome to come with me if you want," I said to my husband the second or third time he said, in so many words, that I absolutely was not going there.

Pete huffed in frustration. I did feel sorry for him sometimes. He'd ruled the Empire since he was fifteen. He had so little experience with being resisted, let alone defied. It wasn't exactly fair to him, being married to a stubborn ass like me.

"You. Are. Not. Going. That's it, Jake. You're not going at all, nor am I. Separately or together, day or night, nothing. We are not going. You are not going."

"How many times do you think you're going to repeat that, darling?" I said, grinning in his direction. I wasn't really amused, but it was fun to bait him sometimes. I wished that was all I was doing now.

I couldn't meet his eyes. I needed for him not to see how much the Duchy of Mexico still scared me. I'd spent most of my life trying to pretend it didn't exist, even when I was a child in Abenez, its worst slum—the most notorious slum in the Empire. And that was before the scandal of the emperor acknowledging me as his lover.

Pete had given the duchy to me in an attempt to do exactly as I'd asked him—to do better for the unclass. What he didn't understand was that I didn't know any more about how to fix their problems than anyone else did. While others didn't look at Abenez too deeply because they were apathetic or actively disinterested, I was afraid of looking too close, of seeing it. Remembering.

Only Dead End and the three days I spent in prison awaiting my execution were experiences in my life worse than being a child in Abenez. And not by much.

"Jake." He took my shoulders and forced me to look at him. "Don't do this. I'm not trying to dictate your life. It's not some silly game we're playing here. 'What you're talking about is unsafe. I promised myself that I wasn't going to lose you again. Do you really think I'm going to let you walk into one of the most dangerous areas in the Empire?"

"I need to do this," I said, my voice strained. "Please. It's— I just need to."

His expression softened.

"I'm not talking about an official tour or anything, Pete. I'll go in disguise. No one will know it's me. And I'll take a guard." I bit out a bitter laugh. "Two of us would be more than a match for anything Abenez could throw at us. They don't have any weapons, and they're too malnourished to overpower two people who eat from the emperor's table every day."

He grimaced. "Jake..."

He buried his face in my shoulder, pulling me tight against him, and said nothing more.

How exactly he got from "too big a security risk" to putting himself there as well, I didn't ask. I think he decided that if something were going to happen to me, it would happen to him, too. It made me feel guilty, but it was his own choice.

It was strange to see him in the disguise. Our clothes were worn and dirty, and we wore no shoes. All exposed skin was streaked with dirt and grime. Our hair was tangled and mussed so that it looked matted.

We went into Abenez in stages. I'd left the actual rulership of Mexico in the hands of the governor who had run the duchy before my appointment. We stopped only briefly at her mansion in Puerto Vallarta, where we acquired a man named Hector—her head of security—who would be our escort into Abenez. With him we traveled on to Mexico City and the slum that had been my home for the first eight years of my life.

We rode in a fairly innocuous transport to the edge of the middle class section of the city. There, we boarded a smaller, older transport that would not look out of place in the low class areas. We took that transport to an old, but reasonably maintained building.

"This is considered the edge of the unclass district," Hector explained. He was a native of the duchy, so, dirtied up like we were, he looked plausible enough, though he was middle class, himself. "We can't take a transport on the surface streets into the part of town where we're going. It would be conspicuous, and that far in, the streets simply won't accommodate it anyway."

"So what's this, then?" I asked.

"A system of tunnels runs under most of the district. They'll allow us to get in and out of sections of Abenez, even the interior, without being seen."

"That's for police and the army?" Pete said.

"Yes, Your Excellence."

"It could be used to get food and medical supplies into the neighborhoods too, couldn't it?" I asked.

The man didn't meet my eye. "I suppose so, yes, Your Highness."

Ironically, the safest place for us within Abenez was deep in the interior. Abenez itself had long ago spilled out of what had once been considered Mexico City, and it seeped northward up the valley. It now covered almost ten thousand square miles, more total area than most cities on the planet. The conglomeration of structures, rubbish, and people was larger than all of Imperial City and the palace together. It was almost impossible to know exactly how many lived there, but estimates averaged twenty-five million people.

The perimeter, where it bordered low class neighborhoods—though separated in all areas by a security fence—was the most populated, and boasted the best conditions, such as they were. It was in one of the perimeter sections that I had lived. It wasn't something I'd really been aware of at the time, but I'd had confirmation of it since. I'd attended school, if irregularly, and been able to find odd jobs, even passing through the security fence at times to work for people in the outlying lower class towns. We'd had water more often than not, electricity at least half of the time, and there was food to be bought when we had money for it.

If I'd been much deeper in, I probably wouldn't even have existed in the Empire's records to have been tested in my eighth year, as all children in the empire were supposed to be, and I'd never have been found to be taken to the Imperial Intellectual Complex.

But it wasn't to those parts of Abenez that Pete and I were going. Deep in the interior, there were areas that rarely had access to water or electricity and where food was scarce. It was where only the elderly and infirm and very young lived, those unable to fight for anyplace better.

Parked in a garage under the building we'd entered was a heavily armored transport. It was small, and outfitted for carrying troops. There were many similar vehicles parked about. Though only Hector would be going above ground with us, at least two dozen guards were accompanying us into the interior. We boarded in silence. After a half hour of travel, we finally came to a stop in a parking area off the main tunnel.

We followed Hector up a set of stairs into a building in obvious disrepair. The dirt floor was a muddy bog and there were gaping holes in the walls.

"Now's a good time, Your Excellence," Hector said.

In tatty scarves around our necks, Pete and I each wore a tiny holo-projector. Its sophistication was such that it could create a false face that would look perfectly real. It was a technology not many knew existed, and which only the ISS was allowed to use. Pete gave me a wry grin and activated his.

With a disorienting flash, Pete's face became that of a stranger, matching the condition of the rest of his disguise: dirt smudges, stained, missing teeth, and dull eyes. I followed suit.

Pete's holo-face frowned. With a small shake of his head, he turned away.

We followed Hector out of a door that hung at an angle in the frame. It was still early morning, but somehow the light in this part of town was dimmer. The buildings stood along the remains of a road like broken teeth, some still four and five stories tall, looking dangerously fragile—leftovers of smaller cities Abenez had swallowed up. Others were long gone, the bricks cleared away or repurposed by the residents.

There weren't many people in the streets. No one begged in this part of town, because they knew no one else had anything to give. There were no homeless, as you'd think of them in other cities, because no one knew who owned the buildings anymore. With no landlord coming to collect rent or evict those who couldn't pay, anyone could live anywhere they could hold on to. What electricity and water people did get was charity from the governor.

Some people scratched out small gardens, though that required that they live outdoors among the plants, otherwise the food was stolen. The children of the neighborhood, and any adults still healthy enough to go so far, would wander out of the area from time to time looking for work. But work was far away, and what there was to be had in other parts of Abenez was usually taken by people who lived closer.

These people lived on ingenuity, charity, and a reluctance to die.

Pete walked beside me as we exited the building. In spite of his disguise, there was something clearly foreign about him. I considered him for a long time before I realized what the problem was.

"You're walking wrong," I said.

He gave me a puzzled look. "How should I be walking?"

I shrugged, trying to put into words something I didn't quite understand.

"You walk... You walk like you eat every day, and go to the doctor when you're ill. And like you've still got some pride left."

He regarded me for a long time without speaking. Then he shifted, stooping his shoulders and holding his arm as if it hurt or didn't work properly, and began to walk again; slow, shuffling steps. I watched him for a few paces before I caught up and continued with him. Something about the sight made me terribly sad.

Just down the street we encountered a small girl standing alone with her thumb in her mouth. She was probably no older than five, and in a devastating flash of memory, I saw Carrie standing in our apartment, watching me leave with solemn eyes.

Pete approached the girl.

"Hi," he said. "What's your name?"

The girl just watched him.

"Where's your mommy?"

The girl shrugged.

"Your daddy?"

With her free hand, the girl pointed to a heap of garbage collected against the side of the closest building. Once I looked closely, I could see that it was a man in rags, buried under the garbage for warmth, though it was summer. A wracking cough scattered much of his "blanket." When the fit passed, he began to gather the refuse around him again with a trembling hand.

Pete stared.

I did too. I wanted to tear my eyes away, but I was stuck, locked in the ungentle grasp of reflection. Would it have been better, I wondered, of all the horrors of childhood among the unclass, to have that father rather than the one I'd gotten? Was there more to be afraid of, or less? Did it matter?

Pete jerked his attention away, finding the girl again.

"Are you hungry?" he asked.

The child shrugged again as if to say, Of course, but what difference does it make?

Pete drew several food pouches from inside his jacket—the kind distributed here sometimes in fits of careless charity, packed with as much nutrition as possible. The girl eyed them warily.

Something inside me felt broken, raw. "It won't work that way," I whispered.

Pete turned to look at me.

"No one does that here, just gives someone else their food. She thinks you're trying to trick her, or harm her."

His mouth tightened.

"Here," I said. "Let me try." I took his arm and steered us away.

Several feet away I made as if to put them in an improvised sack made of my shirt, and dropped them in such a way that it would appear they had fallen out.

We turned a corner. I pulled Pete to a stop and we waited. A few moments later I peeked back down the street. The food packets and the girl were gone.

We returned home, both of us subdued and thoughtful.

"Thank you," I said to Pete.

He gave me a puzzled frown.

"For what?"

"For that. I needed to see that. I know what I need to do now," I said. "Or, at least, why I need to do it. The 'what,' I'm still largely lost on."

Pete smiled. "I'll get you some help," he said. "Administrators and functionaries and all that. People who do this sort of thing all the time."

I nodded, though I wasn't as reassured as I'd have expected.

His expression was thoughtful as he watched me.

"And I'll help you, too," he said. "You're right, Jake. It's important. I didn't understand before." He reached over and squeezed my hand. "Thank you, too."

For once, thinking of Abenez made me feel good, hopeful. I could help them, and I would.

The bomb came later.

CE2

Contrary to all the laws of physics I know, I didn't die when a star went supernova inside my head.

I opened my eyes but I could see only blurry images that moved too fast, and I couldn't hear anything but the whine of matter and energy trying to escape the confines of my skull through my ears. The shape of something I felt sure I had a name for drifted into my sight, but finding the memory felt like an attempt to lasso a passing beam of light. I slipped back into the cool darkness among the stars.

The next time I woke, the images had more defined forms, though they were still muzzy shapes, smears of color when they moved. There were sounds now, an insistent buzz that came and went with the objects. A groan was loud inside my head and the pulsar in my brain objected strongly to the noise. The thing from before came into my line of sight and I remembered the name I'd been searching for with a profound feeling of relief and peace.

Pete.

Sometime later, the buzz resolved into an intermittent hum with the cadence of speech. Pete appeared above me, his face recognizable from memory more than from what I could see. He said something I could almost make out, but comprehension slipped away from me. I shook my head, biting my lips together against the wave of nausea that loosed. Before I fell asleep again, I felt the brush of a soft kiss against my cheek and the solid warmth of Pete's body curl around mine.

When I woke again, the shapes had resolved into familiar, if smudgy, objects. The noise in my ears was no more than a constant susurration, much like the sound of the waves crashing on the shore just outside the door to the balcony. I sat up but a hand on my chest stopped me before I was upright; it took a pitiful amount of pressure to make me collapse onto the bed again. I winced when my head hit the pillow.

Pete's face appeared above me. Pete. My husband. The emperor.

"Did I hurt you?"

"Only my pride," I groaned.

His soft smile and the intensity in his eyes felt like a balm. I didn't mind staying in bed if he would just sit there, looking at me like that.

"What happened?" I asked.

His expression snapped into hard lines, his eyes glittering, though his voice was soft.

"You don't remember?"

I shook my head, which was a bad idea. His brow furrowed but he stroked my face with a gentle hand.

"There was a bomb in your lab."

"Oh." I still didn't remember, but that explained enough.

His eyes were suspiciously bright. "How do you feel?"

"Fine. You?"

He smiled as he pressed his lips to mine. Unconsciousness claimed me again, but the sensation of his kiss pervaded my dreams.

No one stopped me when I tried to sit up again, though Pete was sitting on the bed beside me by the time I came upright. Jonathan—who had been my servant since I first came to the palace—appeared with a tray of soft, easy foods and I made a face at it. He ignored that, though his eyes on me were more intense than usual.

Pete presided over my breakfast before he would engage me in conversation. Finally the tray was taken away.

"It wasn't so bad, then? The bomb?" I asked.

Pete's lips thinned into a white line and he looked away. "It could have been worse. You had Dr. Heinriksen scared for a little while. You threw yourself on top of Greta and took the worst of the blast."

I searched my memory for a face to match the name, a reason I should even know the name, but I couldn't find one.

"Greta?"

"Your lab assistant," Pete said.

I grimaced. "I should have known that."

"She was new," Pete said. "I think you two had only worked three days in the lab together."

I felt like I should have remembered her anyway.

"Do you know who did it?" My gut twisted. Duke Blaine had warned me, hadn't he? At the wedding, he'd told me he meant to get rid of me again. But a bomb? Somehow I hadn't realized he was *that* serious, that I hadn't been nearly afraid enough.

The exasperation in the hard lines of Pete's face told me everything I needed to know about the investigation.

"I will know, soon. I promise. They won't get away with this, Jake." His voice dropped low, laced with black fury. "No one is going to take you away from me. You'd better believe that."

I reached up and stroked his face with fingers that shook.

"I do."

My recovery was frustrating and slow. Apparently, there had been quite a lot of damage that required repair and regeneration.

For all that, there was a disconcerting lack of scars.

I hadn't had access to modern medicine until I was eight years old, so, unlike anyone else I'd met since then, I bore a few scars from childhood mishaps. Dr. Heinriksen had long ago offered to remove them for me but I'd said no. I didn't want to be rid of them for a complex variety of reasons, most of which I couldn't explain even to myself. The scar that ran across the top of my left cheekbone and disappeared into my hairline was what passed, I suppose, as my inheritance from my father.

But I was the emperor's husband now, and his own team of surgeons didn't leave scars. The faint scars I thought I remembered seeing on myself from those bleary, confused first days of my recovery were not there when I was awake enough to see clearly.

It made the situation feel that much more unreal, the weakness and dizziness that much more frustrating. Especially because I didn't remember anything from just before the blast until I woke in my own bed two days later.

I wasn't allowed to go anywhere and it was driving me insane. My keepers quietly sympathized with me but wouldn't budge an inch.

I didn't want to admit they were right, but for much of that time I was too weak to do much more than sleep. Still, a man can only sleep so much. I spent hours reliving the past few months, especially our honeymoon. It had been a full month with Pete, alone. Except for the servants. And the guards. But they were a part of my life that I'd gotten used to again more easily than I'd expected.

For four weeks I'd had him all to myself. No demands of the empire intruded into our time, no protocol, no politics.

"Marco," Pete said one evening as we lazed in the great pool that surrounded the house where we stayed.

"What?"

"Marco," he said, grinning.

"Who's Marco?"

"It's a game. I'll close my eyes and when I say Marco, you say Polo."

I just watched him, waiting for this to make sense.

"Why?" I said.

"So I can try to find you."

"I'm right here."

He laughed. "Well you move around. And I try to find you by listening for your voice."

I shook my head. "I don't get it."

"It's like hide and seek. Only in the water. And I've got my eyes closed. OK, maybe it will be easier if you go first. Close your eyes and say Marco."

I closed my eyes. "I don't understand this game at all," I grumbled. I heard a faint splash and then suddenly Pete surfaced behind me, wrapping wet arms around my shoulders, pulling me against him, kissing the back of my neck.

"Oh, OK," I said, turning. "This game I like."

We traveled around the globe, going places I'd never been before, seeing things I'd never seen, doing things I'd never done: hang gliding and parasailing and cross-country skiing.

In the long days I lay in our bed at the palace, recovering, I was almost grateful to have the quiet time, to remember. Because I had proof enough, in my own body, slowly, slowly healing, that that carefree time we'd had together was something we'd never have again.

CE 3

Eventually I was given permission to spend time in selected, secluded spots. On our private stretch of beach, one afternoon, I sat at the edge of the water, where the waves had diminished to the barest brush against my toes. The ocean was as still as a pond, like glass. Only small, gentle waves rolled apologetically onto the sand, shrinking back again as if ashamed of disturbing so magnificent a thing.

Pete came and stood beside me, his foot pressing against the side of mine.

"I dreamed of the ocean from time to time when I was back at the IIC," I said.

Dreams were on my mind because I'd spent so much time in half-slumbers during my recovery. So many dreams, nightmares, so many of them still clear when I woke. I had too many frightening things to dream about.

"Sometimes they were good dreams," I continued. "But mostly I dreamed of being caught up in the undertow, swimming as hard as I could to reach the surface, only to find that I'd gotten turned around and had reached the bottom instead."

"I wish I could have saved you," he said.

I took his hand and laced our fingers together.

"You did."

After ten days, I was allowed access to the whole of the Imperial Family area. Because the Imperial Wing was so large, and the current family so small, Pete had opened up the hallway bordering the Nobles' Wing for use by the nobility. Some unspoken protocol made it so that only the very highest ranking nobility ever used our shared areas, and not often. I rather thought that missed the point, but I wasn't going to complain about it, particularly now. Of the two garden areas in the section that bordered the ocean, the one open to the nobility was my favorite, and I began to spend my afternoons there.

"May I join you, Your Highness?"

I had set aside the book I was reading and was sitting with my eyes closed, giving in to the damned fatigue that still plagued me. The rush of adrenaline that Blaine's voice provoked was welcome, if the man himself wasn't.

"Why would you want to do that, Blaine?" I said without opening my eyes.

He chuckled. "Not many men can boast of time spent with the Prince Consort."

"You wouldn't boast of it either," I said, cracking my eyes open. "So I'm still not sure what it is you want. If you're trying to make me tired, you already accomplished that with your bomb."

He had been in the process of sitting down and stopped with a jerk.

"I beg your pardon, Your Highness?"

"You should."

Eying me warily, he sank into the chair. "I wasn't aware that the perpetrators of that heinous crime had been identified."

"I don't know if they have or not, but that's not what I'm talking about. No matter who they catch, or don't, you and I both know who is really behind this, don't we?"

He watched me for a long time. I held his gaze without blinking, though it cost me a lot of energy I didn't have. The small surge of anger was already fading.

"Allow me to offer you a bit of friendly advice. Noble to noble." His lips were thin and pale. "There is a great deal of difference between the posturing and power games played among the important people in the empire, and such crass treason as attempted assassinations." He bit off the words as if they tasted bad. "And some people would take grave insult over the insinuation that they would even associate themselves with the latter."

I stared at him, shaken by the passion in his denial.

I lay back and closed my eyes again.

"Thank you for your concern, Duke Blaine. I think visiting time is over for today."

There was a long silence, and my heart began to beat harder, but then I heard the rustle of his clothes as he stood. When I opened my eyes again he was gone.

After that, I didn't venture out much...which brought back the problem that had originally driven me out into the places where Blaine had found me. In my abject boredom, I began researching things I'd never thought to look into before.

My first searches were mostly random, and I ended up only giving myself new things to worry about. I ran across sealed files containing conspiracy theories the palace had long ago buried. One of them detailed ongoing passive and active scans of the palace structure itself, allegedly because anti-imperial groups were believed to have insinuated themselves into the engineering and construction teams that had built the palace.

After all, it had been built in the early, unsettled days of the Empire. It lay on the new west coast of the North American continent. Just after the wars that birthed the empire, an earthquake had dumped most of what was the western coast of the United States of America into the Pacific, and the empire had claimed the new coastline as its own. But at the time there had been a great deal of outrage, and accusations that the fledgling empire itself had triggered the earthquake along the notorious fault line. It was a bare fact that many of the loudest and most influential of the opponents of a global empire had lived in places that had been sloughed off into the sea.

I'd never learned of such rumors in my history lessons at school, and found no evidence of them in any public documents. The empire had closed and sealed any mention of such sedition, and perhaps silenced those who voiced it. I might have had access to the proof one way or the other, but I didn't look. I decided I didn't want to know.

I targeted my searches better, to pleasanter matters. I found records of Pete's childhood. There were a lot of them. I watched hours of vid, read dozens of articles and reports and pieces of nonsense. It was fascinating and oddly disturbing at the same time.

I watched an eight year old Pete standing straight and proper as his father officiated over the announcement of that year's Selected. There were photos of each of us, and brief bios. The other children's photos were from their lives before, full of color and life, bright with smiles and proud families. He detailed names of cities happy to claim them, listed parents and siblings. Precocious accomplishments were read aloud by teary mothers and choked-up fathers. There was a particularly touching account by Anwar's mother of his father's tragic death and how proud he would have been of his son had he lived to know of his Selection.

Sandwiched among them was the brief flash of my picture, one taken for my medical records after my arrival at the IIC. It was a headshot only, where I stood against a white background. I'd been instructed not to smile. In the harsh light, my common brown coloring was a smudge of dirt on the pristine wall. The emperor announced me only as "Jacob Dawes of the Duchy of Mexico," before the next picture appeared. It was one of Kirti, smushed into the middle of a laughing gaggle of girls, her parents standing just behind, holding hands.

Young Pete's brow furrowed in confusion at the oddity that had been my presentation, but quickly smoothed back into polite attention.

It warmed me that he had noticed.

I went further back, tracing Pete's life into a past I could barely comprehend. I watched him playing with toys I would never have imagined, being adored by scores of fancy and important people, standing straight and polished, maybe five years old, but already an emperor in the waiting. I watched him as a baby, toddling precariously across the palace lawn to the adoration of hundreds of onlookers, before he collapsed into the arms of a beautiful young woman, his mother, all honey-blonde hair and laughing eyes. She swept him up with a rippling laugh, the tenderness in the way she looked at him still clear even across the imperfect medium of stored data and long years.

"I don't really remember her," Pete said, sinking to the bed beside me. "I've seen those vids so many times that sometimes I think I do, but I know it's not a real memory of her. I was too young when she died."

I considered that in silence. Pete's childhood couldn't have been more different from mine if we'd tried to make them so. I remembered my mother, sometimes vividly. Real memories, and most of them unpleasant. It wasn't really her fault, but in my memories she was inextricably linked to the hollow gnawing sensation of an empty belly, and the smell of the grime and piss stained walls of buildings we lived in, one after another. Her eyes were always dull, her face strained, or sad, or nothing at all besides the creeping blankness that had taken over in the last years I had with her.

Pete was watching my face, the line of puzzlement drawn between his brows.

"Have you really never seen any of that before?" He gave me a lopsided smile. "You're a researcher. I always assumed you'd looked up my data at some point."

It was hard to explain why I hadn't. I wasn't sure I understood, myself.

"I don't like my past," I said, my hands trembling a bit from the realization and the confession. "I hide from it whenever I can. And I try very hard not to talk about it." I gave him a smile, because he knew this about me, but it felt weak and anemic. "I've never searched for information about anyone else in my life. I let them tell me the things they want me to know."

Pete shrugged. "You can look at anything you want about my past, including the records that aren't public. If I haven't told you about something already, it's because it's never come up. I tell you everything," he said with a small laugh. "You're probably the worst security threat to the empire. You know all my secrets."

I stared at him for a long moment, fighting to keep my mouth closed. I looked away so that he couldn't see too much on my face. So that he wouldn't find there the secrets I was keeping from him.

That was different, though. If he'd had the past I did, he'd keep secrets too. Or so I told myself.

CE<sup>4</sup>

T hat evening's news broadcast carried news of unrest and aborted demonstrations—quashed by the ISS even as they started—among the unclass of Earth's second and third largest slums, Bhadrangi in Mumbai and Liangsitu in Beijing.

To my utter astonishment, the commentators had gone to Blaine for the nobles' reaction.

"It is always troubling," he said, "when there is lawlessness and violence anywhere on any imperial planet. Here at the heart of the empire, doubly so. When it is the unclass, it is both more and less surprising than it might be otherwise. But since the recent attempt on the life of the Prince Consort, who is an unclass by birth, this lowest class of the empire has been dangerously restive. Even before that, since the emperor first announced his engagement with the established order of things so clearly and obviously disrupted, the unclass have been unsettled and unsure of their place."

"What will be done about them, Your Grace?" the reporter asked.

"That is not my place to say. I will do everything in my power to support the emperor and to secure the empire for all its citizens. We will be keeping our eye on the Resets as well," he continued. "There could be similar reactions among them. They would not be wrong to count the Prince Consort as one of their own. They are scattered through the empire and more difficult to pin down as a consolidated group, and that makes any confusion among their ranks, as to the possibility of the sort of

27

miraculous exoneration Prince Jacob received, a security concern that is difficult to address. But I assure you, the palace and my peers on the emperor's council and among the nobility have the safety of the empire at heart and in mind at all times, as is our duty." Here he looked directly into the camera. "And *anyone* threatening the security of the empire, in any way, be it active or passive, deliberate or unwitting, will be dealt with. The empire comes first, always. May the emperor live forever."

Pete returned to our room that night much later than usual. I pounced on him as he stepped through the door.

"How much of that was true?"

"What?" Pete replied with a puzzled frown.

"What Blaine said. How much of it is true?"

"I'm not sure what you mean. That the unclass took grave exception to the attempt on your life? No more than I did, I assure you. But yes, of course that's true. We've been monitoring it. We couldn't prevent it entirely, but we were able to deal with it quickly because we were prepared." He laid his hand on my arm. "Don't worry, Jake. This isn't your fight. There's nothing you need to worry about except resting up and getting better. I'll take care of it, I promise."

"No. That's bullshit. Not my fight? It's my fight more than anyone else's, even yours."

"Jake—"

"This isn't about the security of the empire. Don't you see? Someone is doing this on purpose. They planted a bomb for me. Not for the emperor's husband, but for the unclass who is the emperor's husband. They're provoking the unclass and stirring up trouble. This isn't coincidence, Pete, this is an attack on the unclass."

Pete sighed. "You think I haven't thought of that? I understand what you're saying, and how you feel. But you've just survived a bomb planted in your lab, Jake. Take the time to get better first. Let me handle this for now, at least. Let me take care of you."

I wrapped my arms around him. "We'll take care of each other. But I can't leave this alone. Not now, not ever. You have to know that."

Pete sighed, pulling me to him so tight that I could barely breathe. "Yes," he said. "I do."

I fell asleep that night tangled together with the man I loved, the emperor who understood and was on my side.

A face chased me through my dreams that night. The man never spoke, never came close, but he was always there. I didn't know him, and yet I did, and it was more than frustrating that I couldn't put a name to the face. In light of the discoveries of the day and the emotions they had stirred up, it was extremely unsettling.

Only after I woke up did I remember where I'd seen him. In Capital City. It was the solemn face of the man in the crowd the day of our engagement parade. I hadn't figured out who he was then, either.

I don't remember dreaming of him again.

# CE 5

In spite of my resolve to do something for the unclass, for us, I was stymied by the fact that I was restricted in so many ways until Dr. Heinriksen pronounced me fully recovered. So from my bed I began to plan.

The first thing I did was detail all the problems as I saw them. I jotted down a few ideas for solutions, things I thought I could contribute to the effort from my own lab. I made a list of the many types of collaboration I expected I'd need.

Then I sent it all to Kirti.

At the IIC, when we'd reached the age at which we had to choose our specialties, most of us had already known where our talents were pointing us. By that age, I'd already been on record as a member of the physics department for years. But Kirti's particular brilliance wasn't in any one discipline. It was her ability to store, process, and manipulate data, to see patterns and intuit solutions that no one else—especially no artificial intelligence— would think of. She was brilliant at planning and logistics. In the end she'd chosen engineering as her specialty, and did well there. In reality, her work was wide ranging and rarely restricted to any one area. She wasn't just one of my best friends and one of the few people I trusted, she was perfect for leading my new project.

She sent back an acknowledgment and insisted that I leave it to her for the time being and just concentrate on getting better. I asked in return if Pete and/or Dr. Heinriksen had been talking to her. She didn't deign to reply.

So I went back to my meandering, pointless searches.

I began to find things about myself.

I was searching for information on Mr. Kagawa—the former director of the IIC and my childhood nemesis—more out of a twisted sense of nostalgia than anything else.

The search program was sophisticated, designed to anticipate what I was looking for. It returned results that related to both Mr. Kagawa and me. In one of them, I found a chain of correspondence dated a month after my eleventh birthday, three years after I was taken from my home and brought to the IIC.

*From the Official Records Office RE: Jacob Dawes;*

*Director Kagawa,*

*Following, you will find all the pertinent details regarding the death of Mariquilla Dawes, the natural mother of one of the Selected, Jacob Dawes. As per regulation 197365.8, notification of the death of a parent or sibling is an exception to the restrictions on communication between Selected and their families. Please contact the current liaison for psychological health, Dr. Tillia Ilt, regarding the best way to inform the minor of the death so that his performance and studies will not be negatively impacted.*

\*\*

*Dr. Ilt,*

*I have received notification of the death of the mother of one of the children. Though the regulations permit me to inform him, the child in question is the unclass boy, Jacob Dawes. For many reasons, I don't think it is advisable to inform him. As you know, news of this nature would naturally be upsetting and could have a negative impact on the child's performance here, which, against all likelihood and expectations, has been remarkable and of great benefit to this institution and the Empire itself. But, more than that, in this case, I think that we should do everything possible to separate the child from his origins in the hopes that, with continued and exclusive exposure, he might eventually integrate into the culture of the higher classes here.*

**

*Director Kagawa,*

*I agree with your assessment and advise you to proceed as you have suggested. The nature of the familial bonds among the unclass are nothing like those of the other children you work with; they are not as strong or as important as similar relationships among the other classes. I think informing the child of his mother's death is unwise, as the reminder of his unsavory differences will no doubt prove to be a setback in his successful integration into the upper class group in which he now lives and within which he must learn to operate. His association with the other children might have taught him to believe that his mother would have love for him akin to what the other children's mothers feel, or that he owes her the same sort of feeling in return, and therefore grief at her passing. This simply is not true. She is not, and should not be made to be, as important to him as a normal child's mother would be. It is best not to create a false sense of normal familial affections where this child is concerned.*

"Your Highness?"

I jumped and killed the screen before I turned to Jonathan.

"Is something the matter?" he asked.

"Nothing," I said, willing my voice to sound convincing. "You scared me, that's all. Did you need me for something?"

Without a word he moved past me to switch on my main vid.

"You're going to want to see this," he said.

# CE 6

Jonathan navigated to one of the Empire's officially sanctioned news sources, and the familiar face of reporter Jan Whitman filled the screen. His normally flawless professional expression held a hint of doubt.

"Breaking news directly from the palace. Today, ISS forces raided the home of Niam Gesson, a resident of Imperial City. According to officials at the ISS, this man has been identified as the perpetrator of the bombing of the Prince Consort's lab.

"Gesson was found dead. The cause: self-administered poison. Along with the corpse, ISS officers found a detailed confession of the crime as well as a political declaration. In his own words, Gesson decried the emperor for tainting the noble class and the imperial line by marrying an unclass. Gesson is a native of the duchy of Mexico and middle class by birth, though he has recently come into a good deal of money."

The display blinked, replacing the reporter with blackness that slowly resolved into a starscape. The rushing sound of blood filled my ears.

*People of the Empire, friends and fellow citizens. It is an honor to address you today.*

The voice was artificially constructed. Every now and then, the emphasis fell on the words in an odd way. It made it easier for me to believe that it couldn't possibly be saying what I thought I was hearing.

*I am a loyal subject of The Empire, like yourselves. I wish I could openly tell you who I am, but for now I must tell you only that*

*I am a patriot. It is because of my deep and abiding love for the empire and my duty to defend and protect it, that I bring you this message today.*

*Sources loyal to the ideals of the Empire have brought you this news of the tragic death of one of our own, a brave and deserving man, Niam Gesson, who made the ultimate sacrifice in defense of our way of life and our principles—those on which this Empire was founded. That he attempted to remove from the palace a stain on our noble rulers, was not an act of treason. That he failed, that he took his life to protect others and this most important of causes, is a tragedy. Remember him, my fellow subjects, remember his sacrifice, and know that we will triumph in cleansing the empire once more and restoring order, safety, and majesty to our great society. May the emperor live forever!*

I don't know how long I sat staring at the screen after the vid had gone black again. The picture had been replaced by the seal of the ISS and a generic, reassuring "all will be well" message—the same one that was used from everything from natural disaster to war.

I knew which one this was.

Pete burst into the room and fell to his knees in front of me, grabbing my hands in a grip that was too tight and almost painful.

"Are you all right?"

I stared at him for a moment.

"Of course. Are you?"

His hands dropped and he shook his head, as if annoyed I would even think to ask that question.

"Jake, you know that was an illegal breach, right?"

"Of course."

"You know I would never have allowed—"

I grabbed his hands where they had tightened on my knees. "Is that what you're worried about? That I think you released that news?"

Tight lines appeared around his mouth. "It was a leak. I'll find out how. And the other one..." His eyes clouded with worry. "That shouldn't have been possible, for someone to have gotten that on sanctioned channels."

I nodded slowly. "I know. It shouldn't be possible to get a bomb in my lab either."

He winced.

I slid to my knees and gathered him to me. We clung to each other.

The mattress was hard and the blanket thin and scratchy. There were hands on me, and soft lips that tasted sterile, like manufactured water. Warm breath tickled my ear in a heartless chuckle.

"Jake!"

I was sitting up in the emperor's own bed, tangled in silken sheets soaked with my sweat. There were hands on me. Pete's hands.

"Jake?"

I fell back and buried my face in my pillow, trying not to vomit.

Pete's hand rubbed soft and soothing on my back.

"Are you awake?"

I concentrated on not shivering, not retching, and making him believe I hadn't woken at all.

Eventually he lay back down beside me, putting his arms around me, his head on my shoulder.

I concentrated on not shoving him away, screaming. I concentrated on the fact that this was Pete. That I was safe.

I concentrated on believing it.

In that one horrible day and night, all my fledgling resolve to face my critics and Blaine and any other foes was swallowed up in sick, paralyzing fear. The walls of the palace were closing in on me, and I couldn't breathe, couldn't think.

I had to get out of there.

I set Jonathan to packing, sent Kirti a message, and then went to Pete.

His mouth screwed up in concern that was more worry than logical objection.

"But what can you do at the IIC that you can't do here?"

"I need a space where I can clear my head without—" I threw my arms out to indicate the whole of the palace. "To figure out what I'm going to do about this, about the people who can do these things." How Blaine was doing these things. Because I didn't doubt for a second that he was behind all of it. He had that kind of power and reach. He was one of the few people who could. I already knew he would.

"But Jake, I've got half of ISS intelligence—"

"I don't mean like that. I need to fight back, I need to—" I stopped. "I don't know what I need to do, but Kirti's already been working on things I can do to defend me and mine, and I can think clearer there."

"You and yours?"

The air grew thick with the realization of what I'd just said.

"I don't mean you're not—"

"I know," Pete said, perhaps a little too quickly. "I know what we are to each other. And I know who you are to the unclass, and who they are to you." He stepped closer and laid a tentative hand on my cheek. "I'll miss you."

The journey was quiet and uneventful. Jonathan sat across from me, beating me at chess a lot more often than he should have been able to.

We arrived just before the dinner hour, as planned. When a servant immediately disembarked to make the announcement of our arrival, it hit me, what I should already have known. I wasn't going to be allowed to return quietly. That wasn't how it worked anymore. I exited the transport slowly, anxiety tightening my gut.

I was announced before I entered the great hall. There, the entire faculty was lined up, formal and still, ready to receive me. It made my head swim.

I'd done this, entering a room with all the pomp and ceremony of the Imperial Family. These stiff, stuffy entrances were the way my life worked now.

But here it was wrong. Here where I'd lived as a boy, knowing I was less than everyone else. Here where I'd managed to secure my place as one of them. And where I'd lived in disgrace—less, once again, than my peers.

Now they were all watching me enter the room, as they'd done on more than one occasion before, but this time with reverence and respect where before it had been with malice and hostility.

I was setting foot in the building for the first time since the day that started out as one of the worst of my life and ended one of the best.

I searched the crowd, trying to forget that I was on the wrong side of it. There were the familiar faces of my friends Chuck and Kirti; my old teacher and mentor Dr. Okoro; Sean, my old lab partner; and Sasha. His lip was curled up in a snarl and I nearly laughed with relief. No matter how upside-down things seemed, if Sasha and I could meet as schoolyard enemies, then all was right with the world.

It was mortifying when they all bowed to me. I felt the blood flood my face. Director Harris approached me.

"Your Highness."

"Jacob," I corrected.

He smiled. "If that's what you would like to be called."

I'd never quite understood how Director Harris had always made me feel safe and accepted in his presence, even when I felt the complete opposite everywhere else. Or why he had even tried.

"I would like that very much."

We shook hands and I heard a rushing murmur from the onlookers, which only made me blush harder. Director Harris gave me a sympathetic smile.

"We wanted to prepare a welcome dinner for you, Jacob, but," he glanced at Jonathan, "we were told you would need to rest, being so recently recovered."

I cast a grateful look at Jonathan, who, as usual, pretended he didn't see it.

"Yes, I'm sorry, Director. I do appreciate the thought."

"We want to make sure you're comfortable here," he said. "This is your home."

*Yes.* I thought. *Yes.*

I looked over the crowd again. Kirti and Chuck stood together with Dr. Okoro. I caught Chuck's eye.

"My room," I mouthed at him. He grinned and nodded, glancing at Kirti and grabbing her hand, squeezing it. She smiled back. At him, not me. What did *that* mean?

Pondering over it, I let Jonathan show me to my room.

And so, rather than being subjected to all the formalities and stuffy, uncomfortable dinners, I spent the evening in my room with my best and oldest friends. It was a drink of cool water on a hot day; a breath of planetary air after a long time in space. I could breathe here.

"You know they built this just for you, right?" Chuck said as he gave me a tour of my own room. It *had* surprised me to find such a lavish guest suite at the IIC. Outsiders didn't come here. Pete visiting twice already was an anomaly, and he didn't stay overnight. On the rare occasion a specialist from outside needed to consult with our experts, they stayed in the dormitories. "They couldn't have the emperor or the Prince Consort staying in just any old room, could they?"

I wanted to protest, but it was a waste of breath. I knew Chuck was just teasing me, anyway. His eyes were sparkling. He was saving the real joke.

"OK, and...?"

He laughed. "Director Harris diverted funds from the physics budget to finance some of this. Your old department head was not happy."

I couldn't help but grin along with him. My relationship with Dr. Bartel had been touchy at best when I last lived at the

IIC—I'd been a disgraced Reset he was saddled with, no matter how much talent I brought to his department. It was childish but satisfying to think of his reaction to being told his department was helping finance lavish accommodations for me.

One of the features of my new suite was a private dining room, and I had dinner there with my friends. We talked of their latest projects, the goings of among the people I'd grown up with, the latest class of Selected. Nothing whatsoever to do with politics and prejudice and assassination attempts. And afterward we drank wine in my sitting room and I gave myself permission to feel safe again.

But that night's dreams took me back to the palace, to a vague sense of white, pain-bright confusion and people rushing around me. When I could make out details they were nameless, faceless people in a slum I both knew and didn't recognize, screaming for me to help them. But I couldn't move. It all faded to the image of Blaine's face on the vid and a synthesized voice that said over and over that familial bonds weren't important to unclass.

I scrambled from the bed, as if I could leave the nightmare behind with the tangled sheets. A half-desperate impulse and the muzzy logic of dreamers drove me out the door and down the hallway with the fear-remnants of the dream trailing behind.

I stopped in front of a door and rang the bell. I waited and was just about to ring again when the door opened. Former Director Kagawa, squinting against the light of the corridor, stared at me.

"Jacob?"

I think if he'd called me "Your Highness" it would have broken the spell, but the whole thing was surreal in a way that had put me in front of this door seeking answers from my old enemy.

He stepped back, a tacit invitation, and I entered his sitting room. Only one light was lit, dimmed to match the hour, and neither of us moved to change that. I sat in the armchair, he on the couch.

"Am I really so different?" I said.

I wasn't looking at him, but obliquely I could see his head come up, his gaze on me.

"You've always been different, Jacob."

I shook my head. I hadn't asked the right question.

"They said you shouldn't tell me about my mother, that it didn't matter, because we were different."

There was a long pause and then he sighed.

"You shouldn't ask me this. I was wrong about a lot of things back then. Believe me, the Resettlement authorities made sure I knew it."

"They didn't really tell you that you were wrong about me, did they?"

I heard him shake his head more than I saw it.

"They told me I was wrong to actively oppose the imperial authority that decided you belonged here. Remember that, Jacob. The committee thought you belonged here and wouldn't budge on that stance. You were and are one of the greatest minds in the empire. And now you're married to the emperor. Does anything else really matter?"

I felt ridiculous. What was I here for? Reassurance? A prop for my self-confidence? And yet the words of that expert had made me feel small and dirty in a way no one else had managed for a while. It wasn't about what I had done, what I could do, it wasn't even about what anyone else thought of me. She had been talking about what I *was,* something no amount of achievement or approval could change.

I buried my face in my hands. A gentle hand came to rest on my arm.

"What is the opinion of one person, expert or not, in the face of the evidence? You'd never accept that in the lab. Don't do it with this either. You *are* different, and you always have been. Maybe that's a good thing. None of the other children did, or even *could* have done, what you did. Not just scientifically, but personally."

I snorted. Yes, I'd done a lot of things other people never would have done. Like punching the emperor in open court.

"I don't believe you give in to this kind of self-doubt very often. Why are you doing it now?"

I stared at him. Why was I? He was right. What had changed? I was shaken, though. The mails I'd found, the bomb, the news broadcast, this "patriot." It was so much more personal and vicious than all the other ways people had attacked me in my life. It wasn't even that I could have died. I'd faced that before. Awaiting my execution had been one thing, and something I knew I'd done to myself. This was different. I was afraid, and angry. But mostly afraid.

I stood and offered my hand. Kagawa mirrored the action, shaking it with a strong grip.

"Thank you, sir," I said.

"Thank *you*."

I had already been turning away but I stopped.

"For what?"

"For forgiving me."

I looked at him for a long time.

"You too."

He nodded and I went back to my own room and sleeplessness in my own bed.

I went on with my life as if the strange late-night visit had never happened. One morning, without meaning to, I caught Kagawa's eye as I was leaving the dining hall. A woman ran into him from behind when Kagawa stopped mid-step. I cocked a wry smile at him. He returned a weak one. I looked away and that was the end of it.

# CE 7

The morning after my midnight conversation with Kagawa, Kirti rang my bell before I was finished with breakfast. Jonathan let her in and she sat across from me, tablet in hand, without giving me much more than a glance.

"You realize," she said, studying the data on her tablet, "that there will be a rise in the public criticism of you, the resistance to your efforts as well as your position, in direct proportion to the actions you take that benefit the unclass?"

I put my fork down a little harder than necessary. It made a sharp clank on my plate.

"Good morning to you too."

She looked up with a wry smile. "You really are gone from the IIC, aren't you? You've already forgotten that business comes first here, even ahead of basic politeness?" But she grinned and leaned across the table to kiss my cheek. "Good morning."

I snorted, mostly amused.

"Yes, I do realize people will not be happy if I do anything to benefit the unclass in any way."

"And by 'resistance,' you understand I'm referring to things like that attempt on your life."

Anger was a good way to stave off fear.

"Yes." The word had been clipped off but she seemed to understand that the emotion wasn't directed at her. "I'm not about to let that stop me, though. They're not going to intimidate me into ignoring my own class because it's the polite thing to do."

She cocked an intrigued eyebrow.

"Since when do you identify yourself as unclass?"

I blinked. "What do you mean? I've always been unclass."

"Yes, but I don't think I've ever heard you voluntarily identify yourself as one, to actually identify *with* them."

She might as well have punched me in the gut.

I'd never argued what I was. It would have been ridiculous. I had been born unclass. The move to the IIC hadn't changed that. There probably would have been a rule against an unclass being Selected if anyone had considered the possibility that an unclass could have the test scores to qualify. But there hadn't been, and we'd all simply had to learn to ignore it as something that should have mattered but couldn't be allowed to.

Everything that happened to me after that had been in violation of established rules. Pete had appointed me to a position at the palace that an unclass could not be considered for. He'd taken me into his life and his bed when there were rules that prevented an unclass from even entering the Imperial Wing of the palace. He'd made me a duke, though it was clear and commonly known that an individual could only be promoted by one class level. Even the laws that would have allowed me to move from unclass to low class, still restricted me legally to only a fraction of the things that a man born into the low class would be eligible for.

It was clearly and frankly illegal for me to be a palace appointee, to live with the emperor, to be elevated to the nobility, to be married into the royal family. And yet it had happened because technically, nothing the emperor did was illegal.

That still didn't change what we all knew. I wasn't really a noble or a royal. That was impossible. If the emperor chose to pretend otherwise, then we all had to pretend along with him.

But I was still an unclass. I always had been. Everyone knew that. I'd never argued what my true class was.

But that wasn't the same thing as *claiming* my class. Kirti was right. Maybe I'd started to do that with Pete, but this would be a new change to her. It was still new to me.

She lay a hand over mine.

"I didn't mean it as an insult, Jake. I was just surprised, that's all."

"No, that's fine." I didn't feel insulted. Just blindsided.

She dropped her gaze back down to the tablet. "To minimize the negative impact of any positive actions you take on behalf of the unclass," she said, as if we'd never wandered from the subject, "you need to consider compensatory actions to benefit the other classes that are directly connected to any improvements the unclass experience."

"What do they need that they don't already have? I can't do anything for the unclass unless I give as much or more to the privileged classes as well?"

She shot me a reproving look. "You're the Prince Consort and you cannot afford to act rashly or on emotion rather than logic. And if that's what you'd intended, you wouldn't have involved me in this. You would have bumbled into it in your usual act-first-think-later Jacob Dawes fashion."

"Dawes-Killearn," I grumbled.

She made an amused noise. "If you don't want to hear the truth, then don't ask me to give it to you," she said gently.

"I know. You're right. Just don't expect me not to get upset."

"I don't. Go ahead and have your irrational reaction here with me and not in front of half the empire."

"It's not irrational."

"OK, emotional, then."

I granted her the point with a stiff nod, but then gave her a sheepish smile as well. She shook her head and grinned.

"We'll start in Abenez, of course," she said, back to business at hand. "No matter how much they might hate it, even your loudest critics can't argue about anything you do within the duchy of Mexico. As long as it's within the bounds of imperial law, it's your prerogative—your duty, in fact. Even if it does benefit the unclass. And the real, measurable benefits that will cascade to the other classes within your duchy will give you the perfect set of data from which to argue for empire-wide changes."

We got to work.

In spite of the fact that I wasn't doing this alone, it was still a huge project and felt overwhelming. But I'd seen Abenez with my own eyes, and it was mine in more than just name. Nothing mattered more than that.

Soon, shipments of medicine were being sent into the district, stashed throughout the tunnels for use by mobile clinics, as was food for the mobile soup kitchens. It was a start, a stop-gap measure as longer-term goals in infrastructure and sustainability were put into place.

One of my own ideas was to annex several large factories from the low-class district into Abenez, provide incentives for companies to relocate there, and re-classify the jobs so that unclass workers qualified for them. I also banned the use of Resets as workforce in all of the duchy, setting up a system for transferring unemployed unclass into areas that needed the workforce. In a way, I felt guilty, as if I were discriminating against one group I belonged to for the benefit of another. I was still a Reset, after all. But they had better conditions and more opportunities in the whole of the empire. They wouldn't suffer as a group for being denied a place in my duchy. There were already more people in the duchy than there were jobs. They just had to be allowed to do them.

It would take a long time before there was any measurable improvement in Abenez as a whole. But for now, there would be children who wouldn't go to bed hungry tonight. There would be jobs for their parents, and medicine.

It was a start, and it was very satisfying.

Or it would have been, if it hadn't been for the two mails I found in my box the same morning I got the first status report from Kirti.

The first was a report from the governor of Mexico. I'd met her once, when I'd first gone there as the duke, before Pete and I were married, and then briefly again before we went to

Abenez together. I also had a vague sense of having accepted her congratulations at our wedding. I'd been happy enough to leave the administration of the duchy to someone who knew it well and wouldn't need any help from me.

But it was becoming clear that the governor saw the unclass problem as exactly that: the unclass were a problem. She danced with mincing steps around the fact that I was one of the unclass of Mexico myself. She had emphasized the length of her term as governor more than once, making sure I took note of the fact that she hadn't been in charge when I'd lived in Abenez.

Not that it mattered, I thought, because it was no different now than it had been then. But I doubted she knew that. It was obvious she'd never even seen any of the slums in the duchy.

The other mail was a simple request from Director Harris to have a word with me when it was convenient. I decided it was convenient right then and made my way to his office.

"I'm sorry to disturb you, Your Highness," Director Harris opened after greetings had been exchanged.

"What's going on?" I asked.

"It may be nothing. But I didn't know if you were aware that Oshiro Kagawa is being moved elsewhere. He'll be leaving us this afternoon for his new assignment at a mining facility."

I stared at the director. "A mining facility?" I'd reassigned Kagawa to the IIC myself, years ago, back when I was still young and optimistic and high on my new love affair with the man who was unfortunately also the emperor. There was no reason at all for him to be reassigned now, certainly not without my authorization or Pete's. None at all.

"*Why?*"

A memory of Blaine's face on the vid and a snippet of the interview came back to me.

*We will be keeping our eye on the Resets as well...*

"I was given no explanation," Director Harris answered, "only the orders. I hoped you would know. Or, at least, that you would want to investigate."

"Damn right I do," I growled to myself. I glanced back up at him. "Thank you, Director. I'll take care of this."

"You don't have the authority," Jonathan said again.

"I'm the Prince Consort. How do I not have authority?"

"The order was signed by Lord Laudley himself. Outside of your duchy, you don't have any appreciable political authority. The Head of Corrections may not be able to tell you what to do, but you don't have authority to tell him what to do, either. You could speak to him, of course. This could simply be an oversight."

"Kagawa's last assignment came from the emperor himself. Do you think this was simply an oversight?"

"No, I don't. But that doesn't alter the facts. You can either speak to Lord Laudley or you can go over his head and speak to the emperor."

I narrowed my eyes at him. "Which is exactly what Blaine is hoping I'll do. You think that comment he made about Resets and this thing with Kagawa are just a strange coincidence of timing? It's playing right into his hand, getting the emperor involved in protecting a Reset I have personal ties to."

Jonathan gave me a blank look. "Why are you so sure this has anything to do with Blaine?"

"Don't be thick, Jonathan. Of course it's Blaine. It's too convenient not to be."

Jonathan narrowed his eyes but didn't elaborate. "Then what do you propose?"

I bit my lips together. "There has to be something I can do." I thunked my head down on the back of my chair, rubbing a hand over my eyes. "Let me think."

Twenty minutes later I popped up.

"I've got it. Call Lord Laudley."

"I'm sorry, Your Highness, I didn't realize the criminal was a friend of yours," Laudley sneered.

I gritted my teeth and let that pass. Things hadn't been comfortable between Lord Laudley and me, but I'd had little contact with him before I'd been Resettled, and afterward I assumed it was awkwardness due to the fact that he was head of the department that had sent me to that hellish Resettlement camp.

Clearly I was wrong.

"Whether or not we have a personal relationship is irrelevant. I have need of him elsewhere. I'm requisitioning him for specialized work in my own duchy. I'm sure there are millions of men and women you could pick for a mining job. He has the education and skills I need."

"Many criminals are highly educated and valuable in their situations before they commit their crimes. It makes no difference once they're a ward of the justice system."

"The man's convicted of misusing his authority. He didn't like me and wanted to send me back to the slums. If we're Resettling people for that, half the nobles in the empire would be wards of your system."

His face hardened. "The emperor himself initiated the investigation into Mr. Kagawa's actions that led to his conviction. Do you imply he was in error?"

"Oh, stuff it. We're not going to get anywhere pretending to be nice. I don't know why you're doing this, but I'm asking you to reconsider. It will make things easier for everyone. If I have to go to the emperor about this, I will. And we both know whose side he'll take if it becomes a pissing contest."

"Yes," his eyebrows dropped. "Yes, we do know how he views the rules when it comes to you, don't we?"

My face went hot and, trying to hide my reaction, I looked down. My hands were clenched into fists in my lap. I glared at Laudley.

"Excuse me, Your Highness, but I'm a very busy man. I will consider your request." With an almost imperceptible bob of his head, he cut off the transmission.

Jonathan looked at me, eyebrows raised.

"He may very well call your bluff and insist you bring the emperor into it, after all. You're the one who pointed out that might be their aim."

I frowned. "I know. But maybe he won't. He may not have the balls to push it too far. He's not as powerful or protected as Blaine is. And if he's got any brains at all, he won't trust Blaine to protect him if it's not in Blaine's best interests."

Jonathan shook his head at me and turned away.

"Governor of Mexico?" Kagawa parroted, dumbfounded.
"Yes," I said.
"But why me?"
"Because I forgive you."

It was easy enough to arrange. Lord Laudley didn't block me when I requisitioned Kagawa for my own use. I informed the current governor of her change in status, initiated the shutdown of the elaborate mansion she'd occupied in Puerto Vallarta, established Kagawa in a moderate residence in Mexico City, and hoped for the best.

# CE8

Children raised at the IIC didn't have a lot of free time. An entire day left unstructured and unscheduled was rare. One of the things I would do on those days was go hiking with Kirti. The woods leading up into the mountain were cool and quiet, a soothing place to be. I decided that was exactly what I needed.

"You've just recovered from a bomb blast," Jonathan protested.

"That was almost two months ago."

"It's outside of the established security perimeter."

"This is the IIC, not the palace."

"Precisely. It's even less secure."

"No one here would seriously try to hurt me."

Jonathan raised an eyebrow. "Even if I believed that—"

I growled in frustration. Until the confrontation with Laudley, I had been happily burying my head in the IIC again, pretending and almost believing I still belonged here.

"You know what? I really, really don't care. This is not the palace, this is the *IIC* and I came here to get away from all that bullshit."

"You don't get to take a vacation from security measures. Ever."

"So send some guards out there and have them clear the area of, I don't know, bears or whatever might be out there *in the woods around the IIC*, and then leave me alone."

Jonathan's lips thinned and he stared me down for a long time. Finally his eyes narrowed. "Very well. I'll need at least two hours."

"Fine."

He gave me a curt nod and left the room.

I did get my hike, but I didn't get it exactly the way I wanted it. Kirti came with me, but so did four guards, two ahead, two behind, and they were ordered to keep me in sight. Which meant, of course, that I could see them too. I groaned and rolled my eyes, but tried to focus on ignoring their presence and enjoying the hike that had been so stupidly hard to get.

I'd spent too much of the last few months in bed, and the hike was more difficult than I'd anticipated. Kirti eyed me with concern but I ignored that, forcing my body on.

The guards who were, presumably, capable of hand-wrestling bears or running down mountain lions if necessary, didn't seem to have any trouble. I tried harder to pretend I couldn't see them.

When we broke through the brush into a clearing, I smiled. I'd been here with Kirti many times. It was secluded and small, but big enough for a decent picnic or to lay back and look at the sky through the branches. I stood there, breathing deep and enjoying the peace and the memories.

"I always liked this place," she said with a sigh.

"Yes." There were few times in my life I'd ever felt truly safe, few places that didn't carry the miasma of remembered pain or fear. This was one of them. I closed my eyes, savoring.

There was a sudden sensation of impact on my side, and a sharp pain. I stumbled, clutching my upper arm.

Faster than I would have thought possible, the four guards surrounded us, pushing us to our knees and forming a human shield around us.

I heard one guard on the com reporting and requesting help even as she scanned the forest, weapon held ready. After a moment they all flicked switches on their weapons and shot into the forest in a slow, steady sweep. It was a sonic beam; nothing that would harm the flora but it would hurt like hell if it hit a warm body. Sweeping down as low to the ground as they could, they'd hit the shooter even if he was laying flat. From the right there was a startled yelp and two of the guards sprang off in that direction.

Kirti's hands were already on my arm. It hurt a lot. "Jake?"

One of the guards dropped to a knee to examine me.

"Are you all right, Jake?" Kirti's voice was steady but I could hear her worry.

"I'm fine," I said, though I couldn't seem to get my breath.

I looked down at the guard's hands on me. "What's your name," I asked. It felt like I was jabbing my arm with each word. My head was swimming.

"I'm Kin, Your Highness. I'll have you fixed up in no time."

"Ouch!" The initial tingle of a pain-patch applied to my arm felt more like a bite.

"Sorry, Highness." She returned to her poking and muttering. "Fucking projectile weapon. What the fuck is that all about? Unless..."

I wanted to ask her to go on, but the clearing was revolving around me. I didn't think I'd lost much blood. The clotting agents in the pain patch had practically stopped it. I retched, bringing up my lunch in great heaves.

"Jake!"

My arms and legs were trembling. I started sweating, and I felt so weak, as if I'd been throwing up for hours.

"Your Highness?"

The voices were only hollow, faint echoes far away. Where had they gone? And yet, someone was still poking my arm. It was too much effort to look and see who it was. I didn't much care. It didn't hurt now. Not the arm, at least. A tingling, almost ticklish sensation under my skin had spread from my arm and now I felt it everywhere. It was starting to itch. No, burn. So hot. Pain.

I was on fire.

They were burning me at the stake. A painful, fiery death, reduced to ashes lost among the remains of a bonfire built of intolerance.

Where was Pete? Had he let them do this to me? Did they have him, too?

"Pete!" but the only sound was the roar of the flames, and my scorched throat was too far gone even to scream.

It was cool and quiet when I woke in a room painted in blues, lit only faintly and from somewhere I couldn't see. I squeezed my eyes shut for a minute and groaned but it made no sound. What was I doing here? Then I remembered.

I tried to sit up but my body didn't work. They'd burnt it away.

I forced myself to relax, to breathe. I could do those things. Relax. Breathe. I had to be at least intact if that were true. I took one more deep breath and opened my eyes again. I could see. That was good.

I swallowed, and though I didn't exactly feel the sensation, I knew that something had moved in response to the action.

I focused hard on the feeling of my head on the pillow and there was a sensation I knew meant "heavy." Gravity plus mass. But the mechanism trying to move them had lost force somehow. The little leap my head made when I meant to lift it was pathetic at best. I closed my eyes, suddenly too tired to do anything else. I thought I felt a hand on my forehead, a worried "Jake?" but I was gone again before I could be sure.

53

I dreamed. I was swimming, my movement free and unrestricted, in almost zero gravity. But it wasn't water, it was space, and I was in only a suit, a helmet, and boots that were no longer anchored to the asteroid. I was drifting. Drifting, drifting. My arms, legs, everything moved exactly as I asked it to as I drifted slowly and inexorably into the corona of a star. I burned.

I woke up trying to scream but it was only a garbled noise, swallowed up in the sounds coming from nearby.

"There is no question of my guilt, Your Excellence. I surrender myself to your judgment and ask only to be permitted to turn myself over to the guards."

"Drop the formality, Jonathan," Pete said, "and answer me. How exactly are you to blame for someone else shooting Jake?"

"I allowed the situation that put His Highness in danger. I arranged it."

"When Jake told you to."

"I was responsible for ensuring the proper security was in place."

"No, the ranking guardsman was."

"He could only do so if he had proper notice, and I allowed His Highness to go out there before there had been time to do more than the most cursory of security sweeps."

"You *allowed* Jake to go somewhere? I'm jealous. I can't remember the last time I had the power to *not* allow him to do anything."

Jonathan took a moment to answer and when he did, his voice was carefully neutral. "I didn't mean it that way, Your Excellence. Simply that I didn't delay him long enough or put enough guards in place or insist on stricter perimeters or a larger escort—"

No. That wasn't right. I wanted to say something but my mouth seemed to belong to someone else.

"Jonathan," Pete interrupted. "I'm not happy Jake got into a position where he was shot. I'm not making light of it. But I don't think the blame can be placed on any one person. Particularly not one person who wasn't holding the gun."

Jonathan's silence passed for a sigh. "Please, Your Excellence. Allow me to surrender to the guard. Or at least to resign my position—"

Frantic, I tried to sit up, and this time, with a huge, graceless flop, I turned onto my side.

They made it to me at almost the same time, each grabbing some part of me to haul me back upright.

"Jake!" Pete said. "What are you doing? Dr. Heinriksen said you wouldn't be awake for hours."

I lay there, panting. I concentrated on collecting myself, taking inventory. Everything seemed to be where it should be, though that was based more on the fact that I couldn't prove anything was missing rather than that I could prove anything was there.

"The hell you are," I said in Jonathan's direction. Or really, gasped, as the effort of talking was a lot more complicated than I'd planned for.

It was an effort to coordinate thoughts and actions at the same time, so I let them take all the weight and effort of moving me into a sitting position.

"Jonathan's not going anywhere," I said with a sigh of relief at having remembered this vital message all the way from lying prone to sitting up. Pete sat perched on the bed, his hands fluttering over me, looking perhaps for something to fix but nothing hurt. Nothing was even there unless I looked at it. I didn't feel pain. I didn't feel anything.

I hadn't seen where Jonathan had gone, but apparently it had been to summon Dr. Heinriksen, because she appeared as if from thin air. She sat down beside Pete and he yielded to her, moving to the other side of the bed and taking my hand.

"How do you feel, Jacob?" she asked, as if this were a routine physical.

"I'll let you know," I drawled, "as soon as I feel anything." I pondered for a moment as she silently went about her examination. "What did you do to me?" I asked.

"I put an inhibitor on you," she said, turning my wrist over so I could see the tiny silver device stuck to my skin. "That's why you can't move very well. There was a lot of nerve damage. Nothing irreparable, but nerves are fussy things. Like to make things painful while they heal."

"I can't move, doc."

She grinned. "How come you're sitting up, then, instead of lying still where I left you? Don't tell me you conned these boys," she made a vague gesture toward Pete and Jonathan, "into moving you without calling me first, because I won't believe you."

"OK," I slurred. "I can move a little. Much like Frankenstein's monster. Can we turn this thing off now?"

"I don't think you want me to do that yet."

"Yes I do. Please."

She cocked an eyebrow at me, amusement clear in the quirk of her mouth. "You sure?"

"Yes."

She did no more than flick the device but it felt like she hit me with a sledgehammer. I tried to gasp but my whole body was rigid, my lungs in a vise. Maybe I could move, but I couldn't imagine wanting to. I couldn't imagine wanting to do anything but die very, very quickly.

The pain ceased all at once. I gasped. Nothing hurt anymore, but I knew I was trembling even though I couldn't exactly feel it.

"Jake?" Pete asked, his voice anxious. I could see his hand stroking my forehead and I rolled my eyes up to meet his. I blinked. That seemed to be about what I was capable of.

"So you want the inhibitor on?" Dr. Heinriksen said. With a great effort I rolled my head so I could see her.

"Yes, please," I managed, though with more drool than I cared for.

Her smile was soft, not even gently mocking as her voice had been.

"It's nasty stuff, that Yellow. People have died, not of the poison itself or any damage it's done, but from the sheer overload of pain."

I think I grimaced. Or I would have. It was a grimace-worthy thought.

"What happened?" I managed, slow and deliberate.

I saw Pete and Jonathan glance at each other out of the corner of my eye, but Dr. Heinriksen didn't hesitate.

"You were shot."

I tried to nod but gave it up as a stupid idea.

"Remember."

She nodded and I envied her the ability.

"You were shot in the upper arm. It was a projectile weapon and would normally have been no more than an annoyance and a security nightmare. But the projectile was coated in izellium, or Yellow, as it's called, both for its color, and for the color of the corpses it leaves behind."

I'm sure I would have shivered if I could have. Or maybe I did and just couldn't feel it.

"You were lucky, Your Highness. Izellium is an old one, went out of use a long time ago. Any ISS or private guard carries a stash of counter-agents, but I don't think anyone but the Imperial Guard carries the one for izellium or its ilk anymore. Those are twenty-second century weapons."

"Why?"

"It's messy. Gets everywhere. Too easy to infect your own people with it when you're trying to dump it on someone else. Actually, that's what they used it for, to spray from the air. Coating a projectile with it wasn't done often. Mostly for the same reason: it's too easy to get the stuff on yourself. And no one did that more than once, if they lived."

Oh.

"Guardsman Kin is a fully trained medic, though, and she figured out what it was—or at least, what class of chemical it was—and administered the counter-agent in time. Otherwise, that lovely burning sensation would have been the last thing you felt."

"Doctor," Pete protested.

But she smiled at him. "I'm not making light of it, Your Excellency, I promise. Just bedside manner with one of my more ornery patients."

"Not ornery," I said. She grinned and didn't comment.

"Don't worry," she said, patting my hand, a fact I was only aware of because I could see her do it. "You'll only need the inhibitor for a day and a half at most. You got the counter-agent in time and I've added fancy accelerants and medicines that will have you healed up in no time. I wouldn't expect any lasting damage," she said.

With a few more pats on my hand and a promise to check on me again soon, she left.

"Jonathan's not going anywhere," I said.

Both Jonathan's and Pete's expressions went blank, though Jonathan's had a desperate edge on it.

"That's what I was telling him," Pete said with a deliberate calm no doubt intended to keep me from getting worked up.

I stared Jonathan down. "You're not going anywhere."

He held my gaze for a long time before bowing stiffly. "As you say, Your Highness."

Only after I begged him to stop hovering over me like an anxious mother did Pete finally go to work in the office on the transport the next morning. First he made me promise to rest as I'd been instructed.

"Yes, yes, Mom. I will. Besides, I can barely move. What do you think I'm going to do?"

"You?" Pete said. "I can't even begin to imagine. That's usually the problem."

He smiled at me, but left.

Jonathan stayed, of course.

"I mean it, you're not leaving. Don't even think about going behind my back and getting Pete to reassign you."

"I should be Resettled for putting you in that kind of danger." His voice was harsh and bitter.

"You're not allowed to make mistakes?"

"Not when it comes to your safety."

I rolled my eyes but gave up on getting anywhere with him on that point. "You think someone else could do better?"

He wouldn't meet my eye. "Yes."

I scoffed. "You're crazy."

"So are you, for insisting I stay."

"Why?" I said, swallowing hard. "Why are you so eager to leave? Is it me?"

He looked at me, intense. "I'm not good for you."

I frowned. "What?"

He looked away again, a sadness about his posture that he wouldn't normally have let anyone see, even me. "You should replace me." He turned back, staring at me with some strange expression on his face, as if he was begging me to understand. "I don't make you safe. I—" He dropped his head again. "You're not safe with me."

I was so taken aback by his raw certainty that it was a moment before I could speak. "You're too hard on yourself. It's not your fault."

He sighed. "You don't understand."

But no matter what I said, he wouldn't talk about it again.

I spent a long day in bed, but, with the effects of the inhibitor, I mostly just slept. Dr. Heinriksen came to examine me a few times but I was barely aware of her. When she came the next afternoon, I was very awake. Tired of sleeping.

"So, you've survived two assassination attempts in less than a year. That's impressive."

I shook my head, amused in spite of myself. "Is that a record? Do I get a plaque or something?"

She grinned at me. "Oh no. Only two? That's nothing. Look back a couple of hundred years and the daily life of the imperial rulers was much more exciting." She looked away, frowning in thought. "Though, now that you mention it, this may be a record after all, for the imperial spouse. Not the ruler, certainly, but the spouse isn't usually a target. Not separately, at least."

"Is that supposed to be reassuring?"

She chuckled but, finishing her examination, she sat back. "I'm going to turn the inhibitor off now." She'd dialed down the intensity the day before and it had been fine, but I could remember too well how it had felt when she'd turned it off that first day, and I tensed. She pretended not to see and with a quick brush of her fingers, the inhibitor left my skin. She flourished it in front of me, as if she'd produced it from the air like a magician.

"Were you scared?" she asked.

I huffed. "Yes, actually."

She smiled at me. "That's not a bad thing, sometimes," she said as she collected her things. "See to it that you stay properly scared, Jacob." Her face became abruptly serious. "It would be a shame to lose you next time."

I didn't sleep well that night. I felt fine, if weak, but I couldn't settle my head. Every time I tried to sleep, Dr. Heinriksen's warning sounded in my head, accompanied by vivid flashes of the memory of pain. They mingled in a sickening dance that jerked me back awake.

Pete was sleeping, though the unrestful play of expressions on his face made me think he wasn't enjoying what he found there. At least he was asleep. I didn't know whether nightmares were better asleep or awake and so I left him alone, just lay on my side, head propped up on my hand, watching him.

I loved him so fiercely that when I stopped to think about it, it took my breath away.

But Dr. Heinriksen's words kept coming back to me, and the stark seriousness with which she said them, her normal levity gone. Someone was trying to kill me. I was scared, but not for myself as much as I'd expected. I looked at Pete's face. It had stilled for the moment and was calm, peaceful. Beautiful. I stroked his cheek lightly.

"Should I leave?" I whispered. He didn't stir. "They'd probably leave you alone. If it were just me, I'd tell them all to go fuck themselves. But what would it do to you if they got me? Wouldn't it be easier if I just left? We've done that before." I remembered only too well the hollow despair of those years. "You'd handle it better, I think, if I left you, than if they killed me." I stroked his cheek again, trying to imagine a life without him. I couldn't picture it anymore. All I could see was the longing on his face there at the IIC, when I'd driven him away.

I watched him for a long time. He suddenly flinched, the lines of his face falling into grief, his hands clutching for something that wasn't there. I grabbed the near one and held it tight, watching until he settled again. I lay down, still holding his hand.

"I love you."

It was the next morning, as we lingered over coffee, that Jonathan announced a visitor.

"Sasha Popovich to see you, Your Excellence."

I nearly choked on my drink.

"Sasha Popovich?" I asked in disbelief. "To see Pete?"

"I believe that's what I said."

I couldn't remember the last time I'd been so astonished.

Pete gave me a look, but said to Jonathan, "Show him in."

Jonathan left the room and returned with Sasha behind him. Sasha bowed low to Pete, with a small twist of his body I assumed meant to include me. But once he straightened, no one spoke.

"I wouldn't try anything," I said.

"What?" He turned red and dropped his head, glaring at his shoes. "Your Highness?" he added in a choked grunt.

I don't know what I'd expected it to feel like, to have Sasha call me that, but it surprised me that there was no satisfaction in it. If anything, I felt ashamed.

"You were always good with the quick punch," I clarified. "But I wouldn't try anything with the emperor here. Besides, Jonathan's had some intense martial arts training."

He cast a glance back at Jonathan, who was ignoring us.

"I didn't come here to—I wouldn't attack you, Your Highness." He met Pete's eye with a flinch. His jaw was tight. "There's something I feel obligated to tell you, Your Excellence."

"Yes?" Pete said.

"I was notified in advance of Prince Jacob's arrival."

I frowned, confused.

"*You* were?"

He looked at me with a stiff turn of his head. "Yes. In the same way I was notified you were to be Resettled here after you left your Resettlement camp."

I felt the blood drain from my face.

"Who notified you?"

"I don't know. It was just a mail, with no trace data. And once I'd read it, it was deleted from my inbox remotely."

I knew. Cold anger churned in my gut. Who else but Blaine would make sure my Resettlement was as unpleasant as possible? He'd done it with the Resettlement camp I was sent to. Blaine had been behind the worst things that happened to me at Dead End. He'd as much as admitted it when he told me at the wedding that he knew about Kafe and— That he knew about Kafe. He'd probably been the one who chose Dead End for me.

"Why?" I pressed. "What did the message say?"

"The first time? That I was to make things difficult for you."

"Difficult?"

"He didn't name anything specific, but the meaning was clear."

"You didn't do a very good job."

"Your Highness?"

"Besides the scene in the dining hall the first day, you mostly left me alone."

"I would have kicked the shit out of you for hitting the emperor if things had gone differently." He cast a frightened look at Pete as if he'd forgotten he was there. Pete was watching us, but said nothing.

I couldn't help a quiet laugh. "I believe you. But the two years between?"

He looked down. "There were things I was behind that you didn't know about, and things I planned that never happened." He shrugged. "I'm not a hot tempered kid anymore. I won't say I didn't enjoy needling you that first day, but when Director Harris explained the consequences of continuing, well, it wasn't worth it to me."

"What things I didn't know about?"

His lips drew together but, with an effort, he answered.

"I made sure the stories going around about you were as bad as possible while still being plausible, and I told Dr. Bartel a few things that would make him guaranteed to hate you. I had the vid in your room programmed to show the replay of your sentencing and punishment every few channels, so you couldn't miss it. I tried keeping Kirti mad at you but it didn't last. I even tried to frame you a couple of times for serious infractions, but both times something got in the way." He flushed. "Honestly, I didn't turn out to be very good at the clandestine stuff. It's a good thing they paid me in advance."

"They paid you?"

He nodded.

"And this time?"

He looked away. "It was no more than a message telling me that you would be here, and that I should be ready in case I was given further instructions."

"No ID on this one either?"

He shook his head. "And it's already gone."

I bit my lips together, hard. I cast a look at Pete, but his expression was unreadable.

"Why are you telling us this? You always hated me."

"I still do." With a glance at Pete he added a quick, "Your Highness." I almost laughed.

"Then why did you come to tell him this?"

He stiffened. "I serve the Emperor. And you are...what you are." He turned to Pete, his face red. "I wouldn't question you or work against your interests, Your Excellence. And after what just happened..." he paled and looked back at me. "I never minded the thought of harassing you, making your life unpleasant, and I had no qualms about doing it when you were just a Reset sent back here. But I'm loyal to the empire. I would never be part of treason on that scale. Not even tangentially. I feel it's my duty to confess this, even if it means—" he stopped with a shudder, "bad things for me. I'm loyal to the empire above anything else."

Silence fell again.

"Thank you," Pete said, finally, "for volunteering this information. At this time I don't think any further action is necessary, and I do appreciate the fact that you did not act against Prince Jacob."

Sasha was pale but he nodded stiffly. "May the emperor live forever." At Pete's nod, he left.

I sat back in my chair. "Wow."

Pete was watching me, for my reaction I suppose but I didn't know what it was myself. I frowned.

"You're not surprised?" I said.

Pete shook his head. "No. I already knew about that."

Which shouldn't have surprised, me but it did.

"He was a decoy, though he probably hasn't realized it. As for the actual perpetrators, they've been identified already."

I felt a cold shock in my whole body, a warm rush of relief, and then the icy chill as I wondered if this was like the last time, if there was an illegal broadcast I'd missed. Pete shook his head as if answering the question I hadn't asked and laid his hand over mine.

"The shooter was caught in the woods, though she was already dead of self-administered poison before the guards laid hands on her. The next morning, two men were found dead of the same poison. One was a server in the dining room and the other was one of the guards who had gone into the woods with you."

"And you think that's all of them?"

"I won't rule out the possibility of more, and my investigators certainly haven't, but I think that was probably everyone involved in this attempt. We hadn't even identified the server before we found him. He had no indication he was in danger of being caught, yet he took the poison. I assume that was agreed procedure for this scenario, and that anyone else involved would have done the same thing."

"Thus you don't suspect Sasha."

"That and other reasons. He's too obvious, for one, and we had him under close surveillance. Like I said, I already knew about the mail. But like all the others we've tracked down so far, we can't figure out the source. The trail always snuffs out at some point, as if those mails wrote and sent themselves. None of Sasha's other patterns or correspondence matched the ones we've put together from the four perpetrators we know so far."

I couldn't help but chuckle. Pete gave me a puzzled look.

"You know, I'm actually glad to hear Sasha had nothing to do with it. I think I'd miss him if he were executed."

# CE 11

Now that someone had tried to kill me here too, the feeling of the IIC as a sanctuary was shattered. The way Pete looked at me when we spoke of returning to the palace made me suspect he knew how much of a blow it had been for me, having the IIC violated in that way. I could accept that someone would try to kill me at the palace. But here?

For the short term, it didn't matter so much, because I wasn't willing to part from Pete again. I'd missed him more than I expected to, and I'd expected to miss him a lot And it was a relief to have a reason to want to leave the IIC. I didn't have to leave because my enemies had driven me out. I was choosing to go. We returned to the palace, together.

Chuck and Kirti came with us. It had been Pete's idea, and I was grateful for it. It was a way of bringing the IIC with me. I think he was mostly trying to placate me and have a buffer in place when he told me how much things were going to change for me now. He was right to be worried. When I saw all the new security measures being enacted, I was stunned. Then angry. Not at Pete so much, but at those who had made it necessary.

"You can't be serious!" I spluttered. "These aren't reasonable restrictions. You're just trying to wrap me in a cocoon because you're afraid."

"Of course I am! Two attempts on your life, Jake. Two! How am I supposed to *not* be scared?"

The security at the palace became so tight after that you could almost feel it. I had become used to seeing any one of hundreds of palace employees on any given day, but now the faces became predictable. Part of that was how restricted my movements had become. Before, I had only needed extra security if I left the palace itself. Now it was required if I left the nobles' section at all. Arranging to actually go outside the palace took so long it wasn't worth it anymore. One day, in one fell swoop, all of the common palace employees were simply replaced. I heard about it from Jonathan because it hadn't impacted the servants and functionaries who had been cleared to interact with me since the IIC. I made Pete promise me that they'd all gotten good positions elsewhere and he assured me no one had been penalized unless there had been reason to suspect them.

The only thing that made the perimeter I'd been assigned bearable was my new lab.

My old lab had been a total loss. Not unexpected when a bomb is involved. Though it presumably had been aimed at me rather than the lab itself, it did a thorough job of obliterating the one, if not the other.

That lab had been in the north section of the palace. It was the same one that had been set up for me long ago, among similar facilities, when I had come to the palace as a scientist-in-residence and nothing more. Pete had spoken of moving me closer to the Imperial Family section, somewhere more secure, but I'd never agreed. Now I didn't get a choice.

The Imperial section of the nobles' area was a sacred space, and not open to renovation for so plebeian a use. But there was a great deal of open space around the Imperial area itself that was still contained within the palace walls. So a separate building was constructed.

I think Pete had as much fun planning the design as I did. He threw in wholly unnecessary things, including an observatory on the second level that any astronomer would have given his best eye for. I pointed out to him the difference between astronomy and physics but he just grinned at me and ignored my objections.

The eventual result was no less than stunning, though only parts of it were finished when we got back from the IIC. Even still, it topped the lab Pete had commissioned on his ship by almost ten years, and more levels of social rank than actually existed.

Chuck and Kirti explored it with all the approval and glee that only a scientist from the IIC can have for such a place. They argued good-naturedly over which parts of the space not specifically set up for physics they would claim and I watched them with a smile as much in my heart as on my face.

Until I saw Kirti rest her hand on the small of Chuck's back. And him flash her a quick but private grin. Suddenly it all clicked into place for me, the subtle signs I'd been picking up at the IIC, things I'd noticed but dismissed. I felt stupid for not noticing, and angry with myself for caring now that I had.

It didn't stop my brooding, though. That night, I went to see Chuck alone.

"So is there something between you and Kirti?" I blurted.

He grinned. "Sometimes. I think."

"You think?"

"You know how she is," he said. "Hard to pin down."

I had no right to feel jealous, I didn't. What had happened between Kirti and me had been long ago, and I was the one who told her we were wrong to try to make anything of what had passed between us—that we were only friends, and shouldn't pretend it was more than that. Even when we'd found each other's beds again during my exile, there had been a clear understanding that it was nothing more than companionship and sex. My heart belonged to Pete and she didn't begrudge him that, not even when he came back to claim it.

Chuck smacked me upside the head, startling me out of my thoughts.

"Stop that. You're fine with it if you stop overthinking it."

I stared at him, wide-eyed.

He laughed. "Now snap out of it or I'll start comparing notes on how she is in bed."

I snapped out of it.

# CE 12

**O**n the first morning we were back at the palace, I took Chuck and Kirti on a tour of some of places they hadn't seen. We were in the area between the nobles' and the Imperial section, which housed, among other things, Pete's office and private council chambers. One of my favorite gardens was there.

As I turned into the hallway, I caught sight of Blaine entering the council chambers.

That he was still on Pete's council bothered me more than I could admit to anyone. I could have asked Pete to remove him, and he probably would have, once I told him the reasons. But I'd never told Pete about Blaine's threats at the wedding, never even told Pete I was sure Blaine was the ultimate mastermind behind all the attacks on me. I couldn't. There was no way I could explain this to Pete without him finding out the things Blaine knew about what happened on Dead End. I didn't want anyone to know about that, about her, ever. Even Pete. Especially Pete.

When I was caught off guard, encountering Blaine could still make me flush with anger and humiliation. So seeing him and the others entering the council chambers drew me like a polarized particle.

"Your Highness?" Jonathan asked, as my trajectory turned away from the garden and straight toward the chamber doors.

"Change of plans."

"What is it, Jake?" Kirti said.

I turned to her and Chuck.

"I'm sorry, but there's something I need to take care of. I'll meet you later?"

They both nodded, Kirti frowning with concern, Chuck blithely accepting the change, and they turned back the way we had come.

The doors were closed when I approached and, rather than opening them for me, the guards to the chambers moved unobtrusively, but pointedly, into my path.

"Can I help you with something, Your Highness?" the senior guard asked.

"I'm sitting in on the council meeting this morning," I said.

They exchanged troubled glances with each other and then with my own guards.

"We've gotten no notification of this, Your Highness."

"Probably wasn't important enough to mention," I said, looking meaningfully at the door.

The one who had been speaking colored, but held firm.

"I'm sorry, Your Highness, but I have orders not to allow anyone but the emperor and the council members in this door."

"'The Prince Consort is hardly 'anyone,'" Jonathan interjected.

The guard gave Jonathan a look he wouldn't have dared try with me. "I am well aware of that, but I have my orders."

"I'm sure this matter can be easily cleared up," Jonathan said. "You can check with His Excellence to see if his husband, His Imperial Highness the Prince Consort, is allowed admittance into the room with the emperor and his noble advisers."

I sort of hated Jonathan throwing around all that rank and importance nonsense, but I had to admit, it was effective. The guard mumbled his excuses and ducked into the council room. He returned, moments later, even redder, and held the door open, gesturing respectfully for me to enter.

Several separate conversations were happening around the table, but when I entered, Pete stood, and therefore the rest fell silent and stood as well, most of them with sour looks on their faces. As much as I hated being treated like royalty, I could at least take petty pleasure in the fact that they hated having to treat me that way.

Pete met me halfway across the room.

"Did you need me?" he said in an intimate undertone. His hand settled on my arm. His eyes were filled with questions.

"I'm fine," I said, squeezing his hand. "I just wanted to sit in and listen this morning, if that's OK."

His expression was puzzled. "Of course. If you want."

I smiled for him and his answering look of relief was like the sun coming out. Sometimes it still shocked me to see such unexpected proof of how much he worried about me, how much he loved me.

Jonathan had already prepared a place for me to sit in the corner. It reminded me again of how Jonathan was one of the very few things that made the palace endurable. He didn't need to be told that I didn't want to sit anywhere near the rest of the council, much less at the table with them.

I settled into the chair set up for me and the council proceeded as if I'd never come in.

It was as boring as I'd imagined those things to be, but I didn't consider leaving. I'd come there for a reason, even if I wasn't entirely sure what that was. But I meant for them to see me, to know I was there, listening. I meant for Blaine to know I was there and there wasn't a damn thing he could do about it.

But then Blaine requested permission to bring up a new matter and was granted it.

"Your Excellency," he said, "I'd like to ask for the position of Minister of Social Administration." He nodded to the elderly lord down the table, "I mean no disrespect to or criticism of Duke Shanks. In fact, I discussed this with him before bringing the proposal to you. He agrees that our different talents would better suit an exchange of our current positions."

"I'm old," Duke Shanks said. "Minister of Culture would suit me better than all this unrest going on now. It needs someone younger and more forward thinking than me."

Pete examined Blaine.

"And why would you want Social Administration?"

"I would think that is obvious, Your Excellency. Recent events that concern all of us," he glanced at me. "The continuing unrest among the unclass that needs to be addressed decisively and stopped before it becomes dangerous to the empire as a whole. It's not something we should ignore. You need a minister overseeing that area who can be more useful to you in vigorously rooting out the troublemakers and stopping it."

"Wait, what unrest?" I said. "I thought Bhadrangi and Liangsitu had been handled."

Pete looked uncomfortable. "There was a more recent incident, in Tonga on Valcan."

"Why didn't I know about that?"

"I think you were unconscious at the time," Pete said, both a warning and a promise in his tone. He held my eyes, and I read *I'll tell you later* in them. I shut my mouth, but when I turned back to the rest of the council, Blaine was looking at me.

I glared at him. "You can't be suggesting that the unclass are behind the attempt on my life?"

Blaine spoke to Pete as if he were the one who had asked the question. "No, I'm not, Your Excellence, though there's still no proof one way or another, which is an entirely different area of concern. But we do know that the unclass are agitating all over the empire. Twice now, their unrest has attracted the attention of the other classes and the news outlets. According to the reports we're all reading, the ISS is just barely preventing the same in dozens of other slums across the empire." I snapped another look at Pete, feeling betrayed even though I knew that was unreasonable. He didn't look at me.

Blaine continued, "The simple fact is that Prince Jacob's place in the Imperial Family is an unprecedented inclusion of the unclass where they are not permitted to be. By law."

"You forget yourself, Duke Blaine," Pete cut in, coldly. "If I've done something, by definition it is lawful. But that's not the point. Jake was made a member of the nobility before the engagement was even announced. As such he was most certainly eligible to join the Imperial Family."

"I wouldn't contradict you, Your Excellence, and of course you're right. But it has to be acknowledged that the law stipulates that class restrictions are primarily decided by the individual's class at birth. *We* understand that you have made a one-time exception, but the mentality of the lowest class is so simple. I'm afraid such subtleties are lost on them. The unclass are far too numerous for the empire to withstand misunderstandings among the masses at large."

Pete and Blaine locked gazes and were silent for several tense moments.

"You make a good point," Pete said. I managed to keep my mouth from falling open. "Thank you, Duke Blaine, I'll consider your request."

I bit my tongue so hard I tasted blood, but I managed to say nothing. Blaine didn't look at me.

When the meeting was adjourned and the council dispersed, I waited behind.

"Why didn't I know about this?"

Pete gave me an incredulous look. "You think I was going to tell you anything like this while you were recovering from the second attempt on your life? You didn't need anything else to worry about, and I certainly wasn't going to make it any harder on the rest of us to keep you in bed." He sighed. "Besides, Blaine was also talking about incidents that aren't in the public reports but that were reported to the council. There is a lot of general unrest among the unclass all over the empire. The earliest indicators date back to shortly after our engagement was announced, but a distinct and problematic pattern only emerged after the first attempt on your life. And we can't quell it. Every time I put my foot down in one place, a dozen more are on the verge of rioting."

"I want to know more."

"I know. You will. I'll make sure you get the reports. I don't usually try to keep you uninformed, Jake. But forgive me a little caution right now?"

His smile was weak and the new lines around his eyes crinkled. I didn't want to be angry with him, but I *was* angry. Pete knew this was important to me. Blaine knew enough officially to try to get his hands in it officially, and yet I was told nothing. For that matter, how did Kirti not know about at least the public side of this? She was way too good at what she did not to be monitoring every whisper about the unclass and accounting for it.

I drew breath to say something, to demand he stop hiding things from me, but one look at the worry on Pete's face and I snapped my mouth shut and dropped my gaze, suddenly very aware of all the things I was hiding from him.

I almost ran into the Grand Duchess Aliana, Pete's cousin and heir, in my eagerness to be out of the council chambers. She gave me a wide-eyed look of astonishment before her brows drew down, taking in where I'd just been.

"Why were you in there?" she asked, with her usual bluntness.

"Just trying to keep abreast of current events and imperial policy," I said.

Her eyes narrowed.

"Unlikely. What were you really doing in there, Jacob Dawes?"

I couldn't help but grin. "Why don't you ever believe what I say?"

She looked at me for a moment, considering. "I would say it is because I know you too well, but in truth, it is because you are a terrible liar."

I frowned. "I am not."

"On the contrary, my friend. It is something you must learn to do better."

I didn't have an answer to that. She didn't seem to need one.

"I have been looking for you," she said. "No wonder I could not find you—the council chamber is a place I would never have looked."

"You have servants, don't you?"

"Of course. Do you sit at home and allow your servants to

do everything for you? I think not." She took my arm in what appeared to be an old fashioned courtly gesture. But when she did it, it felt less like she was offering me the honor of escorting her, and more like she was intent on steering us both, and her grip on my arm was a convenient tool.

"I would speak to you," she said, turning us toward her rooms. She brought me to a courtyard that opened off of her sitting room and gestured for me to sit at a table that was already set with chilled drinks and fruits cut into intricate shapes.

"You are truly recovered?" she asked.

"Yes, I promise, I'm feeling much better. And Dr. Heinriksen says I have nothing to worry about. So you aren't allowed to worry either."

Her smile wasn't as genuine as I would have hoped.

"There is always worry, my friend. But this I will not concern myself with any more." She nodded to herself as if to close the matter. "However, it gives me reason to speak to you of other concerns."

"And those are?"

"You must have a child, Jacob."

I laughed, though it was forced. "I'm not sure I want to get pregnant yet. It would ruin my figure."

She scowled at me. "We will not joke of these things. It is a serious conversation."

"It's hasn't been a year yet, Aliana, and I've spent a lot of that time recovering from one attempt on my life or another. I don't get any more time than that?"

"It has been almost eight months. And no, you do not. There must be an heir."

"We have you."

She shook her head. "It is not good enough anymore. The emperor has married. He must have an heir of his own."

I grimaced. "I'd hoped we'd get more time."

"And why should you wait? A child will not inconvenience you, if you do not wish for it to."

Now I scowled at her. "Is that how you would see your own child? An inconvenience?"

76

"I would not. But I am not you."

I stood, needing to do something with the building frustration and fear.

"Is that really what you think of me?"

"Stop these dramatics, Jacob, and tell me what it is that worries you so. Do you think I do not see you go pale at the mere mention of a child. I would understand why this frightens you, if we are to speak productively. You are not a stupid man. You would have known this would be your duty."

I sank back into my chair with a sigh. "Of course I knew. But I'm scared."

I looked away.

"My childhood was..." I glanced at her. Her face had gone impassive again, waiting. I hated talking about him, to anyone. Maybe especially people like Aliana, whose good opinion I actually cared about. I sighed. "My childhood was pure hell for a lot of reasons, but the biggest one was my father. He was a drunk who got his entertainment from beating up whichever of us wasn't fast enough to get away." Her brows drew down in concern but she said nothing. "I'm just...it sounds so stupid, but I worry that maybe I can't be a good father. He was a horrible father, so I will be too."

She gave me a small smile. "You are perhaps not stupid, but you are a fool. Your life is very different than his was. What he was means nothing. Your concerns alone on this matter prove that you will be a better father than he was."

"That's not exactly much to aspire to."

She ignored the interruption. "You must also realize that it will not be permitted for the emperor's children to have less than the best. Even if you could make me believe that you would fail them as a father, there are too many people who would see to it that the child felt no loss."

"Bullshit. Pete's father ignored him. He definitely felt that."

"And yet he was not abandoned or ignored as any other child might have been. Look at the man he became. Would you have him different? He may have felt the loss of a father's love, but he did not suffer for it."

"That's not good enough for me, to be able to say at least my child didn't suffer. I want more for them than that."

She smiled. "Which is why they will have it. Do not allow yourself to fear this, Jacob Dawes. Be mindful, be cautious, be prepared. But, no matter what, this is something you must do. You know we travel to Torrea soon, for the marriage of Duke Blaine to my cousin?"

I nodded, hating it.

"Duke Blaine is very aware of the power of having an heir. He will not wait in this, Jacob. So you must act now."

"I'll think about it," I said.

"You will do more than think," she gave me a wry look, "or we will have this conversation again. That one will more closely resemble a conversation we had some years ago about acceptable dinner conversation."

Quite unexpectedly, I laughed.

Jonathan had waited in the hallway for me, but he wasn't alone when I found him.

"No," Jonathan said, shaking his head emphatically at Blaine, ignoring the man's grip on his arm.

"Duke Blaine, remove your hand at once," I said, my voice tight.

Both men startled, identical flushes coloring their faces before Blaine's expression went hard and cold. He stepped back a pace.

"I see," he said to Jonathan, as if I wasn't there. "I was mistaken, then."

Without another word, he walked away. I stalked over to Jonathan.

"What was he trying to do?" I demanded.

"It was nothing, Your Highness. A misunderstanding."

"He had his hands on you," I said. "I won't let him get away with that. Did he hurt you?"

Jonathan laid a hand on my arm. "Prince Jacob," he pressed

until I was forced to stop and listen. "It was nothing. I know what you think you saw. But not everything is what it appears."

I frowned at him. "You're not trying to protect him, are you?"

"That's not what I mean."

"What do you mean, then?"

He gave me a long look, some conflict warring behind his calm features.

"I mean you shouldn't trust everything you believe," he said, his voice tired. "Sometimes you're wrong."

I found Chuck and Kirti in the lab. She had her hand on his.

"Hey!" Chuck said when he caught sight of me. "You're back. So what was that all about earlier?"

Thrown a little by their closeness, and my irrational jealousy, it took me a minute to remember which "that" he was asking about.

"Oh. Nothing. I forgot Pete had a council session today that I was supposed to go to."

Chuck's brow furrowed. "You go to those things?"

I shrugged, turning to fiddle with a new radiometer on the table so that I wouldn't have to look at him. "Sometimes."

There was no reply. When I looked up, Kirti carefully wasn't looking at me, but Chuck was staring at me, hurt written on his face.

"You don't have to lie to *us* you know. We're on your side. Since the beginning. Before your Pete, even."

"I'm sorry," I said, quietly. But what Chuck didn't understand was that it wasn't just them. I lied to Pete too.

# $\text{CE}13$

**W**hat was that about anyway, you coming to the council today?" Pete asked as we undressed that evening.

I shrugged. "I have no idea, I must have been out of my head. At least one good thing came out of it. I proved to myself those things are just as boring as I thought they would be."

He gave me a soft smile. "You mean you won't be coming back? I kind of enjoyed having you there."

I looked away, uncomfortable and not wanting him to misread it. "I didn't say I wouldn't come again. Just that I'll hate it when I do."

He stepped close and touched my shoulder.

"I didn't mean it like that. If you don't like them, don't come."

I shook my head. "I know. I'm just saying that I might need to come from time to time, you know, to check up on things." I paused, not wanting to say it. "To keep tabs on Blaine and what he's up to."

Pete made a snort of amusement.

"You can't seriously be considering giving the unclass over to Blaine? He hates them," I said.

Pete's brow furrowed. "What makes you think that?"

I gaped. "How can I *not* think that? Haven't you heard anything he's ever said about me? About them?"

Pete shook his head. "There's a difference, Jake, between not wanting an unclass married to the emperor and hating the unclass as a whole."

"He called them simple, said they couldn't understand subtleties and needed a firm hand."

Pete sighed. "It sounds bad the way he said it, but there's some truth to it." I opened my mouth to protest, but he held up a hand. "Let me finish. I don't mean the unclass alone. When you're dealing with any large group of people, you do have to break problems down into their simplest elements, and make changes and policy that are easy to explain to the majority. The larger the group, the more important that is. And the fact remains, Jake, that not only are the unclass the biggest single group in the empire, they're also the least educated and informed. Subtleties are difficult to sell on an individual level. Trying to approach the unclass that way would be worse than useless, it could make things worse."

"He doesn't care anything about them."

Pete grimaced. "I know. But he cares about the status quo, and whether he likes it or not, quelling the unrest among the unclass right now can't be done only with force. He'll have to address their most pressing problems just because it's necessary. Whether the impetus is concern for them or not, the end result is the same."

"He'll try to use force first."

"Maybe he will. Maybe he needs someone appointed to work along with him who actually does care about the unclass, and who can bring a compassionate point of view to his more authoritarian one."

I snorted. "Good luck finding that guy."

"I already have."

I blinked in astonishment. "Who?"

He slid closer to me, running his hand up my chest.

"You, of course."

I took an involuntary step back.

"I'm not a politician, Pete."

"No, but you have an educated perspective and the right motivations. And you're already working on it in Abenez. You know anyone better?"

"You want me to work with Blaine?"

"I'd like for you to."

"Do you think there's any universe in which that wouldn't be a complete disaster? He hates me, and believe me, the feeling is mutual. You know his favorite solution to the unclass problem would be to send me back to Abenez. Preferably in an urn."

Pete slid into the bed, holding the covers up as an invitation to me. I got in beside him, turning down the light.

"Why are you wearing so many clothes?" I said.

"Because it's winter and it's cold."

"These are the imperial apartments. It's never anything but perfect in here. Besides, what do you think I'm for?" I started working the buttons of his shirt and he lay back, surrendering with a leer.

I pulled his shirt away and tossed it to the floor, avoiding his eyes.

He put his arms around me. "Think about it?"

His hands slid down my back.

"This is coercion," I said.

"I know. Is it working?"

I laughed, but my stomach was tight.

"So you're not worried about him?" Trying very hard to sound casual, I said, "He'd get rid of me if he could."

Pete came up on one elbow and considered me. "Jake, I take your safety more seriously than almost anything. I know you've noticed. You've been grumbling about it a lot lately." He softened the remark with a smile. "But I think you're worrying about something that looks scarier than it is."

I frowned, not wanting to argue in case he asked for proof of my assertions, but not wanting to give up, either.

"Blaine doesn't like you, that's not news. He especially doesn't like seeing the established order of things messed with, because that established order is what makes him one of the most important men in the empire. It makes him go cross-eyed that you've gotten where you are. But you *are* here. That's why I married you," he smiled and leaned in for a long kiss. "That and because I love you. But what I mean is, the legal marriage and your patent of nobility and the vows and traditions that bound you as a Prince of the Realm help me protect you. You outrank him now, but more important than that, you're legally bound there. No one in the empire has authority over you now, other than me. He literally can't remove you without taking me out, too. Blaine's ambitious, but he's not suicidal. I've made you safe from the political schemers, at least." He pulled me in so that he was spooned against my back. "As safe as I can, and that's a lot."

"But what if it's not just political scheming? I mean, maybe he agrees with this Patriot." I didn't mention that I thought he was the Patriot, or at least the Patriot's backer. "Maybe he realizes that the manipulation angle didn't work well enough last time and he's willing to go further. Something more permanent."

Pete sat up and looked at me, astonishment clear on his face in the uncertain light. "You think he's behind the attempts to kill you?"

The complete surprise made me angry. "You mean you haven't even considered that?"

He was quiet for a minute. "I have. I have been watching him, just because of this constant pissing contest you and he have going on. But, really, the idea's absurd."

I sat forward, agitated.

"Why is it absurd? He's said in your presence almost the same things that broadcast said."

"I know," he said. "But you said it yourself, it was in my presence. It's sly and petty, but it's all but proof that he had no intention of making—and never would make—those statements in a way that would be considered treason. It would be asking to be beheaded. Besides, he stands to lose more than anyone if he were caught in treason like that, and there's almost nothing he could gain."

"My removal," I said.

"Yes, and by itself, that might be compelling, but he can't get rid of you without bringing down the whole system. It's that system that makes him what he is, and he's the most staunch defender of it. The kind of person who would put out a message like that, who would try to kill you, has more of a theoretical gain and less of a knowledge of what it would mean if he were to accomplish it. When the people behind this are caught, they'll be executed and everything they have would be forfeit to the crown. For a noble, that would include all his titles, everything. He'd not only die as a traitor, he'd have his legacy wiped out. And to do what? Piss you off? Or destroy everything he's supposedly defending and that he benefits from more than almost anyone?" He let out a frustrated sigh. "No way. There's just no way Blaine is involved."

"What would happen if you knew he was?"

"If I knew, I'd have him executed."

"And if you just suspected?"

He paused.

"Because it's Blaine," I said, "it would be different, wouldn't it? You'd have a lot fewer options. You couldn't just execute him and tell everyone who didn't like it to shove it."

"Well of course I *could*. But you're right that I wouldn't."

"Because it would be too dangerous to you."

"It would be dangerous to everyone. It could cause all sorts of rebellion and instability at the highest levels."

"So he might die, but you'd lose, too."

Pete shook his head in annoyance. "No, no. I mean, yes, it would be a nightmare, but there are far too many ways it could fall out, from a short and painful but relatively simple mess to a full-out civil war. It's too complex. It's all too grand-scale and unpredictable with so little payoff. It doesn't make sense."

"Maybe he doesn't need it to."

Pete examined my face, genuine puzzlement creasing his brow.

"Where is this coming from? Why are you so certain it's Blaine all of a sudden?"

I bit my lips together and tried not to look guilty. "It's not sudden."

"And yet you haven't brought him up until now."

"Because this is something you can see. He's scheming and he's doing it right there on the council and asking you to help him. Don't, please."

"Jake—" He stopped, staring at me intently as if he could see into my head and make sense of what I was saying. "I don't—"

"Never mind," I interrupted. "You're right, I don't know where this is coming from. I guess he just surprised me today."

Pete wrapped his arms around me. "Sweetheart, if you have anything to say, you know I'll hear you out, and I'll listen and do my best to understand. Maybe you know something I don't." I managed not to squirm when he said that. "Why don't you come to my office tomorrow and we can really talk about this?"

I tried to relax against him, so he wouldn't think I didn't believe him. Because I wanted to. But there were things he didn't know—that I couldn't tell him.

"No, I'm being silly. You're right, it's nonsensical, I'm tired and not making any sense."

Pete brushed my hair out of my face.

"I love you," he said.

Then I felt his hand somewhere else, and Blaine ceased to matter altogether.

Blaine was made Minister of Social Administration. Pete announced it first to the closed council, a session he'd asked me to attend. Blaine nodded a gracious acceptance.

"Thank you for your faith in me, Your Excellence."

Pete inclined his head in acknowledgment. "I'm confident you'll do your best and do well, Duke Blaine," he said, "and to help you do that, I've appointed Prince Jacob to work with you in an advisory position. I know you'll appreciate and benefit from his unique insights into the unclass."

The silence in the room was palpable. Blaine looked stunned.

"You are wise as always, Your Excellence. I would not have considered such an—" he hesitated, "asset. Thank you."

"I'm sure your differences will complement each other, rather than hinder you from working effectively together."

I suppressed a snort with effort.

"I'm sure you're right, Your Excellency," Blaine replied, in a tone that said he was sure of nothing of the kind.

I lingered in the chambers as the ministers filed out. I meant to leave with Pete, but Blaine was hanging back as well, probably with the same goal. Pete preempted us both.

"I'll leave you two to discuss the new appointments," Pete said, with a smile and a nod, and made his way out before either of us could protest. Blaine and I regarded each other in silence for a long time.

"It wasn't my idea," I said.

Blaine snorted, which may have meant "I doubt it" or "I don't care." I didn't ask.

"I think it's important to make clear that an advisory role has no authority and, quite frankly, I don't care what you think. We can save ourselves time and frustration if we establish that now."

"Can we? Saving you time and frustration, Duke Blaine, isn't something I'm particularly interested in doing."

"Do you really want to give me even more incentive to follow through on what we talked about at your wedding?"

My breath caught in my throat. "You're really stupid if you think anything is the same as it was back then, or that you can threaten me like that now. Do you really think the emperor will let you get away with it?"

"Oh, I don't think I have much to worry about on that score. If for no other reason than that he knows nothing about this, does he?"

"He knows everything."

There wasn't even a flicker of doubt on Blaine's face. "So you've asked him to save you from the big bad bully who scares you? We both know that's a lie."

My fists clenched. "Even if it were, which it isn't, I don't need Pete's help. I can handle you all by myself."

He cocked an amused eyebrow. "So your stay in that Resettlement camp was just part of your plan? Is that how you *handled* it last time?"

I felt the blood drain from my face. It pooled with a sick slosh in my stomach.

He put his mouth so close to my ear I flinched, and for a moment I was afraid he was going to kiss my cheek.

"She told me you were easy," he whispered. I recoiled, sick and dizzy. "She said that once you didn't have a protector to run to, you were weak. A coward."

Shame and grief and hatred washed over me in a disorienting rush. "I—"

"You were easy to get rid of last time."

I dug my fingernails into my palms and willed myself to stay upright. "I'm back, aren't I?" My voice betrayed me with a mortifying hoarseness.

He moved past me, too close, and I couldn't help but move out of his way. I thought of punching him in the back of his arrogant head.

"You're back," his voice drifted behind him. "But not for long."

I stormed back to my room, kicking over a chair in the sitting room. Jonathan stood nearby, silent.

"You know what?" I said, rounding on him. "He's not the only one who can play these games." Jonathan's eyebrows went up.

"Have an encounter with Duke Blaine, Your Highness?" It didn't surprise me that he knew exactly who I was talking about.

"I can kick his ass any way he likes."

Jonathan stared at me, wide eyed. "No. You can't."

It was my turn to stare. "Umm, what?"

"You can't play his game. You're completely wrong for it. You couldn't be subtle if your life depended on it."

"Oh, come on. Like he's so subtle."

He frowned in thought. "Not to you, perhaps, but he can be. When you two clashed before, he wasn't. He didn't have to be. He was one of the most powerful, richest men in the empire and he knew how to throw his weight around. But this man has been playing politics from his cradle. You have no idea how connected and involved he is; what he knows and what he can make happen."

I scoffed.

Jonathan shook his head. "Have you considered the role he might have played in your banishment? How convenient it was that the things Blaine knew would be damning in that specific conversation?"

I felt like he'd punched me.

"Yes! That's what I've been saying for years, but you've never agreed with me."

"I've never disagreed either. I might have focused more on your own contribution to that disaster, for obvious reasons."

"But don't you see, he manipulated me into a situation I couldn't win. He was going to get me banished, one way or another."

"He didn't force you to punch the emperor."

"You know," I said, breathless, "I really wish you wouldn't talk about that."

"Which is why we should. You cannot play Blaine's game against him. You prefer an ostrich approach to problems, which only works when you bury the rest of you as well. You certainly can't plot and scheme with your head in the sand and expect it to be anything but a disaster. You can't engage him in this."

"Well I'm not going to sit back and let him do whatever he wants, laughing about it while I act like his kicked dog."

"You could try talking to the emperor. Your husband."

I grimaced. "No. I mean, I have."

"You could try again."

"No, that's not what I need to do right now."

Jonathan stared at me. "Don't you trust him?"

Sometimes I almost forgot that Jonathan and I weren't one person. He worked so hard to fade into the background that he'd become incorporated into my experience of life, an extension of me. As he stood there talking about the things I tried very hard to hide from myself, I suddenly hated him. "Of course I trust him. I trust him to do whatever he can to protect me and defend me. The problem is that his view of the situation and his idea of how to handle it are very different from mine. This is a stupid water gun fight. I'm not calling in the ISS. Besides, I can handle myself. Blaine's just a bully, and I know how to handle bullies."

From the look on Jonathan's face, if he had been anyone else, his mouth would have fallen open.

"Your Highness, if you can compare engaging Blaine in the game of politics to a water gun fight then you have made my point. You have no idea what you're doing. He would eviscerate you. He wants to get rid of you. Was that so pleasant last time he succeeded that you'd like for him to do it again? He's not going to stop at Resettlement this time."

"How do you know so much about him?"

His face went blank in a way that, for a moment, almost scared me. Then he said, in a flat, even tone, "No one knows the powerful better than the servants. Not even the other powerful people. That's why, other than the ISS, we're the only ones who can be executed just for telling our employer's secrets."

My mouth fell open. "You can be *what*?"

Stark fury crossed his face. "This is exactly what I mean about you having no business playing his game. How can you have been with the emperor this long and *not know that*? Do you mean you've let me see your deepest, darkest secrets and you just *trusted* that I'd keep them?"

"I don't—Of course I trust you. What are you talking about?"

He looked like he wanted to pull his hair out. "No wonder—" he mumbled, glaring at the floor. He locked eyes with me. "If a servant is convicted of telling his employer's secrets, he's not fired or Resettled, he is executed. It's why we're allowed in your bedrooms and to stand attendance while you share confidences. You don't have to trust our conscience or our loyalty. You know that if we don't keep your secrets, we die." I blinked. "Stars and planets and all the space in the heavens, how you're not dead already must be one of the greatest mysteries of the universe."

My face was hot. I turned away from him, embarrassed and angry but not at all ready to concede my point.

"OK. So I don't know some things I need to know."

He scoffed.

"But that's why I asked for your help. You know all the things I don't. You can help me plan this and not screw it up."

He threw up his hands. "How you can be so smart and so stupid at the same time?"

In spite of myself, I laughed. "Aliana says my brain is so full of physics that there's no room for thinking."

He huffed a reluctant laugh. "The Grand Duchess is wise." He turned to me. "Talk to her. If you won't confide in the emperor, seek her advice. She knows these games better than anyone."

I shook my head. "She'll just tell Pete."

I think he was gritting his teeth. "Then why won't *you* tell him?"

There was no good reason, and there were a million good reasons not to, and there was one, very, very big reason that crowded out all the others. But I wasn't going to talk about that. Not with anyone at all.

His jaw locked, his arms crossed, and he turned his back to me. He stood there, silent and rigid until, finally, he relaxed his stance with deliberation, but, without looking at or acknowledging me, he righted the chair I had kicked over and then started to tidy up an already tidy room as if I wasn't even there. I watched him, angry and hurting.

"Are you mad at me, Jonathan?" I asked at last.

He froze. Then resumed his pointless cleaning. "Yes."

"Look, I'm doing the best I can."

"No, you're not."

My jaw clenched. "OK, I'm doing the best with what I know."

"Prince Jacob," he said, which was the closest he ever came to calling me by name, "your best isn't good enough. And that frightens me."

I went to find Chuck and Kirti in the lab. I needed to clear my head. I felt like Jonathan had taken a sledgehammer to it, and I wasn't entirely sure I didn't deserve it.

"Hey!" Chuck said when I entered. "You'll never guess. Your friend Blaine asked Kirti and me to give a presentation on some of the new scientific advances the IIC's cooked up. Unbelievable, right?"

I just stared at him.

"Blaine, as in Duke Blaine the one you know hates me?"

Chuck snorted a laugh. "Yeah, that one. I couldn't believe it when he came here."

"You're not going to do it, are you?"

Chuck's face fell. "Why wouldn't we?"

Kirti piped up, "It hardly matters who asked us, Jake. It's an open presentation to any nobles who want to attend. In fact, he's asked us to do one in your lab aboard the emperor's ship on the way to Torrea."

"We didn't know about that. We're not going to Torrea, are we?"

It took me a moment to gather my thoughts. Blaine was arranging for presentations on scientific advances at the palace, and in *my* lab on Pete's ship? "I would love for you to come with us," I said. "But this thing with Blaine bothers me. That's why he's doing it, he wants to irk me by sticking his nose into my area of expertise."

Kirti frowned. "I was flattered he asked, Jake. Not everything's about you, you know. Besides," she said, turning back to her work. "It's not as if you've ever asked us."

That knocked the wind right out of me. Chuck gave me a sympathetic grin.

"If it bothers you, we won't do it, right Kirti?"

She hesitated a bit too long with her answer. "Of course."

It hit me how little my friends got to do this sort of thing. They were never outside of a group who knew the subject as well as they did. I felt small and petty. "No, that's not what I meant. It's fine. I'm sure you'll do great."

So Blaine wanted to make sure I wasn't needed anywhere for anything? Well, it was a good thing I didn't need him. I read through all the reports the council had been getting on the growing unrest among the unclass. The pattern of escalation was clear, and they cited real and longstanding problems. Hunger, lack of food, shelter, sanitary conditions, medical care, work.

I had a head start on him. I pulled up Kirti's files and set to work.

Much of the problem lay in the sorts of things local government needed to address: lack of distribution channels, rampant unemployment, and crime. Sanitation, food supply, medical care were problems for engineers, biologists, and doctors.

When I found mention of the higher than normal casualty rate in the Tonga slum due to a harsh winter, I got an idea of what I could do. Tonga's location presented challenges in providing the residents with reliable and sufficient power. These problems were annoying but not insurmountable. They would have been given proper time and attention if it had benefitted anyone but the unclass.

Tonga was the perfect place to start, not only because I knew how to help, but because it was the scene of the latest disturbances. I could not only do something, I could make a difference and they would know it. Blaine would know it.

It was probably unreasonable of me, but stung by Chuck and Kirti's nonchalance about cooperating with Blaine, I arranged to work in the lab when they wouldn't be there.

Jonathan was harder to circumvent. But I didn't feel the need to. I never objected to Jonathan being in the lab with me. While I said again and again that I didn't need anyone holding my hand to get through the day, Jonathan took an interest in my work and he asked good questions. He didn't have a scientific brain, but that meant he saw things from a different angle and his questions sometimes made me think of a situation in an entirely new way.

"Energy generation. Specifically for Tonga," I explained. "The analysts claim it's impossible to get sufficient power up there. Too cloudy for solar energy, no hydroelectric or geothermal power to speak of, and the geological instability and extreme terrain are constantly cutting off their supply from anywhere else. The people who live there don't have the technical knowledge or training to run any kind of generator of their own. They're been written off while they're dying from the cold. I was trying to come up with ways we could produce power right there on the plateau with something simple. But then I was thinking, they do get power from outside, just not enough and with no predictability. It gave me the idea of giving them power storage devices that would require little maintenance, and developing some method of energy conservation that could be applied to their circumstances and conditions so that what they did get would last longer and go farther."

"Sounds logical," he said. "No one's ever thought of it for them before?"

"I doubt anyone's thought about them at all, not even Duke 'I want to help the unclass.'"

Jonathan's mouth was pinched but he didn't reply.

And so I filled my days until we left for Torrea.

Whether or not I was happy about the cause of the trip, I was happy that we were going to Torrea. I liked not just the planet, but the culture. They had a frank openness I admired, a stubbornness I identified with. Unlike the silent, backstabbing politics of the palace, the Torrean idea of backstabbing involved a knife and a polite request to turn around.

We traveled with Aliana, Blaine, and the rest of the noble contingent, on the ship that had originally taken me into space, and brought Pete and me together. Chuck and Kirti came as well. We designed a small project perfect for a lab in space and they joined in with an easy eagerness that made me sorry I'd been avoiding them.

At least, until I came upon Kirti and Blaine talking in the hallway. Not just talking; he was leaning in toward her, as if he had just said something intimate, and she was laughing. *Laughing.* Not a forced, awkward laugh, but genuine and carefree, her eyes sparkling, her gaze on him.

My breath stopped in tandem with my body, so suddenly that I nearly stumbled.

They looked up at me.

Kirti colored and took a reflexive step away from Blaine. He didn't move at first, meeting my glare with a lazy, indifferent look. Then he turned back to Kirti and laid a hand on her arm.

"I think it's an excellent idea Ms. Sachar, and I look forward to the presentation."

She made a small bow. "Thank you, Your Grace."

Without acknowledging me, he strode off.

I closed the distance to her, my hand going unconsciously to the same place Blaine's had just been, as if to wipe away his casual claim. When she glared at me, I realized my grip was tight, probably painful, and I forced my hand to relax but didn't move it.

"What was that about?" I hissed.

She cocked an eyebrow.

"You mean the fact that a duke stopped me in the hallway to ask me a question and I didn't ignore him?"

"Yes."

Her eyes narrowed.

"I know it's been a long time for you, Jake, so maybe you don't remember what it's like, but as a member of the IIC, I serve the empire. Unless it contradicts my prime duty or I'm told otherwise by the emperor, if a duke requests my services I'm required to comply. I couldn't say no even if I wanted to."

I pounced on her last words. "But you didn't want to say no."

She crossed her arms, shaking me off. "No, I didn't. This isn't just my job, it's my purpose. It's fulfilling and I like doing it. As much satisfaction as I get out of projects like yours, done among peers, it's also nice to interact with people outside of the field. I get to teach and inform, show people what we're doing and have them appreciate it and be better for it. Why would I want to say no? Just because *you* don't like the person asking me?"

I felt like she'd punched me. "I guess I assumed you didn't like him either, considering what he's done to me. I thought, as my friend, it might bother you that he got me beaten and Resettled."

Kirti gave me a long look. "Don't take this the wrong way, Jake, but you got yourself Resettled." She held up her hand to stop me when I sucked in a startled breath. "I'm not saying he didn't do his best to help you along, but you can't blame him for what you did yourself." Her frown was almost concerned. "You should think about it. If you didn't realize that, you could end up doing it again." Her face softened and she dropped her arms, leaned forward and kissed me chastely on the mouth. "Please think about it. Some of us care about you, you know."

I never did figure out how to respond to that.

We arrived at Torrea and were met by the royal family and Blaine's intended in one of the long, painful greeting ceremonies. My breath caught when Blaine's fiancée was introduced as Hera Laudley. I didn't have to ask if she were related somehow to the Lord Laudley I'd already clashed with. It was too much of a coincidence for her not to be. No doubt it was a political marriage. I wondered if she'd ever even met him. Not that any of that mattered when it came to my opinion of her. I hated her from the moment I laid eyes on her.

She was so damn cute.

Everything about her was petite and pretty. She looked more like a porcelain doll than anyone who would have the name "Blaine" had any right to. She'd probably have gorgeous children. I could already see it: a swarm of Blaine's beautiful spawn, enchanting everyone everywhere they went. The conversation with Aliana about children and heirs suddenly had a new bite.

When I was introduced to Hera she laid her soft little hand in mine and dropped into a graceful curtsy.

"It is an honor to meet you, Your Highness," she said, in a voice with all the peaceful beauty of a trickling brook. She even blushed; not the red flush that would have made her at least a fraction less appealing, but an adorable pinking of her cheeks.

"Likewise," I said, looking away and clearing my throat, trying to break the spell. Unfortunately, that put Blaine directly in my line of vision. He was watching her with a predatory possessiveness. When he caught my eye, he smirked, no doubt knowing exactly the effect she was having on me.

She was seated beside me at dinner. She didn't even have the decency to be stupid or dull. She was bright, funny, and her laugh was pretty and infectious. When she smiled, it was hard not to smile back at her. She asked me about my work, a specific question about a recent project. I admit it took me aback.

"Are you a scientist?"

She graced me with a smile. "No. But you are, and I wanted to be able to talk of subjects that interested you."

She'd studied ahead for a dinner conversation. I didn't know whether to admire her or apologize for not being as considerate.

"What subjects interest you?"

"I am interested in what other people find interesting," she said. I plastered on my smile. It was the perfect politician's answer, the kind I hated. Finally.

"That is," she continued, "I am interested in sociology, and how people interact with each other; how society and tradition shape how we prioritize self above expectations, or vice versa."

Oh.

"I did not look into your specialty so I could flatter you, if that is what you suspected." She gave me a look that said she knew I had, but she didn't mind and had forgiven me for it. "But because I would enjoy hearing you talk about it, especially to someone who is not a scientist."

I flushed. Not as nicely as she had. I suspected not much of anything was as nice as she was. Damn it.

The after-dinner conversation inevitably devolved into politics, and I excused myself. I was tired from the day and from pretending to be nice to people I couldn't care less about—and one I really hated. After the long trip, I was too restless to go back to my room, so I found a garden off the nobles' area. Since the access was restricted and all the important people were clustered around Pete, I hoped this meant I'd have it to myself.

There was a small pond in the middle of the garden, still as a sheet of metal, reflecting the moon so perfectly I could see its craters in the water. It was beautiful and peaceful and just what I needed. I was doing such a good job of losing myself in the quiet solitude that I nearly tripped over someone standing just off the path around a corner.

"Oh, I'm sorry," I said, offering a hand to the figure who had quickly stepped out of my way. "Are you OK?"

"Yes, I am perfectly fine, thank you." I recognized Hera's soft, unaffected tones. She stepped out from under the shade of the trees. "It is my fault, I was in the path."

"No, you weren't," I said. "But I'm sorry if I bothered you."

Her face was even prettier in the silvery light and I felt a stab of pity for her, chained to that man.

She shook her head. "I will go, Your Highness, I did not mean to disturb you."

From anyone else I would have taken it as an attempt to get away from me, but I couldn't shake the feeling that she was just being generous, selflessly accommodating.

"You were here first," I said, fumbling. I didn't like the idea of letting her leave thinking she'd somehow been at fault for such a silly, unimportant thing, or feeling like I was running her off. "Please don't go just because I have big feet."

She smiled, tilting her head down and though I couldn't see it, I knew she had that delicate blush on her cheeks.

"As you say, Your Highness."

I felt stupid again, hoping she hadn't taken it as a command when she really didn't want to stay. I cast about for something to say.

"Have you known Duke Blaine long?"

"Not long. I met him a few times when he visited my father, but the first time was only a year ago."

I hated that. I hated the whole idea of arranged marriages, but that she should be shackled to him, without knowing who and what he really was, burned in me.

"You don't have to marry him, you know." I blurted.

She cast me a look from under her lashes and smiled shyly. "Yes, I know. But it is good for my family, and I do not dislike him. I am sure I will come to love him in time." She hesitated. "I think he is fond of me."

I flinched, disgusted by the idea of Blaine *fond*. I was skeptical, too, that she would come to love him. Though if anyone could manage it, it would be this woman, who seemed so naive, too nice *not* to like people. Maybe she wouldn't see too deeply, or maybe she wouldn't be distressed because she didn't know any better. Then again, the thought of Blaine destroying someone so sweet even if it was only with indifference, made me angry and sad at the same time.

"Listen," I said. "If you're ever unhappy or think you'd like— that is, if you ever want—" I turned so she had to look me in the eye. "If you ever need anything, no matter what it is, let me know. I'll do something about it, OK?"

"You are very kind," she said.

I wasn't, if that's what she imagined was the motivation behind my offer. Oh, I was plenty motivated by simple concern for her. But I also couldn't help admitting to myself that the idea I could save someone from Blaine was intoxicating. Save someone else from him the way I couldn't do for myself.

And I'd be more than happy to make *him* suffer for once.

When I heard the crunch of boots on the path, I took a guilty step away from Hera, though I hadn't been standing that close. Sam, Pete's head guard—the same one who had been Pete's head guard back when I punched the emperor in open court— approached, with several other guards behind.

"Excuse me, Your Highness, but we need to get you inside." He nodded toward Hera, "Lady Hera, as well."

She moved to cooperate without question.

"Why?" I said. Sam had never given me reason to distrust him—once we'd moved past the days when he would punch me on sight—but there was an anxious urgency in the other men that made me nervous, even if Sam seemed no more disturbed than if he were asleep.

"There's trouble outside," he said.

Just then Jonathan joined us. "The Emperor has already re- turned to your rooms. He sent me to make sure you were secure," he said in his prescient way, reassuring me before I needed to ask.

I nodded and let Jonathan show me the way, in that manner of his that managed to lead without walking in front of me. Sam quietly nodded off two guards to escort Hera. She said no more in the way of goodbye than a quick nod and dip of a curtsy as we were escorted away in different directions.

"What's going on?" I hissed to Jonathan.

"A large number of unclass have left their section of the city without authorization and are moving in on the palace, insisting they were promised a part of the festivities and that they would be allowed to see the visitors." He hesitated. "Specifically you."

"Me?" I almost stopped, but was swept along in the momentum of my escort. "Why?"

He gave me a quick look. "I would think that would be obvious."

I wanted to retort. Not because it wasn't obvious to me, too, but because I didn't want the obvious to be true.

Back in our room Pete hugged and kissed me, hard and demanding.

"Thank you for coming without a fight," he said, with only a quick cut of the eyes to Sam to see if that was true. Sam's face was impassive but it seemed to reassure Pete.

"Is everything OK?" I asked.

"Nothing that won't be over by morning. You don't have to worry about it."

Well, what I had to do and what I was going to do weren't often the same thing.

We met in the grand hall for breakfast as scheduled.

"Quite a welcome we had last night, King Rhis," Blaine said to Aliana's father. The king frowned.

"A poor way to welcome our guests," Rhis said, with a nod to Pete. "We do not often have trouble with the unclass here in the capital."

"Hardly surprising that it should happen now," Blaine said, "considering the circumstances."

"What circumstances?" I snapped, and to my horror, felt my face heating. Why was I being deliberately obtuse in front of *Blaine*?

Aliana laid a hand over mine, pressing down hard. I glanced at Hera, who was frowning at the table, concern pinching her delicate features.

"I mean no criticism, Your Highness," Blaine replied. Like hell he didn't. "But as Minister of Social Administration, it's my responsibility to be concerned about these things. I don't think it's an insult to point out that your presence here is a contributing factor in this unprecedented act of civil disobedience on the part of a class that seems to believe their connection to you entitles them to privileges they have never had before. It would be an insult to our intelligence to pretend otherwise."

Which was one of the smoothest insults I'd ever heard. I'd have been impressed if I wasn't so angry.

Aliana's fingernails dug into the back of my hand. I suppressed a wince.

Blaine took in the table as a whole. "Not that it makes it excusable, but understanding the root of the problem is necessary to preventing future incidents. In fact, I believe it was a failure on my part not to make a recommendation to His Excellence that the Prince Consort's inclusion in such public events as this from now on be more closely considered."

I shot out of my seat. "This conversation is finished."

Pete grabbed my hand and tugged. I fell back into my chair and he squeezed my hand hard under the table before letting go.

"I agree," he said. "It's not pleasant breakfast conversation. Especially in light of the reason why we're here, and what we're celebrating." He looked at Hera and smiled. "Are you getting nervous, Lady Hera?"

"Getting cold feet?" I snapped.

Aliana kicked me under the table. Hard.

I leaned closer to her. "Well, she should be," I hissed.

I glanced up and saw Hera concentrating on her plate,

her cheeks red. And I felt like a complete ass. Aliana gave me one scathing look before she changed the subject, all the time squeezing my hand under the table as if she meant to break it.

Aliana pulled me discreetly and not gently aside when the meal was over.

"If you embarrass her again in your feud with Blaine, you will answer to me. Do you understand? No one deserves it less than she does, and I will not see you hurt her, either deliberately or by your carelessness. I will warn you only this once, Jacob Dawes. Are we quite clear?"

"Yes," I said, subdued and ashamed. "We're clear."

It was the morning of the wedding. We were waiting with the wedding party, Pete and I standing aside with Aliana. No matter what we were or weren't to the bride and groom, Pete and I would enter ahead of the wedding party, as would the king and Aliana, to be displayed and seated with honor before the ceremony could begin.

Blaine was also in the anteroom, waiting with many of the other attendants and a man I'd never seen before. Aliana leaned close.

"Hera's father, Grand Duke Laudley."

My eyebrows shot up. "Why haven't I met him before?"

Pete looked at the two of us and winced at the question, but left it to Aliana to answer.

"Because he has not spoken to the emperor in fifty years."

I cast a confused glance between her and Pete.

"Pete hasn't been around that long."

She shook her head. "Not this emperor. Any emperor. When Peter's grandfather did not choose his," here she nodded slightly toward the grand duke, "sister to be the next emperor's wife, the grand duke, who was then only Lord Laudley, declared he would never speak to him again."

It took me a minute to put all that together. "He won't speak to any emperor ever again? How is that even allowed?"

She shrugged. "The upper nobility are excused their eccentricities, and, short of being royal, there are not many who could claim a higher rank in the empire than Grand Duke

Laudley. And there is no one who does not understand his anger at being passed over. The marriage would have put his family back on the throne."

"Back on the throne?"

"The families have intermarried many times in the history of the empire. It was not unreasonable of him to expect it to happen again. The Killearns deliberately maintain the connection, as a means of discouraging the powerful families from attempting to gain power by force."

"So they have to buy loyalty, then?"

She gave me a funny smile. "Loyalty, perhaps. Incentive is perhaps more accurate. Even the grand duke himself would hesitate to give the name 'loyalty' to his position toward the Imperial Family." Her eyes unfocused for a moment. "Laudley's first wife was my father's sister. I did not know Peter for most of my childhood because my father sided with the grand duke in his dispute with Peter's grandfather, and later his father."

"What changed?"

She shrugged. "I became the heir when Peter's father died. Keeping us apart was no longer in my father's power. Also, Peter was too young to have become truly embroiled in the rivalries yet, and is very unlike his father besides. He benefits from that quite a lot."

I snuck another look at the grand duke and found him staring at me, as if he meant to bore through me with his glare. Then he turned his head very deliberately away, as if I had ceased to exist.

For some reason, I shivered.

I focused on Blaine instead, and on the more comfortable role of hating rather than being hated. He didn't look a bit nervous. In fact, he laughed with one of the groomsmen, at ease, not taking it as seriously as he should, I thought. If he was about to marry someone like Hera.

I leaned over to Pete. "He doesn't deserve her. It's not fair. She can't know what she's getting into."

"I don't know," Pete replied, eying him. "She seems to like him.

I'd almost say she has at least the beginnings of affection for him. They might be very happy."

"If she has any positive feelings for him, she doesn't know him at all."

Pete gave me a long, sideways look.

"Not everyone hates him," he said. "In fact, most people don't hate him at all."

"One of life's great mysteries," I grumbled.

Pete shrugged. "Hardly. He's powerful, attractive, and charming."

My mouth dropped open.

He laughed, holding up his hands in mock defense. "I didn't say I wanted him. But if you consider him objectively, he's actually very appealing. You don't see it because you've hated him from the moment you laid eyes on him. But he's powerful for a reason, and it's not simply that he's rich or has titles. He's the model of all that's good and admired about the status quo. He's got the looks, polish, and breeding. He makes the upper classes proud to be part of what he represents, and he is charismatic enough to be appealing to everyone else. Honestly, I liked him just fine before you came along."

"But he's evil and manipulative!"

Pete looked pensive. "'Evil' is a bit strong," he said, "but even evil can be a matter of perspective. He's horrible and threatening to you because the system and philosophy he defends is one that makes you the bad guy. It's also the one that a lot of people benefit from. And for everyone else it's familiar and well established, which some people consider a virtue on its own. From another point of view, you're the one that's evil and a threat."

I stared at him, feeling like he'd not only punched me in the gut, but then stabbed me, reached in and ripped out my innards.

He took my hand and laid his other palm against my cheek. "I didn't say I agreed, I'm just trying to help you understand how other people might think."

I nodded, having no voice to say anything, even if I had anything to say.

After we were paraded in and seated, The Grand Duke escorted Hera down the aisle. She looked beautiful and unspoiled in her simple white dress.

The wedding was officiated by a minister whom many in the empire mockingly called their High Priest. Torrea had held out against the secularization of their world longer than any other planet in the empire. They'd originally been colonists from Earth, like the others, fleeing the devastation and chaos in the wake of the religious wars of the twenty-first century that had eventually brought to power one great general, Seamus Killearn, who had ended the war by taking out the leaders of all the major religions, their most powerful members, and their most cherished monuments in the space of five hours.

Those who settled on Torrea, though, had gone there with the purpose of saving their religion and traditions and being left to practice them in peace. When the Empire began to spread out from Earth, to claim its descendants on their new planets, Torrea refused to give up its religious practices and institutions. It was a brief but costly war, and Torrea eventually bent to the Empire's will. But their culture still had a distinctly religious flavor.

"I still feel sorry for her," I whispered hoarsely to Pete, wanting to make his words from earlier go away.

Pete didn't answer until Hera and Blaine stood together before the minister.

"Look at his face," Pete said. "I think he cares for her. Or at least appreciates what he has."

I glared at Blaine.

"He doesn't. He can't."

Pete took my hand. "You're heartless," he said, but his smile took the sting out of the words, and he held my hand for the rest of the ceremony.

At the ball afterward, I found Pete standing off to the side with a distant look on his face.

"You OK?" I asked.

His gaze focused on me. "Mmmmm," he murmured, lacing his fingers into mine. "Oh yes. I'm wonderful. I was just thinking. Was our wedding like this?"

I shrugged. "I suppose so. Why? Weren't you there?"

He huffed a laugh. "I don't remember much of it. I was in a bit of a daze." He smiled. "You know, once it was done and we were really married, I realized that I'd been afraid all along it wouldn't really happen, that something would take us away from each other again and ruin everything."

"Heh," I scoffed. "Optimist. I'm still afraid of that."

The worry line appeared between his eyes. "You're not really, are you? Why?"

I shrugged, looking away. "History. Me. My life. I guess I expect to lose everything again eventually. Happens to me too often." I tried to smile but it felt weak, and the line between his eyes didn't go away.

"Hey," he said, shaking my hand a little to make sure he had my attention. "I'm never going to let anything happen to you. I promise. I said forever and I meant it. Trust me."

"I do," I said. And I did. I trusted his sincerity, his determination. He was certainly the man who could make those kinds of promises and expect he wouldn't be prevented from keeping them. But I'd already lost him once before, and he hadn't been able to stop it then.

"Jake?" he said.

"Yeah, I heard you."

"You did not. I just said something important and you weren't paying attention."

"I thought everything the emperor said was important." I threw him a cocky grin.

"You heard that one, did you? Funny. How come you never listen to me, then?"

"I listen to you all the time, my darling." I laid a hand against his cheek. "I just don't always agree with or do what you say."

"Oh, well then."

I smiled at him and this time it was genuine. "What did you say that I didn't hear?"

"I said I love you."

"Oh," I said, pulling him close. "Then you're absolutely right, the emperor's every word is of vital importance."

He laughed, "I'm glad you think so. Come on," he said with a distinctly un-imperious leer, "let's go somewhere we can talk about this in depth."

We left the next day. Aliana was staying behind on Torrea. She kissed me on the cheek and then pulled back to look at me, level and stern. "I will hear something of a child soon, Jacob Dawes."

I tried to laugh. "Of course."

"I am not returning to the palace, specifically to clear the way for my replacement in the line of succession. You understand this?"

"Yes." And I did. I knew how this was supposed to go. I avoided making any commitments but the parting look she gave me made sure I knew she was well aware of that and it changed nothing.

Everyone else who had come with us left on one ship. Pete took me to our nebula in another.

It was one of the most wonderful times I can remember. We made love in the lab, a lot, just like the first time. And if I closed my eyes, it was like we'd returned to those days, and that new and hopeful feeling, when you know nothing will ever go wrong.

One afternoon I stood at the window wall, just as I had the night he gave the lab to me, my face so close I could feel the chill on my cheeks, my hands at the level of my face, pressed against the poly so that all I could see were my own hands and the universe itself.

Pete came up behind me and wrapped his arms around my waist. I leaned back against him and he put his chin on my shoulder, tilting his head against mine. We stood like that for a long time, just staring out at the nebula blooming before us.

"I want to give it to you," he said.

"What?"

"Everything. The universe." I felt him smile against my neck. "But since I can't quite manage that, I want to give you the nebula. I'll have them rename it. The Dawes Nebula."

"Dawes-Killearn."

I felt more than heard his chuckle. "Yes, you're right."

"It's a good name," I said.

He hugged me harder. "It is."

For a while longer we stood there, looking at our nebula.

"You know what I wish?" he said.

"What?"

"I wish that after I die, you could bring me out here and put me there," he loosed one hand to point at the purple-blue center of the cloud.

"Me? I'm not bringing you anywhere. I intend to die first."

"Oh? Why?"

I had just blurted out words without considering them, but when I thought for a minute, I realized I meant it.

"Because I don't want to have to live through losing you. Doing things like that," I waved in the direction of the nebula, "disposing of your remains?" I couldn't help shivering. "No. I'm definitely going first."

He laughed. "OK, we'll go together. That way, they can bring us both out here, put us into the cloud, and it'll really be the Dawes-Killearn nebula then." His gaze wandered back to the cloud. "And our remains will become part of a star someday."

His breath on my neck made me shiver.

"That's a good plan. We'll do it."

He sighed. "It's a nice thought."

"So we'll make sure it happens. I mean, not a suicide pact or anything, but we can leave instructions for what to do with our remains. If one of us goes first, we promise to bring the other out here."

He shook his head. "I'll do it for you, if you want. But you won't be able to do it for me. Emperors are interred in the Imperial Mausoleum."

"So just tell them you don't want to be."

"Doesn't work that way. That's just how it's done. It's not something I can change." He shrugged. "It's OK. I'm sure I won't care at that point."

We didn't say any more about it, but as I stared at the patterns in the cloud, I couldn't get out of my head the image of Pete's remains moldering away in the imperial shrine and me floating out here in the cloud, all alone.

# $\underset{CE}{\times}16$

We planned to stay in the vicinity of the nebula for two weeks, but nine days after we arrived, Pete was called back to the palace. The unclass were rioting.

The planet of Tlo had been the first non-human addition to the Empire, and even though they were in some ways completely different culturally from most other Imperial worlds, they had taken easily and early to the developing class-based social policies of the early Empire, as it fit well with their own beliefs and practices.

So when Pete told me that their slum of Nri was where the violence had erupted, it was a shock that sat heavy in my gut.

Nri wasn't even a particularly large slum, nor historically significant. It was under the jurisdiction of a minor city called Tri. They'd had no more than the most common troubles all unclass districts experienced and no more than the normal portion of hardships.

"About 150,000 people, or half of Nri's population, have left their district and converged on the mayor's mansion in Tri," Pete said.

"What do they want?"

"They're demanding to be allowed access to city services in the low class section of the city."

"Well that's not unreasonable."

Pete gave me a serious look. "Aside from the fact that the addition of 300,000 more people eligible to use the services in the low class district would completely overwhelm them, their approach to this 'request' is in violation of Imperial law, and the Tlo place their own restrictions on top of that when it comes to social order. There are at least a dozen deaths and hundreds if not thousands of injuries among the city's ISS forces, caused by the rioters. They're not going to be rewarded for their rebellion by meek acquiescence to their demands."

"Only a dozen killed, by a mob of 150,000? They're clearly not intending violence, Pete. Maybe this was the only way they could get heard. Kirti's been monitoring the unclass in the empire for months and she never even mentioned them. How long have they been asking for services and not getting them?"

Pete examined my face, almost as if he was wondering if I were serious. "As long as they all have, which is pretty much always and regularly. Jake, every unclass district in the empire is under-served and in need. Isn't that what we've argued about? Isn't that what you've been working on? I gave Blaine the target of improving each district with more than 100,000 inhabitants by ten percent over the next ten years, but every time he reports to me there are new reasons why the target's unreasonable, so many complications and obstacles. Not least of which is the general resistance in every duchy to allocate any time and resources to the unclass, beyond the bare minimum to keep the casualty rate below the maximum level allowable for that district."

"The maximum allowable casualty rate in some of those is 40% annually," I bit off.

"I know that. It's why we're trying to make things better, isn't it? A sudden and drastic cut of that allowance won't make it instantly better; there are real reasons the death rate is so high in those areas. You can't just pass a decree to fix it. That would just breed resentment and make things worse in the end."

I hated that it was a logical answer; that I knew he had a point. I knew it from my own studies and efforts.

He hesitated. "They've mentioned Abenez, and you, as the basis for their demands. It puts me in a tough position, Jake. There are too many powerful people who are already claiming you influence my decisions in a way that's compromising the empire. I have to think about how this will appear to the nobility."

A heavy emptiness settled in my chest. "How bad's it going to be?"

He took my hand, squeezing it as if willing me to understand. "They'll be ordered to return to Nri. Anyone who goes peacefully will not face additional repercussions, but anyone who resists and those identified as the ringleaders will be executed for treason."

I heard him suck in a breath through his teeth and realized I'd tightened my grip on his hand so hard that it was hurting *me*, never mind him.

"It's a better offer than they'd get from anyone else and you know it. A plain reading of the law would justify executing everyone who left the district. It's the best I can do, Jake."

"So they can go back to their inadequate services and lack of food, clothing, and shelter."

"You know we're working on that. But they can't be seen to benefit from their illegal actions and the death of ISS men and women. It would be a disaster for the empire if I gave in to that even once. Honestly, Jake, there's a very real chance that allowing them this much will make things worse for all of us, not just make things for them as bad as they were before."

I gave a slow, reluctant nod, the taste of bitterness in my mouth. "Yeah. I know. You're doing what you can." He was. It was a concession no one else would have made to them. It was probably better than they'd even expected. I couldn't imagine they believed they'd accomplish anything with their illegal protests. Hope wasn't something the unclass had in any better supply than food or clothing. It churned like nausea in my gut. And it wasn't fair to feel as angry at Pete as I did just then.

"I'm not ignoring them, Jake."

"I know," I said. I stood but I couldn't look at him. "Thank you." He didn't try to call me back when I walked away.

I went back to the lab, because that's what I did when I wanted the world to make sense, to conform to logic, to feel safe. I'd been there a few hours when Jonathan came in and switched on my vid. Icy fear squeezed my throat.

It was the same starscape and artificial voice as the last time.

*A mob has taken to the streets in the city of Tri, in the Southern Hemisphere of Tlo. A lawless and dangerous group of unclass, in direct rebellion to the laws of both the Empire and the Kingdom of Tlo, have invaded the city and threatened the lives of peace-loving citizens. In the wake of the emperor's marriage to an unclass, it was perhaps not surprising that the slums grew restive. Were we not all confused and troubled? But it has escalated now into full-scale rioting and has resulted in the deaths of imperial security forces. This is unacceptable. The unclass have forgotten their place since one of their own was placed prominently at the Emperor's side. The Patriot was not alone in grieving this alliance in his heart, even as he loyally refused to criticize the decisions of our Emperor. But in light of consequences such as this, can we keep silent? The Patriot cannot and will not. Take heed, fellow—*

The feed screeched and died, going black and silent for a moment before the preempted signal reappeared in a flash of color and sound that made me flinch.

"Off," Jonathan said, and it mercifully went away.

I stared at him.

Jonathan pursed his lips. Quite frankly, he looked sick, which unnerved me almost more than the message had. "Perhaps you should return to your room," he said. "I'm sure the emperor will be looking for you."

Pete did come to find me, but had little to say that I didn't already know. I didn't need him to tell me that I had to stay out of this. I was cycling between anger and fear, but mostly I just felt stunned. How could this have happened again? Who could *do* that? Pete didn't have any answers. And that scared me most of all.

By the time I contacted Kirti she was already back at the IIC.

Yes, of course she had seen the broadcast—she and the rest of the empire. Yes, she was factoring it into the long-term calculations. No, it didn't change anything right now. Yes, things were on track and going well in Abenez.

I disconnected the call, not feeling reassured, but useless. And, with a shiver, I realized: powerless.

When we got back to the palace, I was unpleasantly surprised to learn that Blaine too had come back in response to the situation on Tlo, cutting his honeymoon short by months. I was neither masochistic nor stupid enough to try to remind him of my supposed position as adviser to his Minister. I knew he was doing this somehow; inciting the riots, helping the Patriot. Maybe he even was the Patriot. But I knew he wasn't careless enough to give himself away to me if I tried to stay close to him. Which was a relief. I wanted nothing to do with him.

Maybe I had to stay out of Nri, but that didn't mean I couldn't start working for the unclass outside of Abenez as well. I just had to do it somewhere else. I retreated to the lab and my energy conservation project for Tonga.

I started taking the long way from my lab back to our rooms, the way that took me through the nobles' section. I hated encountering people there, but it helped create the illusion that I had more freedom than I really did; that I wasn't still restricted to such a small slice of the palace.

I was rounding a corner when, for the second time, I nearly walked right into Hera Blaine. I grabbed for her before we both fell over. She looked at me with wide, startled eyes.

"I'm sorry," I said, releasing her with a jerk, reaching out again when I realized I'd tipped her off balance. But she steadied herself, and I pulled my hand back before I touched her again. "I'm sorry," I repeated, "I didn't mean to grab you, I just didn't want you to fall."

She gave me a smile that was like a benediction. There was no need for forgiveness because I couldn't possibly have offended. It would have been suspicious, coming in my direction from anyone else, but from her, it was so natural that I didn't doubt it.

I found myself smiling. She was so easy to be around. I wondered that she didn't have half a dozen people buzzing about her all the time. When I thought about it, I realized I'd never seen her with anyone like that, not outside of groups that were already formed. Even then, she was usually with her husband or somehow separate.

"Where are all your followers?" I said, before I could remind myself that was rude. "I'd expect to see people flocking around you. They usually do, in this place."

She nodded once. "I think they are perhaps hesitant, because of my father's and now my husband's rank being so very high. I am sure you know what I mean."

I knew about people avoiding me but I doubted it had anything to do with rank, not my current one, anyway. People had always avoided me. Now they just bowed when they did it.

"Or perhaps I am not as likable as I thought," she said, with a smile that said she didn't mean anything unpleasant by it, that she wouldn't be resentful if it were true.

"It's impossible not to like you. Believe me, I've tried."

She laughed. When I flushed again, she reached out, laying a hand on my arm, frowning with concern. "You must find it... distressing, in this place, to be so naturally honest," which would have been a laughable description for my tendency to blurt out whatever I was thinking, if it came from anyone but her. "But I find it charming"

Well there was something I'd never been accused of before.

"Endearing, even," she continued. "I can see why he was willing to risk so much to keep you."

I stared at her, not at all sure how to take that. Yet I couldn't imagine a barbed comment coming from her. "I—"

She blushed, maybe thinking she'd been too forward again, so I rushed on, "Have you ever had lunch in the aquarium?"

"I have not," she said. "I have eaten in the dining area with the aquarium wall, but not the one you mean, I think. The small room with no furniture that is not part of the tank itself?" I nodded. "That room is in the Imperial Area."

Was it? I thought about that. "No, it's in the area where the nobles' section joins the Imperial, but I'm sure the nobles are allowed to use it."

She nodded. "The emperor has granted permission for the upper nobility to make use of it when the Family is not, but I did not want to presume."

"Would you like to have lunch with me there sometime?"

She gave me her smile. "Yes, I would like that very much."

We arranged to meet for lunch three days later. I was looking forward to it, feeling like a giddy little kid. But I gave myself permission to feel that way, reasoning that between long days spent in the lab and my truncated freedom, I was allowed to be excited about any break in my routine.

In the meantime, I really was putting in long days in the lab, working myself to exhaustion every night. After two days of that, I decided I wasn't up to spending time forcing myself to be social with the nobles after dinner. I excused myself and Pete made no protest, only frowning with concern and then kissing me lightly. Just outside the door of the lounge, I stopped short before I ran into Hera.

"Oh, Your Highness, forgive me," she said.

"I seem to have a habit of running into you, literally," I said, smiling. It went a long way to relieving some of the pressure building behind my eyes. "Are you all right?" I asked, looking more closely. She was pale. A swell of anger at Blaine surged within me. Whatever was wrong with her, I was confident it was his fault.

She blushed and smiled, lowering her eyes, but there was no pretense in the gesture, only a quiet pleasure.

"I am tired, perhaps," she said. "But I am well." There *was* something she wasn't saying, but I had no idea what.

"OK," I said, not wanting to call her a liar. She was entitled to her secrets, after all. But it dampened the happiness I'd felt at seeing her. Why had I thought we were that sort of bosom friends that she would share her secrets with me? I didn't even want to like any Blaine that much.

Her face, as she examined me, took on a tinge of concern. "Your Highness—"

"I wish you'd call me Jacob," I said.

She gave me a shy smile. "Thank you, I would like that. If it is not presumptuous of me to ask, I would be pleased if you would call me Hera," she replied.

"I would like that very much. Thank you." I held out my arm. "Let me see you back into the room," I said. "Unless I can convince you to retire for the night; you do look tired."

"I will soon," she said. "But I should rejoin my husband." I tried not to let my smile slip but I didn't succeed. She took my arm and I laid my hand lightly over hers as I escorted her back into the room. I had a moment of pleasure at seeing Blaine's obvious *dis*pleasure when he saw us together. He stood and not-very-discreetly claimed her by taking her other arm so that she relinquished mine.

"Speaking of heirs," he said, and she looked up at him, blushing.

"Enryn," she said, a quiet protest in her tone. It took me a minute to realize that was his first name. "Not here."

But he gave her a sickeningly fond smile and stroked her cheek. "I can't help myself, love. How can I not shout from the rooftops that I not only have such a charming, beautiful wife, but that she's carrying my son?"

Though the words suggested a private conversation, they were pitched to carry, and so they did. The news caught like a blaze in dry kindling and the room was soon crackling with it. Pete came to my side and slid his arm around my waist.

"I hear you are to be congratulated, Duke Blaine," he nodded to her, "and Duchess." He slipped his arm away from me long enough to take her hand and kiss it in an uncommon and dashingly gallant way. "You must be very happy."

Blaine put his arm around her in what I thought was more of a possessive than an affectionate gesture.

"Thank you, Your Excellence," Hera answered. "We are."

Pete's arm returned to my waist and I let myself quirk a smile at Blaine when he took note of it and frowned. Dueling husbands and their possessive body language. It was funny in its way. And I felt a petty triumph over it.

"Now I know you're not just tired from your trip," I said to her, "and I'm going to insist that you let me see you back to your room, Hera." I held my arm out to her again.

"I *am* tired," she said, but she looked up at Blaine. "If it is all right with you?"

I kept my face turned away. I didn't want to see them being affectionate.

"Of course," he said. "We'll go together." He bowed slightly in Pete's direction. "If you'll excuse us, Your Excellence?"

Pete waited, silent, until Blaine tacked on, "Your Highness?"

Pete's return nod was gracious and poised as always. "Of course. Good night."

I watched them leave, not sure how I felt at all. Angry? Jealous? Sad? Pete's whisper in my ear startled me. "Let's go, too."

He was oddly quiet as we got ready for bed, the line between his brows flickering in and out, his eyes and thoughts far away.

"Is something wrong?" I said.

He gave me a sheepish, almost guilty look. "Just thinking."

"About what?"

"The Blaines," he said, his gaze drifting away again. "How happy they must be." He sighed. "I love babies."

I had no answer to that. I was honestly shocked, and lost in a wash of shame that I hadn't known that already. Especially when I knew how important it was that he have a baby soon. How had I not known that he actually *wanted* one? No, I knew the answer to that. I hadn't *wanted* to know.

"Is something wrong?" he said, startling me out of my brooding.

"No," I said. "Just thinking."

He chuckled and grabbed hold of me, tumbling us into bed together. He didn't ask what I'd been thinking about. Instead, silently, he let his hands ask all the questions that I always answered "yes" to.

I lay awake long after we finished, sated and yet almost squirming with unease. At last I rolled onto my side, coming up on my elbow so I could look down at Pete.

"Do you really want to be a father?" I asked.

He made a half-asleep noise. "What?"

"You want to be a father, don't you?"

He raised his head and looked at me. "Yes. I want to." He hesitated. "But you don't."

I grimaced. "That's not exactly true. It's not that I don't want to, I just don't *want* to."

He raised a wry eyebrow.

"Besides, how do you know that?" I asked. "We've never talked about this before."

"That's how I know," he said. "Because you've never brought it up before."

"Why didn't *you* bring it up, then?"

"Did you want me to?"

"No."

"That's why."

I lay back down, staring at the ceiling. "I'm sorry I didn't know that."

I heard him shrug.

"It's OK, Jake. You've had a hell of a year. It's all right to be a little self-absorbed."

I gave him a look. "Because I'm not usually?"

He laughed and lay back down, curling into my side. We lay in silence for a while.

"I'm afraid," I said.

He came up on his elbow now, looking down at me. He ran the backs of his knuckles down my cheek.

"I am too, if that helps any."

"You shouldn't be afraid," I said. "You'll be great at it. You're good with people. You'll be really good with your own kid."

He was quiet for a moment. "I always thought I would be. But I think you will be, too. I think you'll be a great father."

"You're just saying that."

"No," he said, sitting up. "Don't you see? Look how worried you are about this. You're afraid you won't do it right. But the thing that matters is that you *want* to do it right. The rest of it we'll figure out."

I didn't have any reply to that. I didn't believe him, but he was so earnest it didn't seem nice to say so, and I didn't want to talk about it anymore. Finally he settled back down, pulling me to him.

"I love you," he said.

I kissed his cheek.

He pulled me even tighter against him. Soon his breathing became slow and steady. I lay awake for a long time after that, feeling sorry for the poor kid who was going to get stuck with me.

# CE 17

The next morning, I went to visit Dr. Heinriksen. She lived in a gorgeous house, just beside the Imperial medical center and hospital. Pete's father had built it for her. He was too much of a traditionalist to allow her to live within the nobles' section, because she was only high class. But he was ill too often and wanted her closer than the high class section. Thus the house.

I saw her coming out of the front door of her home and heading for the medical building. Her house connected directly to the building, so seeing that she took the long way around, that symbolic distancing of home from work, made me smile. I'd always been comfortable with her, from my first night in the palace, and had seen her quite a lot in the past few months, what with the assassination attempts, but this morning I was nervous.

I waited a few minutes, telling myself it was to allow her to settle in before she had to deal with me. Finally, I entered the outer room of her building and found a little girl sitting there on the floor, alone. I looked around, confused.

"What are you doing?" I said, and could have kicked myself. What did I think this was, an interrogation? It was just a little girl. I'd only started to believe a very little bit that Pete could be right, that I might be an OK father. That fledgling opinion was nipped in the bud.

She glanced up at me. "Playing." She held up the doll in her hands as if for proof, and then went back to her game.

I glanced around the room again, but still no one was there.

"Where are your parents?"

She cast a look at Dr. Heinriksen's door but shrugged. "Daddy's talking with the doctor."

I frowned. "And he left you alone?"

"He wanted to talk to the doctor in private."

"But... He left you by yourself?"

She glared at me. "I'm seven years old."

"Ummm, yes. That's what I meant."

She made a huff of annoyance. "I'm not a baby. I don't need someone watching me all the time." Her self-righteous disgust at my obtuseness was funny, in a way. Then I realized that *she* might be allowed to sit alone in a semi-public area with no one keeping an eye on her, but *I* wasn't.

"But is anyone—"

A woman entered the room and, catching sight of me, dropped into a palace-worker's practiced bow. "Your Highness," she said.

The girl looked up at me curiously.

"He's the prince?" She looked decidedly unimpressed.

The woman rushed forward and pulled the girl upright with a hissed, "Bea, your manners!"

"It's OK," I said, my hands up. I was surprised but amused that she didn't recognize me.

"We've not been at the palace long, Your Highness," the woman protested. "We showed her pictures, but she hasn't seen you in person, yet."

I smiled in what I hoped was reassurance. "She has now."

"We'll do better, Your Highness," the woman flushed.

"No," I said, both hands out, trying to fend off the assumption. "She's fine."

The door to Dr. Heinriksen's office opened and Hamish, one of my servants, exited. He took in the situation with well-trained stoicism, and bowed to me. "Your Highness."

The girl went to him, slipping her hand into his and glaring at me protectively.

He bent and whispered a few words in her ear. She scowled at him but returned to her mother. He nodded to the woman and the two of them left with a quick bow.

I looked back at Hamish.

"Is there something I can do for you, Your Highness?" he asked.

I frowned. "Isn't it your day off?"

His opaque expression would have made Jonathan proud. "Nothing is more important than seeing to your comfort, Your Highness."

I felt a rush of...something. Anger, mostly. Embarrassment, guilt.

"No." I said, fighting to make my tone sound less harsh. "A whole lot of things are more important than that. Including whatever you were here for, and especially them." I gestured in the direction his family had left in.

He nodded acceptance of my correction, but with no more emotion than he'd showed before. "Thank you, Your Highness."

Still he waited, because I hadn't actually dismissed him. Sometimes I hated this game.

"You should go with them," I said. "It's not your day to worry about me."

He bowed, thanked me, and left.

I watched him, scowling at his back, angry. When I turned back, Dr. Heinriksen was studying me with a pensive expression.

"Why was he here?" I asked. I hadn't meant to sound combative but I still didn't have a handle on what bothered me. "What did she mean they hadn't been at the palace long? Hamish has been here for...well, he was here when I got back, so at least that long."

"I believe she meant they're living in the palace now. They lived in Imperial City until recently."

"But he lives here." That much I knew. All our servants lived off of a hallway that connected to our sitting room.

"Yes," she said. "But he only recently could afford to bring his family here, and with security the way it is, it took quite a while to get clearance for them."

"What do you mean they couldn't afford to live here? Isn't that part of his job? To live here?"

"His job. Not theirs." She seemed to take pity on me, seeing I was still completely confused. "In most key Imperial positions, having a family is not encouraged. In some, it's not even an option. Hamish can have a family if he wants, but it's not set up for it to be easy for him to do so, to encourage the emperor's household staff to remain single and dedicated to their duties."

"He does just fine!"

She raised her eyebrows at my vehemence, but didn't comment on it. "I have no doubt of it." She gave me a considering look. "I'm surprised you didn't know about this. Surely at the IIC the topic came up. You wouldn't be permitted to have children of your own if you were still there."

I stared at her. "Not permitted..." Her eyebrows climbed. "They told us about the repro-control at our checkups, but I didn't know they meant we could *never* have kids."

"You never noticed that there were no children at the IIC other than yourselves?"

I shook my head, but more to clear away the fog of stupidity than as an answer. "I was a teenager. I guess I assumed the adults weren't having sex. And we were too young to worry about it." My head snapped up. "But wouldn't they be the perfect ones to have children? The genetic mix of two people selected for the IIC would be ideal."

She nodded. "Yes, and for that reason they're encouraged to donate their reproductive cells. Many high class and noble families pay a lot of money to have one of those children. Even the Imperial Family." She waved away my incredulous look. "Oh, the legalities of adding a donor directly to the imperial line are too problematic, but there have been times that noble families have used a donated egg or sperm to conceive a child, and that offspring has then been married to the next imperial heir or ruler."

I stood there, trying to get my bearings and wrap my head around all of this. It was too much. Going from being bullied into having a child of my own in the interests of the empire, to finding out that, if I'd stayed at the IIC, I wouldn't have been allowed to have a child even if I'd wanted one. In the interests of the empire. In fact, the interests of the empire were what had taken me to the IIC in the first place, as a child, whether my parents wanted it or not. The empire came first. Which apparently included making sure the emperor and his family were never even inconvenienced, if one of more than a dozen people who did nothing more than see that my life was as easy and comfortable as possible (those obviously being relative terms), was discouraged from having a family of his own just to better serve one full-grown, capable man. I scowled.

"Why was he in here?"

Her face clouded for a moment.

"I'm sorry, I didn't mean to pry. I know it's none of my business why he came to see you. I just mean I didn't realize he saw you. I thought that was for the nobility only."

She cocked a grin. "You're wrong about whether or not it's your business. That's another thing about being a servant to the imperial family. He doesn't have the privilege of privacy from you. But back to your question, he comes to see me because all of your servants do. It's something your husband started when he was young. One of his servants was severely injured saving Peter from a fall. The young Prince wouldn't hear of his servant being seen by anyone but the emperor's own physician. There was a bit of a row about it between father and son, but over time it was put into place. And since Peter came to the throne, his household staff and personal guards all see me for their medical care."

I smiled to myself. I liked that mental image, a young Pete who wanted everyone treated equally. Or, at least, within the framework of what he understood. He still did that, it was just that his worldview was more narrow and insular than he realized. What an emperor like that and I could *do* together.

Of course, that was the root of most of my problems, and his, right now. I wasn't the only one who realized that.

"He's dying."

Dr. Heinriksen's words nearly doubled me over with a gasp. "What?" *Pete?*

She nodded in the direction Hamish had gone.

I blew out a huge breath of relief. She gave me an odd look.

"I'm sorry," I said, "That's awful. It's just that, for a minute, I thought you were still talking about Pete."

"Oh," she said, grimacing. "No. That's not what I meant. Hamish has a degenerative condition. We're treating the symptoms, but it's only a matter of time."

"How long?"

"A few more weeks."

For a moment, all I could see was that little girl, holding his hand like a hissing kitten, too young to know how really small and insignificant she was in the face of almost any danger at all. Too small to be anything but brave.

My voice was hard to find. "Why?" There were so few things a doctor like Dr. Heinriksen couldn't fix anymore. Most of them were genetic, which made it hard to believe he'd gotten a position as my servant, if that were the case.

She scowled. "He was Grand Duke Laudley's servant for five years. The former Grand Duke, I should say. He was using Gillian treatments in his last years, trying to stave off the inevitable."

"What? I thought those were illegal."

"It's illegal to sell or administer them as a medical treatment. But none of the components are banned by themselves. And there's no law against administering them to yourself. Which that man was crazy enough to do. It's lethal more often than not. But his father used them and lived to one hundred fifty."

She sighed. "Anyone  exposed to the radiation and the chemicals without the proper combination and timing of the doses will suffer the worst of the side effects, and die young. That's simply not in doubt." She looked at me. "Hamish would probably be dead already if Jonathan hadn't arranged to have him transferred here a few years back. When Bea was born, actually."

It didn't surprise me that Jonathan would do something like that. "Did Pete know?"

She arched an eyebrow at me. "Of course."

I smiled, though it was a bit subdued. "He likes to protect people." I said. "He's going to make a good father." But the stab of fear in my gut at the word took the smile away.

She gave me a speculative look. "Yes. He is." After a meaningful pause she added, "Is there a reason you came to see me this morning, Your Highness?"

I scowled at the title. She was one of the few people who would call me by name, but most of the time, she didn't.

"Yes, actually. Do you have time to talk?"

"I always have time for you," she said as she led me into her office. "Are you feeling all right this morning?"

"I'm fine, really. I didn't come for me. At least, not exactly."

She sat down behind her desk, folding her hands calmly in front of her, an expression of polite interest on her face. Far too studied and bland. I narrowed my eyes.

"Aliana told you."

She smiled. "The Grand Duchess did have a word with me several weeks back."

"She told you I'd be coming."

"She told me if you didn't come to see me before long, that I was to let her know so she could drag you in here herself."

"It's nice to know everyone's conspiring behind my back."

Her grin widened. "Only the Grand Duchess and myself."

"So I suppose if I said we were ready to have a kid right now, you've already got everything set up and ready in another room?"

She laughed. "It's not quite that easy. There's only so much I can do on my own, and without authorization."

A sudden suspicion crawled through me.

"Has Pete talked to you about this?"

"Many times," she said, without hesitation. "Both before and since you."

"Oh."

"Why does that surprise you? Producing an heir is a part of his duty he's known about all his life."

I nodded, stifling a sigh.

"So I guess this conversation is superfluous, then. You probably don't even need me."

Her face became very serious.

"Not only is that untrue and you know it, but none of us, especially your husband, would want you to go into this without feeling comfortable and knowing everything you need to know."

I scoffed. "If we waited for me to feel comfortable about it, we'd die childless."

Her expression softened. "It's not as scary as you think. You have a lot of support, not only personally but on a grand scale. The whole empire cares very much about this."

That was part of what I was afraid of.

It was a relief to meet Hera for lunch in the aquarium room. Even more so because the tranquility I always felt around her was no less in this setting than any other, and conversation came so easy.

"I knew things at the palace would be different," she said, "but in a way, they are not. I was often isolated on Torrea, but there it was due to my father's deliberate efforts. Here, living in the emperor's palace, I think I am still isolated, only for different reasons."

"I just can't believe," I said, "that you haven't been bowled over by some of the characters around here. Duchess Xian, for example, I can't imagine her sitting back and waiting for you to approach her."

Hera smiled shyly. "Aliana did tell me that she warned the nobles they must not approach me with overtures of friendship unless I indicated they should. She knew I sometimes have trouble fending off pushy people. But the problem is, of those who do not seem to be the troublesome, overbearing type, there have been none so far that stand out to me as anyone I would particularly like to know better. I do not want to be inundated all at once. Yet if I show favor to one and not another, I may be causing trouble or making a statement I do not mean to make." She sighed. "It has just seemed easier to keep to myself for a little while longer, until I have a better idea of the personalities and politics involved."

"Good luck with that," I grumbled.

She laughed, like the tinkling of bells. "But perhaps I will not need to do any of that. I have always kept the number of my close friends small. I have my husband, and you. That may be enough, I think."

"Me?"

A brief frown crossed her brow and her smile dimmed.

"I do not mean to be presumptuous, of course," she added.

"No!" I nearly yelled the word. "Stars above, that's not what I meant. It's just—" I frowned at the table. Tact and diplomacy were not my strong points. "I just mean, I didn't realize you considered me a friend."

Her smile recovered, though it was still shaky. "But of course I do. I thought we understood each other on that point."

"Duchess, I never pretend to understand anyone around here, and I certainly don't assume that what they say and what they do mean anything of substance, especially if it is in any way nice to me. Especially—"

I bit off the end of the sentence, glaring at a big orange fish swimming in lazy circles under my plate.

"Especially a Blaine?" she finished for me.

I didn't have an answer to that, not wanting to test the hypothesis that it was physically impossible for me to say anything nice about Blaine.

"Jacob," she said quietly, "I do not know all that has happened or been said between the two of you. Enryn has spoken to me about you, but we do not talk about you, if you understand the difference."

I nodded.

"What I choose to think and feel are privileges I reserve for myself. I will not have my friends chosen for me, or be told who I may not like. Whatever happened between you and him, it need not be a part of our relationship, if you do not want it to be."

"I wouldn't want you to have trouble with your husband, just to be friends with me."

"If there were to be trouble, it would be because he did not realize that who I spend my time with is not his decision to make."

And so, unexpectedly and from the strangest source, I had a friend at the palace.

Hera and I didn't even talk about her pregnancy that day, and yet, just enjoying her company made me feel relaxed and hopeful in general. Watching her, knowing she was carrying a child and that she wasn't frightened or concerned, had an effect on me.

The hungry way Pete looked at her at dinner that night, even if it was brief and quickly smoothed away, was the final thing I needed to strengthen my resolve.

I went to Dr. Heinriksen to arrange it.

We were dressing for dinner the next night and again Pete was quiet, lost in his own thoughts.

"I'd like to do something for you," I said. As always, no matter how preoccupied he was, he gave me his full attention once I spoke to him. He deserved better than he got with me, but I was glad, at least, that I realized how amazing he was.

"What's that?" Pete said, waggling his eyebrows suggestively.

I laughed. "Later. Actually, I was thinking it was more something I wanted you to have, for us to have."

"Yeah?"

"Yeah. I want us to have a baby."

He went very still. A rush of emotion lit his eyes. "You really mean that?" His voice was unsteady and I realized with a shock that hit me between the eyes that this was something he'd wanted even more than I'd realized. He stepped closer to me, raising a trembling hand to my cheek. "Are you sure?"

It took me a moment to catch my breath.

"Yes," I said, only a little shaky.

He grabbed my head with both hands and brought my face

to his in a hard, fierce kiss. When he pulled away, he laid his forehead to mine, eyes closed.

"Thank you," he breathed.

You're welcome seemed a ridiculous thing to say, so I said nothing. The way he held me, radiating quiet happiness, said more than enough.

And so it all started. The process of producing a child from the male emperor and his male husband wasn't something that happened quickly. Not that the science of it was that difficult. The technology was centuries old. But the matter of who would carry the emperor's child was an issue given an importance beyond even what I'd feared.

It was a production that lit up the empire like a bonfire lit in an overwhelming rush of excitement and speculation. Word leaked from the palace before the official announcements were even made, and so when the statements were released, that the emperor would be choosing the young woman who would carry his child, half of the eligible women in the empire were already scheming.

There were entire committees and task forces assigned to the selection process. The physical and situational requirements were rigorous. Anything less than perfect health and circumstances would disqualify a candidate. It was narrowed even further to only considering the high class.

It had been decided that allowing a noblewoman to carry the child could be seen as favoritism and give a powerful family undue leverage and influence with the emperor. But the surrogate couldn't be considered lowly. The high class it was.

As a way to narrow the pool and protect the emperor's interests, the candidate selected would not be eligible to be elevated to the nobility by either Pete or his heir. This wasn't as much of a deterrent as it sounded like. Only a fraction of the high class, the richest and most influential, those who had been so for generations, had any chance of being raised to the nobility.

The young woman who would carry the heir now could build wealth and influence for her own family from the honor, and a few generations down the road, it might well pay off.

Once the pool of candidates had been narrowed by as many variables as possible, the woman would be selected by lottery.

We decided we didn't want to create embryos and then shop among them for the best one. We wanted to create a child, our child, and have him or her be who they were meant to be, without us mucking about in the process. Eggs were created that contained my genetic material, and then one of them was fertilized with Pete's.

There was genetic testing, of course, to ensure that the embryo carried no defects, but Pete wouldn't allow more than one embryo to be created at a time. "It's a little piece of the two of us," he said. "And I'd never agree to discard anything made by you and me together."

Such a romantic.

Pete and I were at breakfast when Dr. Heinriksen came to see us. Pete offered her a seat and tea, both of which she accepted.

She took a sip and set the cup back down.

"Implantation is confirmed," she said.

Pete and I both stared at her for a moment. Comprehension clicked faster for him than it did for me. His hand tightened on his own cup.

"It is?"

She smiled fondly at him. "Yes. Congratulations. I know you two will make wonderful parents."

I spent that day in a sort of distracted half-shock, half-excitement. I was surprised by the fact that I actually seemed to want this now, at least, peripherally. It was so important to Pete. He was so excited. I kept seeing the look on his face when she told him. I could be happy for him, at least. It kept the fear at bay.

# CE 18

That night I dreamed of Dead End, but it wasn't a Resettlement camp on that rock on the edge of the solar system, it was Abenez. All the unclass in the empire had been dumped there, discarded. We were sent outside, day after day, with no grav-boots, no tethers, nothing more than a suit and an oxygen tank between life and an icy death. Any wrong move and you simply floated away, to die alone in the cold vastness of space. Every work detail was solitary. No coms, no companion but the sound of your own panicked breathing. Nothing but the ground beneath your feet, and the stars.

Inside, there was Kafe. Waiting. And every night it happened again; first as it had been, alone with her in the dark, restrained by nothing more than her threats and my fear. But then it was in the common room with all the inmates gathered around, laughing and jeering. Or in a quiet corner where the guards didn't go, held down by her goons who chuckled and watched with a wicked gleam in their eyes, waiting for their turn with me.

Helplessness and powerless desperation gripped my throat like a pair of hands, squeezing, cutting off air and life.

I woke up, my breath loud and too-fast, too-hard.

"It's OK, Jake." Pete's hands on me were warm and gentle, but they felt like the hands in the dream, a crawling, nauseating sensation on my skin. "It's OK. Just a nightmare. You're all right."

I concentrated on my breathing, forcing it into a more normal rhythm, concentrated on Pete's hands, on believing they were

Pete's and not jerking away.

He pulled me against him, put his arms around me. "What was it about?" he murmured into my hair.

I waited, as if thinking. "I don't know. I can't remember."

There was nothing to tell. It hadn't happened.

"You don't remember it at all? Even a little bit? Sometimes it helps to start talking, and then the rest comes back."

"I don't remember. Not even a little bit." I focused on relaxing into his embrace. "It's all right. Let's just go back to sleep. I'm OK."

His lips moved against the side of my face. "I love you."

I bit down hard on the urge to beg him to prove that I'd never be so powerless again, that he wouldn't let Blaine get any more power over the unclass, because I was unclass and he knew it. That there would never again be in my life someone who could hold me down, force me, hurt me, make me terrified and ashamed, knowing I had no way to fight back. Like my father. Like Kafe.

I breathed in and out with deliberation until I had the impulse under control.

He hummed tuneless nonsense as we settled back down, tangled together. I didn't sleep again that night, brooding alone to the rhythmic sound of his breathing.

When I met Hera for our lunch that afternoon, Blaine was in the room as well.

I stopped short just inside the doorway.

Blaine's head jerked up, Hera looked at me as well, her cheeks coloring.

"Enryn, I told you this morning I had my usual plans for lunch. It would be rude to cancel now," she nodded in my direction. "Unless you would like to join us?"

Blaine and I shot each other startled looks.

"Otherwise," her voice came, soft and conciliatory, "since your afternoon is free, I can meet you when I am finished here."

Blaine glared at her now, but she held his gaze, unapologetic.

"Enjoy your lunch," he said stiffly and left without another word.

For a long moment, neither of us spoke.

"I am sorry about that," she said. "He had a difficult meeting with his advisers this morning and he came to find me."

"It's all right," I said. "If you want to have lunch with him, it's fine with me."

She shook her head as she smoothed the napkin in her lap. "No. I look forward to our lunches. I will see him this afternoon and this evening and all day tomorrow. He is not lacking opportunities to spend time with me."

"Just so long as you're not spending time with me?" I said, not really a question.

She gave me a tight, strained look. "He knows I do not share his opinion of you." She picked the napkin up off her lap and shook it out again in an uncharacteristically fidgety gesture for her. "And I would like to enjoy this lunch that I look forward to every week."

She gave me a smile that wasn't up to her normal standard, but I couldn't blame her for that. I sat down and, both doing our best to pretend nothing had happened, we were served lunch. For a long time neither of us spoke of anything beyond the most unimportant blandishments. Nonsense. I don't think she was thinking of the actual words we were saying any more than I was.

Finally, my natural talent for blurting out exactly what I shouldn't say asserted itself.

"How can you do it?" I said. "You have to be one of the kindest people I know. How can you stand him?"

She glanced up at me, and her expression softened, her eyes no longer pinched and tight.

"Perhaps that is why," she answered.

I frowned in confusion. "What do you mean?"

She looked at me, but then away again.

"You are not the first person to tell me I am kind. I have thought about that many times. I suppose it is easier to be kind when you look for the things to like about a person rather than the other way around. I have always been that way." She looked back at me. "He does have redeeming qualities, you know."

I was quite sure I didn't want her to elaborate on that. And I felt awful. Not for what I thought of him, but for saying anything to her about it.

"I'm sorry. I shouldn't have said that. It's none of my business." I grimaced. "I guess I'm the opposite of kind."

She shook her head. "It is not your fault. You have such difficulty trusting people. I do not think you are truly unkind, but you think you need to keep everyone at a distance."

I made an effort not to gape at her.

"It is not a criticism, Jacob," she added quietly. "You have good reason to feel that way."

I wanted to say "Your husband is one of them," but I didn't. It wasn't her fault, and wouldn't be fair.

I examined her, poking around inside myself to see why her words calmed me.

"I trust you," I said, finally.

She ginned from under her lashes again. "That is because I am kind," she said.

"No," I said, abrupt and certain. "I mean, you are kind. But that's not why."

"No?"

I shook my head. "It's a lot more than that. You're—" I met her gaze straight on. "You may be the only genuinely honest person I've ever met. Not the way I do it, by accident because I can't hide what I really mean. You truly mean what you say. It's the strangest thing I've ever seen. But I like it."

Making her laugh hadn't been the point, but it was a wonderful feeling all the same.

There was nothing to do now but wait. Renewing my focus on the Tonga project gave me something else to think about. I mentioned the work to Hera over one of our lunches. We'd established a

137

routine that we both fiercely protected from interruption, so that we met at least once a week. Hera's eyes lit up as I described the project to her, questions tumbling from her like an overexcited child. It was so wonderful to have someone else get enthusiastic about my work for the unclass that I was almost giddy. She wanted to know everything and when I offered to show her what I was doing in the lab, she wanted to go right away.

When I finished the tour of the project, she sighed.

"Back home I was working with children in the low class section of the nearest city. Their needs are different. I did much with improving their educational opportunities. But my father did not permit me to work with the unclass. The work I did was very fulfilling, but it saddened me to know of children with much more pressing needs so nearby that I was not allowed to help."

"You're always welcome to help me," I said.

She beamed at me. "You would not mind?"

I snorted. "No, Hera. I would not mind."

While Kirti still managed the meta project, Hera became her liaison for logistics on my end and I was surprised at what a difference it made. It was a big project when it came down to it, arranging for the necessary equipment to be delivered and installed, locals recruited and trained, and the necessary repairs and expansions of their current infrastructure. Hera and Kirti managed it all.

I handled the science. It was simple in the end. Building off of ideas that had come of my work with the Dawes Laser, I devised a neat and effective way to compress the energy being transmitted into a tighter band that tripled output and reduced energy loss by a factor of ten.

It was an amazing feeling, watching it all come together, something I had done that was going to improve the lives of millions.

We all judged it best, and Pete agreed—even Blaine agreed, though I don't know how much Hera had to lean on him—

that the project should be kept quiet, implemented without advertising it to the empire at large. In truth, I didn't care if anyone ever knew about it at all. I had done something that would actually matter for the unclass, and not just the unclass of Abenez. I didn't want to share, or sully it, by letting the rest of the empire know and express their opinion on the matter. And besides that, it was safer. No one could oppose a project they didn't know about.

Kirti came to the palace to coordinate the final details and to accompany the implementation team to Tonga.

"That's a great idea," I said to her, when she brought it up. "I'm sorry I didn't think of it myself."

Kirti grinned at me. "To be honest, I didn't think of it either. That is, I thought of it, but I didn't think it was an allowable option so I dismissed it. Duke Blaine suggested it, practically insisted on it."

"Blaine?" My skin prickled. I hadn't realized he was involved, beyond giving it the official go-ahead from his department. I hadn't realized Kirti had been dealing with him. That *bothered* me. "When did you talk to him?"

She shrugged. "I've talked with him many times since Hera became involved in the project. He asked for weekly reports, and has followed up for details more than once."

"Why didn't you tell me?"

She cocked an eyebrow. "I wasn't aware I had to report to you every conversation I had."

I huffed. "Not every conversation, but didn't you think I might want to know that you were *regularly* talking to Blaine about my project?"

She brushed off my irritation. "I thought you knew."

"Why didn't you at least say something, just to make sure?"

She cut me a quick glare, but I didn't miss the fact that she dropped my gaze quickly.

"Honestly, Jake. I thought you trusted me."

"It never occurred to me that I couldn't."

This time her glare could have bested any laser I'd ever designed.

"When you're ready to apologize to me for that asinine remark, you know where to find me."

But she departed Earth before I got a chance to, and that, too, shocked me. Why was she avoiding me? What didn't she want me to know?

# CE 19

**S**till discomfited from my unresolved fight with Kirti, I attended one of Pete's private council sessions the next morning.

It was a habit I'd decided to get into. There was too much going on, too much that impacted me, for me to not to go, no matter how much I didn't want to. And I needed them to see I wasn't afraid, that I was watching and paying attention. I decided it was best to do it without advance notice and with enough variation that they wouldn't be able to predict whether I was coming or not. I meant to keep them on their toes. I meant not to be trapped.

But that was exactly how I felt when I walked in and caught the end of something Blaine had been saying to Duke Shanks.

"There should be no need for such measures," he said in an exasperated tone, not as if he meant to contradict. "The unclass being pampered like this will only make them think they have the power to make demands, to expect the empire to cater to them now." His head turned in my direction, his eyes widened in surprise for only a moment and then he looked away, though he didn't turn his head, and I couldn't have missed what he said next. "No matter how much power they may think they have now, it's all nonsense. It's been proven time and time again that allowing such thinking only leads to disaster. But, you're right, perhaps they need a reminder of how truly powerless they are."

I took my seat in the corner and stayed for the rest of the meeting. What else could I do? I wasn't about to run out now. I couldn't have said later what they discussed, though.

I didn't mention it to Pete. There was nothing to tell him. It was Blaine's petty bullying again. It was nonsense. Pete noticed I was quiet that evening, but when he asked I gave him a vague, meaningless answer as to why. He frowned but didn't ask again. That did nothing to help my irritation.

I was still brooding the next morning, flicking through my mails with only half my attention on them, when a strange message header caught my eye. The preview was indecipherable, as if the data had been garbled along the way. I knew I should do the sensible thing and send it to the security team unopened. But when have I ever been sensible?

It was a video that opened onto a mélange of light and sound and activity. Dozens of moving bodies in the camera's field, all wearing brown prison-issue suits, milling around in the bit of free time between the meal and the return to the cell for the night.

One figure broke away and turned down the hallway to the cells, alone. I didn't even have to look to know it was me. I'd done that so many times in my months on Dead End, retreating to my cell so I couldn't be accused of breaking the rules again and sent off to another eternity in solitary. A sick lump of inevitability settled in my gut as I watched three men follow me out of the room.

*I was backed into a corner and a big, bald goon punched me. I tried to pull away, but he grabbed my hand, which I'd curled instinctively in a fist, and slammed it into the wall. Then he punched himself in the nose and I watched in horror as the slow line of blood trickled into his grinning mouth.*

The playback cut to black just as the guards came around the corner.

A video that shouldn't have existed. A video that *hadn't* existed when I'd needed it to prove my innocence.

*The other inmates who "found" us swore that we'd been fighting, and my bruised, scraped knuckles, and the fact that we'd been in a corner where the surveillance devices had been malfunctioning, were testimony enough against me.*

*I served my last eight days of work detail in solitary.*

*I began to think I was really alone, left adrift in a universe void of any life at all, so that mine too was just a fading nothing. I began to think I was going mad. I began to want to.*

The screen hadn't gone black but was slowly revealing a vast starscape with a soundtrack of nothing but filtered, panicked breaths.

Eventually that faded away too. Leaving only the sound of mine.

When I was sure I wasn't hyperventilating, I did something I thought I'd never do: I canceled my lunch with Hera that day. I sent a message saying I wasn't feeling well. I couldn't face her yet. She would know something was wrong.

Naturally, since I'd claimed illness, Dr. Heinriksen showed up. I gave her enough vague symptoms that she frowned at me and packed her diagnostics away.

"Do you want to tell me what's really wrong, Jake?"

"I already did," I lied, not meeting her eye.

She sighed.

"How's the baby?" I said.

She moved into my line of vision and forced me to meet her eye, to make sure I saw her "I know what you're doing" face before she answered.

"The baby's just fine, as is Tina. The worst symptoms of early pregnancy are usually nausea, which I can do something about, and fatigue, which she can do something about. She can sleep all day if she needs to."

No doubt. She'd been moved into one of the Family bedrooms down the hall from us, and was probably the most protected and pampered person in the empire at the moment. No one was taking any chances with the emperor's baby.

"Are you sure you don't want to talk about it, Jacob," Dr. Heinriksen said, in a tone that clearly said she'd changed the subject.

"Nothing to talk about, doc."

Pete didn't believe me either. There wasn't anything either of them could do about it.

The next day I had my postponed lunch with Hera. She asked too, and for a moment, I had the powerful urge to really answer her. To tell someone, to get rid of the ball of fear that sat like a stone in my middle, that clenched in my chest. I took in her sincere expression, the concern in her eyes. It didn't even matter that she was married to him. She would keep my confidences.

I didn't tell her, either. The moment passed and life went on.

Six weeks after Dr. Heinriksen confirmed the implantation, the pregnancy was announced to the public. There was a festival air about the palace, and reportedly all over the empire.

The mother miscarried two weeks later.

"It's always a possibility," Dr. Heinriksen said, when she told us. Pete's face had gone blank, but Dr. Heinriksen was no more fooled by it than I was. "As advanced as medicine is, we can't control everything. Miscarriage is rare in planned, well-managed pregnancies, but it does happen. We'll simply try again."

"Of course," Pete said, his voice flat. "How soon can we start?"

"Today," she answered. "The next surrogate can be brought in and we can begin immediately."

Pete nodded, one quick jerk of the head. "Do it."

Dr. Heinriksen shot me a worried look when Pete turned away, marching briskly out of the room. I grimaced at her before hurrying after him.

Pete slowed to allow me to catch up, but it felt more like politeness than willingness to bear company at the moment. We walked together in silence until we were in our own rooms. He walked past me into the bedroom and out onto the balcony. He stood there, bracing his hands on the railing, shoulders and back rigid.

"It's just a setback," I said.

I could see the flinch in his body.

"Yes." His reply was ragged, hoarse.

"We'll try again."

He stared out over the ocean, his hands gripping hard on the railing. "You're right. Just a setback." Nothing in the line of his body or even his voice agreed with me. I suddenly realized that this was different for him than it was for me. I'd been trying to pretend it wasn't happening. Pete wanted this. He'd had the promise of a child and it had been taken away from him.

I came up behind him and wrapped my arms around him, kissed his neck. "I'm sorry."

He turned in my arms so quickly he nearly chinned me, his arms tightened around my neck, a sudden explosion of what I thought at first was shivering and quickly realized were quiet sobs.

"It wasn't just a setback. It was a baby." The words were choked and wet.

I held him so tight I could barely breathe.

"I know. I'm so sorry, Pete. So sorry."

He clung to me until he stopped crying. It took a long time.

Pete's loss was a palpable thing and I felt helpless in the face of it, made worse by my own guilt that I didn't feel the same. I was disappointed, a little angry, even sad to some extent, but Pete was grieving. I began to regret that we had restarted the process so quickly. It was almost as if he wasn't aware of it this time.

I would have given anything for something to distract him.

I sorely regretted that sentiment two weeks later when we got the news from Tonga.

# CE 20

**C**atastrophic explosion," Pete said. Or I thought he said. My head had filled with white noise the moment I realized what he was talking about.

"Imperial representatives were still there when it happened." He stopped and took my hand in his. I gasped a strangled breath.

"Don't say it," I begged, shaking my head. "She wasn't still there. She couldn't have been." Pete just watched me, holding my hand tight.

"I didn't get to apologize," I croaked.

"I'm so sorry, Jake."

"It wasn't a volatile design. There wasn't anything that could just up and explode."

Pete nodded. "I understand. But something did explode. It took out the facility and all the people in it, and wiped out everything in a one-mile radius."

"How many dead?" Because I wasn't going to think about *my* dead. Except they were all my dead, weren't they? Hadn't that been the point?

"More than 80,000 unclass, and the twelve facilitators, including," he hesitated, but plowed on, "including Kirti."

"But it's not possible," I said. Pete just held my hand in silence. I looked up at him, desperate for him to understand. "It's not like that. There's nothing there that could cause a reaction like that. It's *not* possible."

"I know," he said quietly.

"Someone did this," I ground out from between my teeth. Pete squeezed my hand, looking down.

"I know that, too."

I almost didn't care that The Patriot managed to broadcast, in its entirety, a response to the events on Tonga.

*There is emerging evidence that the explosion was triggered by the locals, in retaliation against imperial officials for the many deaths in that area the winter past. The unclass seem to claim that the local government did nothing to help them obtain adequate heat during the cold months when, in fact, they had sabotaged and destroyed the authorities' efforts in the past. Perhaps they didn't intend the large scale destruction this incident caused. The Patriot can't help but think that whatever the consequences of their lawlessness in this incident, it is no less than they deserve. The imperial government has been entirely too generous and lenient with the unclass everywhere in the past year. How much longer will this go on? Twelve loyal and hardworking imperial representatives were killed. How many next time?*

*A troubling pattern is emerging. With Prince Jacob's subversive efforts on behalf of the unclass, overturning the very order of things not just in his home district of Abenez, but now on Tonga, and undoubtedly elsewhere too, can we expect his kind to ignore this blatant disregard of the rules of our society?*

*The unclass will continue to be a problem so long as these confusions and contradictions exist. Rules of society are meant to bring order and stability. When they're ignored at the highest levels, what can we expect of those below? Inconsistencies breed chaos. The emperor uses a firm hand when real trouble starts, but when things quiet again he forgets caution. Our emperor is a good man and an excellent ruler. But he's being compromised and undermined by those he keeps closest to him. For all the pardons and platitudes, Prince Jacob was once convicted of treason. And now he sits at the emperor's side, whispering in his ear. The Patriot can't be the only one who sees the danger in that.*

*Can we really expect the people to remember and keep to their place and role in society when Prince Jacob's mere existence not only flies in the face of that, but flaunts the rewards of lawlessness? It is a volatile situation. We should all be concerned.*

The palace did not remain quiet this time.

"There is a dangerous and seditious element forming within the empire," old Lord Sifer said in a formal release. "Treason of this kind will not bring stability, or solve problems we must face together. Legitimate concerns brought to the imperial ruler in formal petitions have always been given serious concern by this emperor, and are the only legal means of addressing issues. This so-called Patriot is a traitor and a threat to the empire, and will not be ignored. The palace will root out the perpetrators and deal with them as the law requires. Anyone who aid and abets them, even by perpetuating this kind of talk among their acquaintances, is guilty of treason and, when found, will be executed.

"May the emperor live forever!"

# CE 21

The explosion in Tonga blew me back to Abenez. I'd been content before with making a difference from afar, riding the feeling of charity and accomplishment from Kirti's reports. Tonga was now a bitter reminder of my own impotence. Of Kirti's death. I needed to do something. See it done. Do it with my own hands.

And this time, I wouldn't be in disguise. No more hiding. I meant to go there as their duke and prince, distribute food and medicine and hope as myself, as someone they knew and could depend on. If I was going to be a symbol, I would do it on my own terms.

Pete was determined that I was not going to take the risk. I vented to Hera about it one afternoon and found, quite suddenly, all obstacles and objections cleared away.

Hera was going with me.

She was hugely pregnant, already in her ninth month. But Dr. Heinriksen was confident she was not ready to deliver and in no danger traveling to Mexico City and engaging in light activity. And, quite opposite my expectations, the risk assessments for the entire venture, once a very prominent and much loved pregnant woman was added to the equation, decreased dramatically. She announced her intention to join our team, and all of the major objections melted away.

But before I went to Abenez, there was something else I had to do. And so first I went to the IIC, for Kirti's funeral.

I didn't get to bring Kirti's remains home. There were none. Walking empty-handed into the IIC felt like another way I'd let her down. At least I managed to avoid the arrival ceremony. My transport parked in the IIC's garage and I got out there, met only by Chuck.

His eyes were red and swollen and as I drew closer, they filled with tears. We met halfway and I threw my arms around him, hard, an embrace he returned with equal ferocity. He pressed his face into my neck with the force of a punch, as if he meant to hurt me. I wished he did. I wanted him to hurt me, to blame me, even though I knew he wouldn't.

"I wish you weren't here," he choked. "For this reason, I mean. I'm glad you came, though."

"You think I wouldn't?"

He shook his head, still buried in my neck.

"Nah." He lifted his head and met my eye. "You wouldn't dare miss it. Kirti'd have killed you."

The momentary light in his eyes dimmed again, let down by his own attempt at a joke that didn't help. I squeezed his shoulders so tight that he winced, and he gave me a watery smile.

"Let's take the waterworks inside," he said.

I wanted to go to the lake, where the stream we liked to sit beside fed into the deep waters, where the stones were small and shiny, where Kirti and I had walked the night I told her I was leaving the IIC. But that was outside and I'd pushed my security restrictions enough lately, gotten farther than I'd expected, and I didn't want to deal with the hassle and get angry at being told no. Instead Chuck steered me down the hall, into the dormitories and through the door into his room.

No, not his room. Kirti's.

He took in my expression with an apologetic shrug.

"Most of my stuff's still in here," he said. "I haven't had the heart to take it back to my own room yet."

I sank to the couch with a sigh, burying my face in my hands. "You'd moved in together."

It wasn't a question. He'd just told me as much.

"I hadn't given up my own room, so, not technically. But I haven't actually stayed in my own room for months."

"I didn't realize it was so serious."

"What was there to realize?" I looked up at him, he was smiling weakly. "You know how she was. It wasn't anything official. We didn't talk about me moving in, it just happened."

I tipped my head against the back of the couch, closing my eyes against the pain. Yes, I knew how she was.

"I argued with her the last time I talked to her," I said. "Practically accused her of conspiring with Blaine or something ridiculous like that."

Chuck huffed. "I told her I loved her."

I looked up at him in shock. His expression was half-surprised as well.

"I'd never done it before. I hadn't planned it, either. She was heading off on her big project and she was excited and distracted and she kissed me, said she'd see me in a few months, and was already halfway to the transport and I said, 'I love you.'"

He chuckled, looking off into the distance, into the memory. "Stopped her dead. She turned back and looked at me like I'd lost my mind. Then she laughed. Her good laugh, you know, happy. And she came back and kissed me again and she said, 'Hold that thought. Three months. I'll be back.'"

"She loved you, too," I said.

"I know." And he did. Chuck didn't have it in him to doubt people he loved.

I sighed as if something inside me were breaking.

"I feel like it's my fault."

The next thing I knew, Chuck stood and smacked me on the side of the head. I stared up at him in astonishment.

"That's from Kirti," he said. "She'd have done it if she heard nonsense like that come out of your mouth." He shrugged. "I'll just have to do it for her, from now on."

An unexpected laugh popped out of my mouth.

"You're right. She never did put up with me being stupid, did she?"

He sank to the seat beside me and slung his arm around my shoulder, though the gesture was more exhaustion than camaraderie.

"One of the things we loved about her," he said.

"What are you going to do now," I asked.

He gave me a funny look and laughed. "The same thing I did yesterday, and the day before, and last week, and last year. The same thing I've been doing since I was ten and will be doing for the rest of my life." He shook his head at me. "I was about to say you really have forgotten what it's like here, but you never even knew, did you? You were too young when you left. You never lived this life."

"Of course I did. And then there were the three years I was Resettled here."

He waved that away. "Those don't count. You were so lost in your head most of that time it was like you weren't even here. I don't mean anything bad by it. It's just strange sometimes when you say things that make me realize how much you really don't understand." He softened the words with a grin. "I'm a scientist at the IIC. That's what I'm going to do now. That's what I was always going to do." He sighed and with a sadness that was so startling in Chuck, he said, "I'll just do it alone, now."

I met Hera at the new governor's mansion in Mexico City, where Kagawa had set up operations since I'd given him administration of the duchy. I wanted to make Mexico City the official capital again, but both Kagawa and Pete suggested waiting and tying the change to the next anniversary of the duchy's founding. It was to be a special celebration anyway, coming as it did only weeks after the empire's third centennial.

It was nice that neither of them objected to making the change itself. The capital had been moved by the second Duchess, who had wrinkled her nose at the spreading despair that was Abenez, and had left it behind for the ocean. I was going to move it back, put Abenez back at the heart of the duchy, force Mexico to claim its own, make it impossible to turn their eyes away and pretend they didn't see.

Hera hugged me when I arrived.

"If you want to talk, or anything, I'm here."

"Thank you," I said, meaning it. But I felt strangely possessive of my grief over Kirti. I wasn't ready to share it outside the IIC.

We went into Abenez the next morning for a large-scale and intensive medical clinic and food distribution effort. Skilled workers were brought in from all over the duchy, and paid full wages for their services. All of the unskilled work, no matter how it was categorized typically, was provided by the people who lived in Abenez and they were paid the going rate for jobs they wouldn't have qualified for in any other situation. It was twice and three times what most of them could expect to earn in a day. Residents were also organized into a paid citizen militia for the day. They were given no weapons, of course, and were largely symbolic and show. But I could see and feel the sense of pride, both in those employed for the day for the benefit of their own, and those who came for services and saw their fellow unclass in such an important role.

The turnout was overwhelming, and yet Kagawa and his team had planned meticulously. It wasn't the first such event they had run in Abenez and other slums in the duchy since I'd put him in place as the governor. In almost every case, there were no troubles, and no one was sent home without food and medical care.

The only detail of the arrangements I didn't like was that we were accompanied by a crew that would record the event so that later it could be shown to the empire at large. Blaine was behind that, and it grated on my nerves that he would get positive publicity for all the wrong reasons, from this thing I was doing for all the right ones. But, with Hera's participation as his leverage in the negotiations, he got his way.

As part of the security arrangements, it was advertised as previous events had been, and no mention was made of my visit. It was good in that there was no stuffy welcoming ceremony, no hullabaloo that made this about me rather than the people we'd come to help. And yet, there was the uncomfortable itchy feeling of being watched, of the rush of whispers as the news spread.

*"The Prince Consort!" "It's Prince Jacob!" "It's him, the one who went to the Complex place. And then he married the emperor. Remember?"*

I almost laughed when I heard that one. I liked that they remembered me for something other than being married to Pete. Or the really bad things that had happened between me leaving the IIC at fifteen and him proposing to me years later.

Somehow, because it was never officially announced who I was, it gave people permission to pretend they didn't know. They took food packets from my hand with only a red-faced giggle, or a pale, breathless "thank you." My line was always longer than anyone else's. And even when they took food from the others, usually their eyes were on me. I could handle that in a way I couldn't at the palace; I could like it, even. They knew why I was here and, even better, I was *proud* of why I was here.

Hera was a well of kindness and patience, refreshing and pleasant to be around. Gradually, I began to notice people flocking to her in almost the same proportion they were to me. I liked that very much. I looked over at her just in time to see a small boy, two or three years old, tug on her pants leg. She looked down and crouched in front of him with a mother's alacrity— in spite of the swell of her belly. She took the boy in her arms before pulling away to listen, with her full attention, to whatever he spoke to her about, with all the grave earnestness of his years.

Over the course of the next half hour, I looked over from time to time as Hera presided over a medic tending to the boy and the collection of people clustered around him—family, presumably. Each was given a thorough assessment, inoculations, treatments. And Hera made sure each ate a full meal before she sent them on their way with arms stuffed with food packets. She kissed the boy's grubby cheek, as his chubby arms clutched her around the neck, before he ran off into the growing dusk. Hera stood for a long time watching him before she turned away, subdued, and went back to her work.

I was still watching her when one of the documentary team came up to me.

"Excuse me, Your Highness. Do you have a moment to give us a comment for the record?"

No. Pete had warned me this would happen and I was prepared, but I didn't have to like it. I gritted my teeth and plastered on my best serious face.

"As important as it is to do this, to bring the unclass the food and medicine they need right now, we shouldn't have to feed and clothe them when they could do it themselves, and would do it for themselves if only they had the opportunity. We're forcing them to live off of our charity because our laws, and our resistance to change, deny them the dignity and right to provide for themselves, to make positive contributions to society."

The prepared words that had felt so hollow and insincere in the palace took on a weight and emotion here where I could see the faces of the very people I was talking about.

"Anyone who thinks they live off of handouts because they choose that over honest work is fooling themselves. No one wants to live like this. They would work as hard or harder than any higher class person if they were allowed to. But they're relegated to jobs that were replaced by automation centuries ago, or only exist in places they can't go." I turned and indicated the crowd behind me with a sweep of my arm. "This is our fault, not theirs. And it's our responsibility to fix it, not with occasional charity, but real, lasting change."

I nodded to the man that I was finished and they thanked me, moving away. I took another look around me, feeling both deflated and hopeful at the same time.

There was a tug on my sleeve and I looked down to find a small boy, no more than five, I guessed, glaring at me.

"You're not really the prince, are you?"

His indignation made me laugh.

"I'm afraid so."

He crossed his arms. "Then you're not really from here."

"Do you not want me to be?"

He shook his head. "You can't be unclass and a prince too."

I sighed. "So I've been told."

He gave me a doubtful look. "So, are you one of us or not?"

I examined his offended expression, the stiff, angry posture. I remembered feeling the way he did, being so certain. Even after I'd been taken away, hardly daring to believe it was true.

"I am. I was born here in Abenez, just like you."

He shook his head at me, livid.

"*Verdad.*"

His eyes widened in surprise, quickly narrowing into suspicion, and I realized what I'd said. I'd forgotten this, as I'd forgotten as many things as I could about my time in Abenez. But the boy's accent, one peculiar to this place, a lilt of the old language before Standard, brought one of our hoarded words to my lips.

I watched his expression soften in concession. People outside of Abenez didn't use our words.

"Does that mean," he hesitated, struggling with conflicting flickers of disbelief and curiosity, "that I could leave too?"

My throat tightened. "I hope so. That's what I'm trying to do." I looked away, afraid of the hope I saw lighting his eyes. "I can't promise anything. But I'll try."

He allowed me a smile. Even without promises, it was more than he'd before.

"OK," he said. "You can be the prince, then." As if granting me his permission.

"Thank you," I replied. He cast me one more pensive glance before he ran away.

"Your Highness?"

The voice was hesitant, almost apologetic, but it snapped at my attention like a whipcord. At memory that didn't surface but was just there, nudging me. I turned to find a withered old man watching me with wide, hopeful eyes.

No, not old, no more than middle aged, but Abenez made everyone look older, drank life and vitality fast and early. Something about his face, the way he held his mouth maybe, the tilt of his eyes, more than the look of him, pushed harder at the memory I still couldn't reach.

"Yes?" I replied.

He exhaled a long breath, relief perhaps. Had he been afraid?

"I'm sorry to bother you, Your Highness, but they," he cast a look behind him, a vague gesture at a large and growing group, "everyone asked me to let you know, tell you that your mother and sister never went hungry while they were still here. We made sure of that, after you left."

My heart seized, the breath catching in my lungs. No. Surely not. I looked around.

The crowd of faces. It was familiar, more in aggregate than because I recognized the individuals. The buildings...I turned. Backed up. The colors were fresher, but I could see them the way they had been, sad, washed out, dirty. So much more starkly neglected and crumbling when compared to the shining transport that had been hovering over the muddy street, the IIC's logo bright on its gleaming door. I wasn't sure I was capable of turning around and looking at what I now knew I would find. I closed my eyes. It made it easier.

When I opened them again, I was facing the building, recently scrubbed and painted, but undoubtedly the same crumbling building where I had lived. There on the ground floor was Mr. Sacks' store. Three floors above, at the back, would be the apartment I'd shared with Ma and Carrie when Director Kagawa showed up at my door to take me to the IIC.

I looked back at the man, so much smaller than I remembered.

"Mr. Sacks."

He beamed.

"I didn't think you would remember, Your Highness."

I shook my head, though I didn't know if I meant "'of course I would'" or "'I can't believe I did.'"

"I didn't realize," I said, finding the breath hard to come by, "I didn't realize where we were. I'm sorry."

He looked stricken that I'd apologized.

"You took care of Ma and Carrie?"

"Yes," he said, gesturing again behind him. "We weren't in the habit of abandoning our own anyway, but we were so proud that they wanted you at the great place, there wasn't anybody who didn't see to it that your ma and sister lacked for nothing. Well, nothing we had to give them, at least."

I felt broken and raw. It had been my greatest fear for years, worse than being sent away from the IIC, or of what anyone there could do to me: the fear that back home, without me, my mother and sister were starving, in need, hurting, and there was no one to take care of them.

"Thank you," I rasped, looking past Mr. Sacks at the growing crowd behind him. "Thank you. You don't know what that means to me."

Pleasure rippled through the group, smiles sweeping over them, murmurs. Someone giggled. It felt like the world was tilting out from under my feet.

I focused on Mr. Sacks again. "You knew I was stealing food sometimes, and you let me get away with it, didn't you?"

I'd been impressed with my stealth at the time. I'd come to doubt that ability later, when it worked nowhere else.

He gave me a sheepish grin. "Well, if it had been a while since you'd come in with money to pay, I'd look the other way if a sack of beans slipped out the door with you. Couldn't do it often, but I tried to keep track of the kids who needed it the most, make sure my back was turned."

My throat tightened.

He chuckled. "Funny thing about you. Other kids would take tins of meat, the sorts of things they couldn't afford to buy when they did have money. You always took the beans."

I stared at him. It seemed so clear at the time, so obvious. We needed food, as simple as that. I hadn't been thinking of anything so outside of my experience as tins of meat. I laughed too.

"I don't think I even knew where the tins of meat were. I didn't know anything about tins of meat."

He gave me a soft smile. "Your sister did. I'd take them to her myself, when I could."

Tears burned in my throat and behind my eyes. I dug frantically in my pockets for the coins Jonathan had put there; a cold shock to my sweaty hand. Without even looking at them, I pressed them into Mr. Sacks' hand.

"Thank you," I said. "I'm sorry I stole from you. Maybe this will make up for it, and for what you gave my family."

He was already shaking his head even as he opened his hand to see what I'd given him.

"It wasn't like that. You don't have to—"

The words just stopped and he stared at the glinting pile of coins in his hand. He picked one up, large and heavy, shiny and new. He stared at it as if he had no idea what he was looking at. I didn't either, for that matter. Physical money was considered quaint anywhere else, but in the slums, where many would never even see a working vid in their lives, there was no other currency besides trade. I hadn't realized how very long it had been since I'd used coins like that. I didn't even recognize the one he was holding.

He gasped and turned pale.

"A thousand?"

Scalding embarrassment swept over me. A thousand dollar coin. One of a handful I'd given him. I felt cheap and tawdry, as if I were teasing them with this largess, as if I were one of those privileged nobles who would throw coins like that at starving children, never realizing they were worthless in a place where people would never see a hundred dollars together at one time, let alone ten times that. Mr. Sacks wouldn't take, let alone keep as profit, enough money in five years to make change for something like that.

"I'm sorry," I blurted. "I didn't mean—"

He met my eye, his face glazed with astonishment.

"Thank you," he breathed. He looked at the pile in his fist again. "We'll cherish them, Your Highness." His bow was stiff but heartfelt. He turned to the nearest person in the crowd. "Look," he said, handing her one. "Aren't they beautiful. From the Prince Consort himself."

I didn't know whether to laugh or cry. Mementos. He was handing them out to the crowd, not as money, but as shiny gifts received from the Prince Consort's own hand.

I looked around for Jonathan in despair. He was standing just behind my shoulder. He held my gaze and gave me a small nod. I didn't even know what that meant, but I knew that he would take care of it.

I practically ran to the transport. Once I was behind three different closed doors, I sank to a chair, curled up into myself with my arms over my head, and gave into the shuddering.

I was left alone until I heard the ruckus of people loading back onto our transport. Jonathan knocked once on my door.

"Your Highness."

It was only then that I realized I'd locked it.

"I'm fine."

"We'll be underway, then, if you approve."

"Yes, thank you."

"May I unlock the door?"

"No." I hesitated. "Please, not yet."

Back at the governor's residence, Hera hugged me tight, planting a kiss on my cheek. She gave me a long appraising look, but didn't ask.

"Thank you for this," she said.

It took me a moment, and then I remembered the little boy, the way she'd held him, the look on her face as she watched him go.

"I wish people understood the good you do," she said. "But

even if they don't, I do, and I want you to know how much I appreciate you letting me be a part of it."

I think I fell in love with her that day, in a way that was no threat to her husband or mine. There were only a handful of people in the universe I truly cared for and trusted, and Hera would be one of them forever.

We went home and, after a brief flurry of reports about our trip, public interest waned more quickly than I'd expected. I wasn't sure how I felt about that.

I was having lunch with Pete when a servant came to tell us that Hera was in labor. Pete paled at the news.

I laid my hand over his.

"Do you want to get out of here?" I said. "Walk on the beach?"

Pete shook his head. "I have work I need to get back to."

I gave him a long look. He didn't avoid it, but his eyes begged me leave it alone. So I did.

I went to see her. I meant only to visit her rooms and get an update from her servants, have them tell her I had checked in on her. But when I got there and delivered my message, I wasn't given an update on her status, I was invited into her room.

Blaine wasn't there; I'd guessed as much from the fact that I was invited in, but I was relieved to see that guess confirmed. Hera was propped up in the bed, her face grim but focused. I approached her slowly, as if she were a wounded animal.

"Jacob!" she said, and I went to her side with alacrity.

"I'm sorry, I didn't mean to intrude."

She shook her head. "Not intruding."

The words were clipped off and terse. It was odd, because pain management had long ago become sophisticated enough that a woman like Hera Blaine would never have to feel even the first twinges of labor. But there was a definite sense of something happening. She was tense, focused. Anticipation was thick in the air. She took my hand without looking at me and held it—too hard for her on a normal day. I held on right back, and watched her.

For more than an hour I sat there. I said nothing, unless she asked me a question, which she did at odd intervals in a pattern that meant nothing to me. Each new question that emerged from the silence was something different and profound. As if in this process of bringing life into the world, everything was shrouded in meaning and significance.

But eventually Jonathan leaned down and whispered in my ear, "Duke Blaine is on his way."

I squeezed Hera's hand once and stood. She looked up at me, frowning. "I have to go," I said. "But your husband will be here soon."

The look on her face said clearly that she knew the proper phrasing there would have been "because" rather than "but." She smiled and squeezed my arm, though her lips were still pressed firmly together, and her attention went immediately back to whatever she had been doing in her silent, tense watchfulness.

I left quickly. Because Jonathan and the other servants had timed it so well, I didn't encounter Blaine at all. I wandered back to my own room, lost in the muddle of thoughts and emotions the last hour had churned up.

When I woke in the morning, there was a messenger waiting to tell us that Hera's son had been born in the night. Pete nodded to the servant, and for once left it to me to thank and dismiss him.

"She may want to rest," Pete said, not looking at me. "I don't suppose she'll want visitors right now. I'd hate to go and make her feel obligated to see us. Maybe we should wait."

"It'll still be there later," I said, and the tone of my voice made him look up at me.

"What will?"

"The fact that she has a baby and we don't."

He caught his breath. "I know that," he protested in almost a whisper.

I went over to him, put my arms around him.

He just shook his head against my shoulder. Which about summed it up.

Jonathan did all his servant magic and within the hour we were in the room where I'd last seen Hera. This time, she sat serenely in the bed, presiding over her new family. Blaine stood at her shoulder looking down at her and the baby in her arms. For once, he had little attention for even the emperor.

"Congratulations to you both," Pete said. "He's beautiful. What did you name him?" Pete's tone and expression were the very picture of the emperor's mask: exactly suited to the situation, with all of his real emotion hidden away.

Hera flicked a look at me.

"His name is Owenton," Blaine said, "after one of my great ancestors." Blaine gave an absent-minded nod to Pete. "And yours as well, I suppose. The man who almost was an emperor."

Pete went still. "Yes," he said. "A fine name."

"We plan to call him Owen," Hera said, in a calm, diplomatic tone.

Pete smiled at her. "I'm sure you're very proud of your son, Hera. Congratulations."

"Yes," I added, "you're amazing, Hera. Congratulations, he's beautiful." I stepped forward and placed a quick kiss on her cheek, Blaine be damned. She gave me a small but genuine smile.

But Blaine didn't even notice. He sank to a seat on the bed beside Hera, tracing the lines of the baby's face with a gentle finger. I looked away. I didn't want to see Blaine being...tender.

Pete cleared his throat. "We won't disturb you any longer. This should be time for you as a family, not an official reception."

"Thank you, Your Excellence," Hera said. She smiled at me. "Thank you too, Jacob, for coming."

The look on Pete's face as we left hurt, and I slipped my hand in his and squeezed once. He shot me a look of gratitude and held on tight.

When Dr. Heinriksen stopped by our room as we were eating breakfast the next morning to tell us that the implantation in the second surrogate had been successful, I could have kissed her for her timing. It was a bit of déjà vu, in an unpleasant way, and I think it was only in that moment she realized that telling us elsewhere might have been better. But Pete gave her a smile and thanked her. I caught her eye as she turned to leave, and I knew she'd seen it too, the cautious distance, the way Pete's smile had moved his mouth but stayed out of his eyes. He was going to be careful this time.

There was something terribly sad about that.

I had to meet with Blaine later that week. It had been his idea to take footage of our trip to Abenez and make it into a documentary to distribute throughout the empire. I hated that it had been his idea, but I couldn't argue the power of a visual image. And with Hera involved, Blaine couldn't try to make it look like a propaganda stunt, or use it to make me look like I was overreaching. Really, there were very few ways this could go wrong, I could hardly say no. And I was definitely going to make sure I knew what they were putting in it every step of the way.

Blaine had scheduled a meeting for me with the director and his editing crew. Unfortunately, he was there too. He smiled at me when I came in.

It was not a nice smile.

"I was reviewing some of the footage earlier, Your Highness. Very touching moment with the storekeeper."

I glared at him. "Yes, it was lovely, wasn't it. I don't think we should use it in the film, though." I turned to the director. "Do you?"

He cast a look between Blaine and me. "It depends on how you want this to go. It's a nice human interest piece, but it would put the focus on the Prince rather than the people. Unless we edit it carefully, which would take away much of its charm, I think."

"We could make it about his sister, then," Blaine said. "The little girl left behind in Abenez, and the shopkeeper who brought her canned meat. Probably shouldn't include the bit about Prince

Jacob stealing, though. We wouldn't want to remind people of his criminal tendencies."

A wave of fury carried me across the room and I grabbed the front of his shirt.

"What's wrong with you, Blaine? A few days ago you were almost nice. You're already back to being a jackass?"

The entire room held its breath.

Blaine pulled his shirt out of my grip and took a step back.

"Forgive me, Your Highness," and the humble note he put in it was a stinging reminder of who had just attacked whom, "Owen hasn't figured out the difference between day and night yet." There was a ripple of sympathetic chuckles. "I'm short on sleep and have misspoken, I think." He turned to the others. "If you'll excuse me, gentlemen, ladies, I seem to be disrupting the session. I will meet with you at another time."

He turned to the director. "On second thought, it might be best to leave the sister out as well. That story had its own tragic end. The point isn't to make people depressed. We want them to leave feeling introspective and motivated to act," he locked his gaze with me, "even guilty, perhaps, if their actions, or inaction, caused such suffering."

Before I could stop him, he was gone.

I returned to my room just before dinner, tired and frustrated, Blaine's words still rattling around inside me. I thumped into the chair in front of my desk, flicking on my messages for auto-play. There was a burst of noise, garbled and incomprehensible, and then the message, voice only, began to play.

"Jake?"

I'd been eight years old the last time I'd heard that voice, and she'd only been five. But I'd have recognized Carrie anywhere.

"Is that you?" the watery voice continued. The room was spinning. I clutched the armrests of the chair as if they were the only thing holding me up. "I don't know, maybe I'm wrong, but—" her voice cracked, "I don't have anyone else."

I stabbed at the message info, but there was nothing: nonsense and the voice.

"Ma said you were dead, but Mr. Sacks and some of the others, they said that couldn't be true. I keep seeing the news vids, and…I don't know, it was so long ago. But I think…I think it looks like you. Ma said they came and got you, and that you died, but I remember that man, and I'm not sure. Maybe he was from the IIC, like they say you are. Anyway, I guess if it isn't you, you won't even get this. I just know that I can't go on like this, and no one will help me. No one believes me. They're all high class and they know where I'm from. Is…if it's you, you know what I mean. We're just…what we are."

Her voice caught on a sob. "I'm scared. I'm so scared and alone and I know they all just wish I'd go away, but there's something—I don't understand anything about it but I hear them yelling about how they can't get rid of me. Something to do with why I'm here. And since there's someone at the palace with the same name as my brother, well, I just wonder if maybe that's what it is, that it's you up there. Did you let them put me here, Jake? Do you know about it? Did you—I mean, I don't know. I hate it here. I hate it. The things he does… Get me out of here. Please? Are you my brother? Do you remember me? Do you care? Please help me."

I barely had the wastebasket in hand before I threw up. Even as I retched, I couldn't stop thinking that if I'd gotten any on the floor, someone would clean it up. That there were a fucking legion of someones who would be there to wipe my ass, and my sister had been scared and alone and she died believing I'd ignored her pleas. Believing I didn't care.

I was still on my knees, dry-heaving into the bin when I heard him.

"Jake!"

Pete fell to his knees beside me, pulling me roughly against him, holding me too tight. Didn't he worry I was going to throw up on him? He didn't seem to think of it, or care. He just clung to me. I realized I was trembling; shaking so hard that even his solid strength pressed against me shivered with the force of my spasms.

He was mumbling. "It's OK, Jake. It's all right. We'll take care of it. It's OK."

I shoved him away from me.

"Take care of what? She's dead! What the fuck is there to take care of? She's DEAD!" I stumbled to my feet. "She died. She died after she sent me—and she thought I didn't fucking care enough to—"

My throat closed around the words and I couldn't finish. Pete was on his knees beside me again and only then did I realize that I'd fallen too.

"Let me hear it, Jonathan," he said. Jonathan. Jonathan had sent for Pete. But what was he going to fix?

I tried to get up, get away, but my body jerked—more like a seizure than a movement. Pete held me tight and didn't let me rise. He murmured nonsense noises and stroked my neck as he listened to the message in its entirety. I shuddered as if somehow I could shake off the knowledge, the guilt, the responsibility for my sister's suicide.

Pete was silent for so long after the message ended that I knew he'd realized what it all meant, and a new panic seized me.

"I never got it," I protested, trying to pull away. "I didn't know. I just found it. If I'd known back then. Pete," panic seized my muscles, "I never would have abandoned her. I never would have left her there. I would have told you. I would."

"I thought you told me Chuck gave you the nickname."

The complete non sequitor startled me out of my hysteria. "What?"

"Didn't you tell me that no one had ever called you "Jake" until Chuck did, when you first met him?"

I cast my thoughts around, trying to figure out what he was even talking about, clinging to the change of subject like a lifeline. Trying to grasp what this could possibly have to do with the fact that I'd abandoned my sister to abuse and death at her own hand, out of the despair of knowing she was all alone, that no one cared enough to help her. Not even her brother...

I spasmed with the need to get up, to run, to throw myself off the balcony, to run and run into the waves on the shore until there was no more running, until there was no more anything.

"Jake!"

Pete jerked me hard, gripping my arms so tight I began to realize it hurt. It might have been hurting for a while. I couldn't think.

"Jake. Answer me. Who gave you the nickname?"

My eyes darted about the room, looking for the answer in places it didn't exist.

"Chuck." My voice felt rusty, harsh. "Chuck. I told you. Chuck."

"So Carrie never called you Jake?"

"I—" Had she? I couldn't remember. My memories of her were so scattered, so jumbled with dreams and nightmares and all the times I'd tried to picture her life since I'd abandoned her, all the ways I'd imagined her. How many of my memories of her were really memories? The last time I'd seen her had been in our apartment as they'd led me off to the IIC. She was five. Standing in the apartment, sucking her thumb. Alone.

"Think, Jake," Pete said, his voice not harsh but demanding all the same. Steady. Like a rock. "What did Carrie call you?"

"I— I don't know. I don't remember."

"If Chuck was the first person to call you Jake, then she must have called you Jacob, right?"

"I— Yes. Probably. I guess. I think so."

Stay with me," Pete said. "Chuck gave you the nickname. Before you met Chuck, everyone called you Jacob."

I nodded before my brain realized I was agreeing.

"Then why does the girl in the recording call you Jake?"

My breath caught. "Did she?"

"Yes. Do you want to play—"

"No!"

"So it can't have been from Carrie, if she called you Jake."

His voice was calm, slow, quiet. Patient. I got the sense that he was talking across a great distance. My brain felt slow, sluggish. A layer of ice clung to my mind, my heart, seized up my lungs.

"But—But why?" I said. A thought struck me. "She heard it on the vids. On the news vids. Maybe she never called me Jake, but she knew that people called me that."

Pete shook his head.

"Outside of the IIC, I'm the only one who calls you Jake. Every vid, official or otherwise, calls you Jacob. Believe me. I—" He pulled me close and I felt his cheek pressed to mine, warm as if he were blushing. "It matters to me that I'm one of the few people who call you that."

I pushed back enough to look at him. He *was* blushing. "It makes me feel special," he said, growing redder.

"You are."

He dropped his eyes and pulled me tight against him again. "It's not her," he said. "I don't know what it is, or why, but the message isn't from your sister, Jake. You didn't let anything happen to her."

"I let everything happen to her," I said. "I failed her."

"Jake—"

"No," I cut him off. "I failed her."

He hugged me so hard that I couldn't catch enough breath to protest further. And he held me for a long, long time. "I'm going to find out who did this," he said.

"It's Blaine."

He was quiet.

"It's Blaine."

"Is there some reason you believe that, besides the fact that you two don't get along," Pete said.

I pulled away. *Don't get along?* "It *is* Blaine."

"I believe you," he said, holding my gaze. "That is, I believe you believe that. And I take that seriously. But you have to look at it from my viewpoint, too. Besides your certainty, I have no evidence to suspect Blaine above anyone else." His hesitation was thick in the air. "Is there anything you haven't told me, maybe?"

This was why I handled things alone. Pete wanted things I couldn't give him.

And yet I was coming to the horrible realization that Jonathan was right. I was way out of my league.

Pete stayed very close over the next few days. His quiet presence was often nearby, and he touched me frequently: affectionate caresses, wordless reassurance. But I couldn't shake the echoes of the horror I'd felt. I was twitchy and restless, and the worry line between Pete's eyes made a frequent appearance.

Pete's investigation found nothing, As I knew it would. But I found something: I found out that it was possible to hate Blaine even more than I had before.

The night the documentary was broadcast to the empire, we went to a special showing in a historic theater in Imperial City, a grand event that had been arranged for the emperor and the upper nobility. Even I was allowed to go, something I hadn't been at all sure would happen. It was one security scenario to show up as a surprise in Abenez, and quite another at an event like this. I felt like a kid let out of school.

In truth, I was also excited and proud of the documentary. Pete and I had seen the final product several days before and given our approval. It was better than I expected. Just the right tone, the right focus. It wasn't about me or Hera, it was about the unclass and their plight. The swelling of optimism and hope I felt was nice, and something I could get used to. I settled in beside Pete, with Blaine and Hera behind us, with a smile on my face.

Which died when I appeared on the screen and said:

*We shouldn't have to feed and clothe them when they could do it themselves.*

And then the scene cut to something else. I don't remember what.

My jaw locked in fury. Hera gasped behind me. Pete cast me a look that was as much concern as anger before he rounded on Blaine.

"I want to know how that happened," he demanded in a whisper that couldn't have been more authoritative and imperial if he'd been wearing his crown and addressing the court.

Blaine looked genuinely taken aback, his knuckles white where they were locked together with Hera's. It threw me for a minute before I reminded myself that Blaine had to be an excellent liar to accomplish all he had so far.

"Yes, Your Excellence," was his only reply. Pete turned back to the screen and, somehow, the waves of fury rolling off him and the silence from Hera behind me gave me the strength not to stand up and punch him in his shocked, innocent face.

The film went on, no different than it had been in the version I'd approved. Only my quote had been changed. In the worst possible way.

The moment it was over, I catapulted from my seat and, with a degree of self-control I'm not known for, I ignored Blaine completely as I bullied my way out, Pete close behind me. But outside the theater, in the crowd gathered to watch us leave, a face caught my eye and I stopped dead in my tracks. Pete had to grab my shoulders to keep from running into me.

"Whoa," he said. "What's the matter?" And when he got no response, "Are you OK?"

Already the face was gone, faded back into the crowds, but I had seen enough of it. It was the man I'd seen the day of our engagement parade, and later in a dream; the man whose face had troubled me with its nameless familiarity.

"Did you see him?" I asked Pete.

"Who?"

I looked at Jonathan, the same question on my face, but he only looked puzzled.

I shivered. "No one. Never mind."

By the time we woke up in the morning, Blaine had a report prepared for Pete. The data trails clearly showed the version marked with Pete's seal, sent by Blaine to the broadcast hub. It was, in fact, still there. But another version had also been uploaded, from the same frustrating non-source I was coming to hate, the same disappearing trail the Patriot's messages used. And, the instructions that would have broadcast Blaine's upload, had been quietly rerouted to use the other instead.

Blaine accepted an official, if sealed, reprimand from Pete, delivered in a private council session. He listened with appropriate gravity and responded, "Thank you, Your Excellence." He met my eye, "And you too, Your Highness, for your mercy. Excepting yourselves, there can be no one more horrified by this error than I am." His fellow councilors nodded and murmured sympathetically.

The correct version was rebroadcast. It was prefaced by a message from Blaine pointing out the correction: "Let no one in the Empire doubt Prince Jacob's dedication to the betterment of the unclass. His full statement is as follows." And then it was played word for word, as I'd said it.

The documentary followed. The right one.

I didn't feel vindicated, though. People would remember what they had seen, and Blaine had come out of it looking like a hero.

# CE 24

Three weeks later, we learned of the second miscarriage.

"Why?" Pete asked, his voice raw.

Dr. Heinriksen shook her head. "I don't know. I admit, one shocked me, but I could accept the possibility. Two is so unlikely as to boggle the mind. Especially for two different women, both perfect candidates for a successful pregnancy, under the best medical care in the empire. For both of them to spontaneously abort? I'd have said it was impossible."

"So you have no idea why either of them miscarried?" I said, holding Pete's hand tight.

"None whatsoever. They were both in excellent health, with textbook pregnancies."

Pete put his head in his hands and I slipped an arm around his shoulders, pulling him against me.

"What does this mean, Doctor?" I said.

"Hell if I know."

"Can we try again?" Pete asked.

"Yes, of course."

"But this might happen again."

Dr. Heinriksen sighed. "Your Excellence, I suppose in an infinite universe, anything is possible. But I would honestly question everything I know about biology, genetics, and medicine if another woman were to miscarry your child."

Pete nodded slowly. "We should wait, though," he said.

"There's no reason—"

"It's not—" Pete stopped himself, took a deep breath. "I just think we should wait. A month or two. It's just—" he carefully schooled his expression. "I just want to wait. Not very long. But at least something."

Dr. Heinriksen shared a quick glance with me.

"Of course. Forgive me, Your Excellence. You're right. It's a good idea. In the meantime we can reexamine all the data on the possible surrogates, make sure the alternate candidates are still the best choices. We can analyze everything we have on the last two women." She hesitated. "I also think every member of my staff and anyone who has been involved in this project should go through another security screening. I can find no medical reason why this is happening. In light of all that has been happening in the empire, I think we have to consider deliberate sabotage."

"Yes, of course," Pete said, his voice wooden. "Thank you, doctor."

She nodded once. "It's my job, Your Excellence. I'll do the best I can."

"You already do," he said.

The 'and it hasn't been good enough' wasn't even implied, and I don't think it even occurred to Pete, but the brief flash of something in Dr. Heinriksen's eyes made me think that it had occurred to her. She only smiled at him.

"Thank you," she said.

Pete suffered my hand clutching his all the way back to our rooms. There, he stormed past me out onto the balcony, clutching the rail hard he raised his head to the bright blue sky.

"Why!" he screamed, the echo of his voice chasing itself down the beach.

I put my arms around him and he melted, collapsed like a puppet with his strings cut.

"Come to bed," I whispered. "You need to rest." He shook his head but didn't resist me. "Let me hold you."

He gave in, allowing me to move him, undress him, lay him

down as he trembled, staring into the distance, his gaze both far away and oddly focused, flickering between anger and grief.

"We'll fix this," I whispered against his skin, when I'd curled around him. "I'll fix this for you, Pete. I love you."

He turned in my arms and clung to me, shuddering but silent until he dropped finally into an unquiet sleep.

*Today the emperor's second attempt to conceive a child with his unclass husband ended in tragedy. For an unheard of two times in a row, the attempts to combine the most nurtured, most noble of genetic lines with the unclass has proven impossible to bring to fruition. The Patriot is hardly surprised. The order of things that has kept our society in peace and prosperity for so long has put those two groups as far from each other as possible. They were never meant to mix, even casually, much less to mingle the bloodlines. Even our genes have adapted to reject such a combination. The unclass as a whole continue to escalate their lawless behavior, and the unclass in the emperor's bed stands between us and an imperial heir.*

*How long will this be permitted to go on?*

I woke before Pete in the morning, glad at least, that he had some relief, in sleep if nowhere else. I pulled up my mails and my heart stopped. The same blank, garbled preview, the same scrambled sender data. I knew I shouldn't open it. Not again.

The screen was black and silent. But just as I was about to turn it off, the volume began to adjust to compensate for the low level of sound and I could hear faint noises. The picture sharpened, resolving into a long line of cots at regular intervals.

*The feel of the guard's hand on my shoulder—human contact after days without it—and the puzzled sensation of trying to figure out how this worked, all the beds in a row but no walls...*

My hands were sweating. I rubbed them hard against my pants, trying to slow my breath.

*He steered me to a cell and pushed me inside. That was when I realized there were walls, each a transparent force-field. He released my wrists from the cuffs.*

*They left me alone. But I'd just spent a week in solitary and I found myself wishing they'd come back.*

I found myself wishing the poor fool on the screen would just go to sleep; maybe he wouldn't be awake later when she—

*I heard the sound of footsteps and stood, looking around.*

*The woman from the common room strolled down the hallway, watching me. She stopped in front of my door and examined me.*

My stomach clenched and I clamped my hand over my mouth.

*"I'm Jake," I offered, to break the silence.*

*"I know who you are," she said.*

*"That makes one of us. I don't know who you are."*

*"I'm K52. My friends call me Kafe. You can call me K52."*

*"Well I'm not here to stay," I said. "So, no offense, but I'll stick with Jake."*

*"Will you?" she smirked. The laughter in her voice was nothing like amusement. "The guards won't care what you're planning to 'stick with.' And they," she jerked her head back toward the common room, "will call you what I tell them to call you. I know it didn't work that way for you in your pretty little life at the palace, but welcome to the asshole of the solar system, Your Highness."*

My hand trembled as I reached out to kill the feed, but something moved in the foreground and I stopped, not wanting to watch but not able to stop myself.

*I heard the muted beep and pop of my door opening. I sat up. I could barely make out the figure in the darkness but I heard the door close again and the figure approached. I was pushed onto my back and the intruder swung over on top of me. Lips, too soft and small to be a man's, pressed against mine. They tasted slightly sterile, like manufactured water.*

One dark figure lay down on top of the other in the silence.

*I tried to cry out but I couldn't get enough air. I grabbed her upper arms but she pushed harder. Her other hand grabbed my balls and squeezed, hard.*

The voices were barely discernible, but I didn't need to hear them.

*"Now here's what we're going to do. You're going to lie here, quiet and still, and I'm going to fuck the emperor's piece of ass."*

*"No, I don't think so,"* I rasped.

*"You don't seem to understand,"* she said. *"Either we do this now, just you and me, or we do it tomorrow, in a quiet corner where the guards don't go, with two of my men holding you down. If you make me do that, I'll let them have you when I'm finished."*

I felt dizzy.

*I didn't fight when her hands went to my waistband.*

My head throbbed, filling with white noise and it was just like I remembered. Guilt and shame washed over me.

*When it was over she put her mouth to my ear and bit the lobe, hard.* *"Was I as good as your emperor?"*

*My throat was tight.* *"Fuck off."*

She'd smiled at me, then.

*"Don't forget this, deserter. You're no one again. A nameless, powerless nobody. Get used to it."*

The screen went dark and I doubled over, burying my face in my hands.

"No, no, no, no, no, no, no."

"Your Highness?"

I catapulted out of my chair, only when I turned around realizing that the voice had been Jonathan's and not Kafe's.

"Are you all right?"

"Yes." I slammed my hand over my mouth again as I gagged and fell to my knees.

"I'll get Dr. Heinriksen," he said.

I grabbed for his wrist. "No!"

He frowned at me.

"No. I'm fine. I'm just—I'm fine. I just need a minute."

His lips thinned and he walked away, but a moment later he returned with a cool cloth, laying it on the back of my neck. With another he began to wipe the clammy sweat off my face. For once, I let him.

That night I dreamed of the cold, pitiless void stretching to infinity around me as I drifted, drifted, drifted. Alone with my regrets and my death.

I clutched one of the blankets around me like a shield and for the first time since I left the IIC, I stumbled out of the bed toward the closet. One look at the dressing room nearly made me cry in despair. At the IIC, the close darkness of my small closet had given me the illusion of security, safety, because I could feel all four walls at the same time. There was no such place here, in the emperor's own rooms. There was nothing "small" at all. There was nowhere to hide.

The doors off the main room stood open, revealing their contents: shoes in one, overcoats and formal garb in another. I stepped into the quiet of the smallest room, the place where all of the Imperial jewelry and crowns were kept. There, across from the door, was a low shelf.

I crawled under it. There, surrounded by all the glittering symbols of imperial wealth and power, I curled into a ball, pulling the blanket over my head, and fell into a restless, helpless sleep.

I woke later to the realization that something warm was pressed against my back. I rolled over far enough to see the back of Jonathan's robe where he sat, his shoulders propped against the shelf, his back pressed to mine. I just stared. Choking on a sob, I turned my face back to the wall, and finally, finally I cried, long and scouring.

Jonathan didn't move.

# CE 25

We were at dinner when a functionary came up beside Pete, kneeling beside him, whispering urgently. When Pete excused himself and stood, I followed him out of the room.

"What is it?" I said.

He didn't look back but slowed enough so I could catch up. He sounded tired.

"I don't know yet."

"What did she tell you?"

He sighed. "Trouble in Delf."

I knew the name but it took me a minute to remember why. "The unclass district on Sed?"

"Yes."

My throat tried to close on the words, but I forced them out. "What's happening?"

"Demonstrations. So far they're still within their district, but they've sent a list of demands and ultimatums to the mayor."

My mouth was dry. "Why?"

"All I know right now is that a lot of people have died and a lot more are very sick."

I frowned. "An epidemic?"

"That's possible."

"But not likely?"

He shook his head. "No. The only report out so far speculates that it's poison. Some of the residents are claiming that a donation of food brought in a couple of days ago was poisoned.

They're saying we did it to them deliberately." He sent a wry look in my direction. "There's speculation that the empire has been encouraging the local governors to do the same; that the documentary was just a ruse to make the people trusting."

"Was it?"

He stopped in his tracks. I felt a stab of guilt for saying it, but I couldn't stop the fact that I'd thought it.

"No, Jake," he said, with a weary patience. "It wasn't poisoned."

I ducked my head from his gaze, flushing with shame. He slid his hand into mine as we continued toward his office.

"Where was the food from?"

He shook his head. "A number of nobles donated it directly to the mayor."

"Could it have been an accident?"

"Of course. It could always be an accident."

"Someone's murdering the unclass and trying to make it look like we're doing it."

He slowed but didn't stop. "That's possible, too."

"We have to tell them it wasn't us."

He shook his head. "The last thing we want to do is acknowledge that poisoned food may have been sent. Then no one will believe we weren't behind it. We have to make it appear to be something else. A tragic accident."

"It *was* a tragic accident," I said.

He sighed. "Tragic, yes. I only hope it was an accident."

Pete was pulled out of the after-dinner entertainment as well, and no one was surprised to learn why.

*The Patriot is encouraged by the latest news that indicates the Emperor might finally be attempting to deal with the unclass problem. Reports from the planet of Sed indicate that the Empire sent a shipment of poisoned food into one of their slums that has killed, to date, over two hundred thousand unclass.*

*As heartening as this news is, the Emperor needs to take control*

*of the situation with more direct methods—with a show of force—*
*demonstrating to the unclass that he himself, and the rest of the*
*empire, won't tolerate treason. He should be dealing with the unclass*
*using soldiers, not poison.*

*We can only hope this is the next step.*

I buried myself in my work. I was a physicist, and I had
that over and above everything else. I had been that first and
longest and it was simply who I was. Science didn't scheme or
manipulate, it didn't judge, it couldn't betray, or die, or leave me,
or send me away.

In spite of the tragedy at Tonga, or perhaps because of it, I
continued my work with practical applications of the power
conservation methods that would give major slums better access to
electricity. I'd narrowed my vision, though. I no longer thought of
grand plans for all of the empire's unclass. I'd work on small projects.
Not ambitious, sweeping solutions, but simple ways to ameliorate
the suffering. Smaller benefit, perhaps, but smaller risk, too.

I still met with Hera for lunch once a week. Owen was growing
like a weed. She brought him, wrapped snug against her chest, silent
or squirming; later cooing and burbling, flailing his little hands.
Sometimes he wailed too, but usually he didn't. We stopped rotating
the location and always met in the aquarium room. As Owen became
more aware of his surroundings, the meanderings of the large fish
behind the glass, or the rush of a school of little ones, drew from him
infectious smiles and later heartbreakingly adorable giggles.

Even in the face of her total dedication to Owen, she still took
an interest in my life as well, and we often discussed my work. I
rattled on one afternoon about how well the energy conservation
work was going.

"Even beyond the slums, there could be many applications
where better conservation of energy would have a huge impact.
Everything from more efficient use of energy resources to space
travel and weapons pro—"

I choked back the word, suddenly very aware of just exactly what it could be used for.

Her face tilted with concern. "Are you well, Jacob?"

I faked a cough. "Still working on this eating thing," I said.

She giggled prettily. Owen looked up at her and blew bubbles.

Pete answered my message within the half-hour.

"What wrong?" he said, as he entered the lab. "Your message sounded bad."

"Yeah," I said, "I'm sorry about that. I was a little upset when I sent it."

"Why?" he asked, stepping close and running his hand down my arm. "Is everything OK?"

I let myself enjoy the caress for only a moment. "Something's come up."

Pete whistled low. "You're right. This could be a problem." He glanced up at me with a quick smile. "I mean, a good problem, for me." His smile faltered in the face of my glare. "Jake, you have to understand what something like this can mean for me. I'm not asking you to—"

"No, you have to understand what something like this means for me, Pete. I know what you are and what you do, but you can't seriously consider that I'd develop weapons technology to help the Empire kill people."

His face went carefully blank. "The Empire, Jake, in this context, would be me."

We stared each other down for a moment.

"Developing new weapons technology immediately after The Empire is being accused of poisoning its own citizens would look bad, anyway," I said.

He gave me a wry look. "Well I wasn't planning on announcing it, Jake. I usually don't discuss military strategy with the general populace."

"You know how I feel about this," I said, my protest sounding weaker than I wanted. There was an edge of pleading in it that I didn't like, but it seemed to work. His expression softened.

"I'm not interested in starting wars or killing people, if that's what you're worried about," he said, a slight, tentative teasing in the words.

"I know," I said quietly. "But I wouldn't be the first scientist in history to find himself responsible for developing the technology that wiped out millions of lives."

"So trust me?" he said.

I sighed, closing my eyes. "I do."

"Then you'll work on this?"

I was shaking my head before he even finished the sentence. "No."

"Jake, this could be—"

"I know exactly what this could be. Better than you do."

He pressed his lips together. "Just because you don't develop this doesn't mean someone else won't."

I stopped.

"Surely you're not the only one who would see the potential of this work."

My stomach sank. No. Of course I wasn't. And too much of my work on the Tonga project was already accessible to the scientific community.

"So you develop this first," he said gently, "and you and I together get to control what comes of it, right?"

I sighed. "OK," I said. "I'll keep you updated."

I slammed the door into my room in a frustrated huff, but stopped short at the sight of Jonathan, bent over my desk. He startled, but turned slowly, calm.

"What are you doing?" I blurted.

"You left your mails open. You've been so private about them lately, I assumed you'd want me to remedy that."

It was perfectly reasonable. I might have. And it's what he would have done.

It bothered me, though.

Pete decided he was ready to try again, to see if this time we could get a baby. Dr. Heinriksen set to work, and less than a month later, implantation had been confirmed.

We told no one.

Some weeks later, Pete came to the lab in the middle of the afternoon and asked if we could talk. He was closed off, hiding behind the imperial mask. The childish, cowardly part of me wanted to say no, as if I could hide from whatever was happening by sticking my fingers in my ears.

He didn't say anything until we were alone in our sitting room. There, he sat stiffly in front of me and told me of the report of new uprisings on Carolis. The name ran ice up my spine.

It had been quiet since Pete had moved the unclass out of Wildflower Hill and razed the sector, years ago. The plan had been to disperse the population throughout the planet, but, over time and in bits and pieces, the people of the areas they were sent to complained and finagled and bribed their way into moving the unclass back out. The same group of people who had been broken up to end their rioting had slowly been moved back into one giant slum city, if no longer Wildflower Hill. The valley's original name had been Terra Duenna, but with the unclass newly grouped there, the people of Carolis had dubbed it The Dump.

If anything, the fact that they were settled in a fresh, unspoiled area was worse for the people than old, crumbling Wildflower Hill. At least there they'd had established—if often inadequate or unsanitary—infrastructure and methods of bringing in water and disposing of waste. They had structures in which to live and shelter from the elements. Terra Duenna had nothing like that. The one compensation, the fact that edible flora and fauna inhabited the area, quickly became irrelevant as the new residents stripped it bare. The authorities made a token effort to provide some basic infrastructure, or at least the materials for it. But it was all quickly commandeered by gangs of thugs. Things to be built were never built, and most people went without.

When flash floods wiped out everything they'd established, killing tens of thousands, the survivors flooded down the mountain as well, as a mob. They were underfed, underclothed, and they were angry. The city of Dens was in their path, and the residents fled before the savages descending from the mountains. No doubt knowing they wouldn't be allowed to keep what they captured, the rampaging mob destroyed it instead. By the time enough troops were assembled from around Carolis, over half of the city had been taken over by the rioters. Half of that was in ashes.

"What are you going to do?" I asked. This was the part he dreaded telling me; not the cause, but the solution.

"The city has already been isolated inside a force field, and they'll fill it with a gas that will kill the people inside quickly and painlessly."

I gaped. I'd known it was going to be bad, but this was much worse than bad. It was horrifying.

I shot out of my seat. "You're going to *kill* them?"

"Yes" he said. "It's what you do, Jake, when an invading force captures one of your cities and drives out or kills the inhabitants and proceeds to destroy what's left. You kill them and retake your territory."

I was frozen in place, stunned and angry and *scared*. "It's not an invading force, Pete, these are citizens of the empire!"

"They're armed rebels who have gained a foothold through force, and I can't just ignore that. Would you expect me to ignore it if the Prussians took the city?"

"You can't be serious. Armed? With what? Debris? You're comparing a mass of starved, desperate people to the military of a rival nation?"

"It's only different in the details. It's the same in principle, and in the realities of the situation. I can't just ask them nicely to surrender the city and go back up to the mountains, please."

"Have you tried it?"

He stared at me. "You can't be serious."

"Of course I'm serious! Haven't we had this conversation before?"

"Yes," Pete said firmly, "which is why I came here, to have it in private."

"So you just came to tell me. You're not asking me for my opinion or advice, like you said you would."

He closed his eyes for a moment.

"Jake, I was talking about consulting you for improvement and prevention, not military strategy."

I dropped down in front of him, taking both his hands, desperate for him to hear me. "Then prevent."

"Jake—"

"No. Listen to me for one minute. Please, Pete. I know you see this as some kind of fucked up war, but maybe they don't. I don't know if it will do any good, maybe it won't, but couldn't you just try? Give them a chance to leave the city. At least a chance, before you have them put down like a pack of wild dogs."

Pete's face was rigid. "I've already given the order."

"Then ungive the order."

"I can't do that. I'd appear indecisive. It's probably already too late, anyway."

I squeezed his hands so hard he winced and tried to pull away. I considered not letting go, of just squeezing until he hurt as much as I did, until he felt as sickened and disgusted with me as I felt with him.

I let go of him, stood, and backed away. I closed my eyes so I couldn't see him, then turned and walked out of the room.

I stormed into my lab and grabbed the first thing that came to hand—a glass tube—and threw it against the wall. It shattered with a not-satisfying-enough crash. So I grabbed something bigger. There weren't many things in the room that would shatter the way glass did, but I grabbed everything I could lift, taking whatever comfort I could out of slamming it into the wall to join the pile below.

An hour later I was still at it when Jonathan came in, completely ignoring the mess and the contributions I was still making to it, and turned on the vid.

I watched with Jonathan in horror as the Patriot's broadcast clearly showed a series of bombs obliterating the city of Dens.

*New weapons technology, developed by the Empire in recent months, was tested today on a mob of unclass rebels who took over the city of Dens on Carolis only yesterday. The Emperor has finally addressed the unclass threat with the degree of severity it deserves.*

*Does this mean that he will soon address the unclass threat in his own household?*

I stared at Jonathan in disbelief.

Pete had betrayed me.

Pete was in the lab before I'd had time to properly react. He was panting, as if he'd been running.

"I didn't do it," he gasped.

I stared at him, still in shock. Out of the corner of my eye I saw Jonathan bow and leave the room.

Pete watched me, his face screwed up with anxiety. He took a step closer.

"I didn't do it."

"Who did?" I croaked.

"I don't know." He waved an arm. "The same person who's been doing all of it. I don't know, Jake. But I didn't do anything with your weapons research, I swear." He came closer and took my hand. "I swear." He squeezed it, as if to somehow make me understand.

"I believe you," I said.

I wanted to.

He knew me too well.

"Jake..."

"You have to do something," I said. "You have to tell them you didn't do it, that you didn't kill all those people."

He winced. "I can't," he said quietly. "What good would it do? I was going to kill them anyway, just not like that. To make any statement about it would just advertise a security breach, for no benefit."

I rounded on him. "You have to *do* something! Don't you see? They're using me against you, and the unclass against both of us. You have to do something they won't expect, something that will undermine their position."

His eyebrows drew together. "Like what?"

"Eliminate 'unclass' as an official classification. Merge them with the low class. Change the qualifications so that more of the current low class become middle, middle become high. Everyone will benefit."

Pete's mouth fell open. "You've got to be kidding me. Eliminate an entire social class designation? Do you realize how much of the current social and economic welfare depends on the structure as is? The formation of the empire itself was predicated on cementing each man's place in society under a strong central government. Before that, we nearly destroyed ourselves!"

"I didn't ask you to eliminate the structure, just change it."

"You're asking me to break something that's worked for hundreds of years, that's brought us peace. Hell, Jake, this is what my very authority is built on."

"Not break it, fix it! This is institutionalized oppression. A huge segment of the population is being systematically disenfranchised, and the empire's doing it."

"I know. But what can I do besides try to improve their situation as best I can?"

"Change it. It's changed before. It's not the same as it was when it was implemented. There wasn't even an unclass at first. Even when it was established, it was a small fraction of the population, and now it's 25% of the empire." I took his hand, holding it tight.

"By the Empire's definition, I'm worth nothing. Fit only for dangerous manual labor and the sorts of jobs even the low class wouldn't deign to do. Do you really agree with that?"

"No, of course not, but you're dif—" He bit the word in half trying to keep it from coming out.

"No. I'm not. The unclass aren't contributing their share because they don't have a chance, not because they don't have anything to contribute."

"You don't understand what you're asking me."

I barked a mirthless laugh. "Oh, I understand. Better than you do."

He just shook his head. "I don't know," he said quietly, answering some question I hadn't asked. "I don't know."

The next morning, we learned about the third miscarriage.

"Your Excellence," Dr. Heinriksen said, sounding tired, "at this point I would recommend removing me from this project."

"No," Pete said flatly.

"It's the only commonality between these three women: me and my team. You need to eliminate that factor."

"It can't be the only commonality," I said.

"Your Highness, believe me, I've done everything I can to differentiate this pregnancy from the others, without compromising the standard of care, and still this happened. I don't think you have any other choice."

"I don't believe you're causing this," Pete said.

"I hope you're right," she said. "But hope won't give you a child. If you're going to try again now, move this project to another location and another team. There's obviously some element here that is causing these miscarriages, and as much as I hate to say it, the most likely possibility is sabotage."

"But you were all just recertified by the ISS," I protested.

She shook her head. "They can miss something. I'm clearly missing something. Eliminate this factor. Get a new team and put them somewhere else. It's the only thing that makes sense."

"I don't think any of this makes sense in any way," I grumbled.

"Nor do I," she sighed. "But that doesn't change anything."

I followed Pete back to our rooms. The worst part was how quiet he was. He'd cried the first time, screamed the second, but now he made no sound. He went straight to his desk, stabbing hard at the display, growling in frustration when the computer couldn't interpret his jerky, angry jabs.

I came around behind him, slid my arms around his shoulders. He was shaking. No, sobbing. Crying in gasps and gulps, even as he shoved and smashed at the desk vid.

"I don't understand *how*. It's not possible. Why can't we stop them? Why can't we *find* them?" He was trembling so hard I saw him stab three times as the same area of the display before he slammed his fist into it with a roar.

I pulled him tight, dragging his chair back from the desk and sitting down in it, pulling him with me.

"We'll find them," I said. "I promise."

He went still for a moment, then started to laugh. It wasn't a pleasant sound. "'This is all wrong," he said, shoving a hand through his hair. "That's my line."

I took his shoulders in my hands. "No. There's you and me, and we do what needs to be done for each other. And fuck whoever this is. We'll beat them."

Pete started trembling again. I got him undressed and into bed.

He let me hold him, saying nothing. I didn't even mention trying again.

Neither did he.

# ✳ CE 27

As with all things, life didn't stop for my problems, or even Pete's grief, and the world spun on around us.

The Empire's Third Centennial was approaching. An air of celebration and anticipation spread throughout the empire. Two full weeks of festivities were planned at the palace. The last thing I felt like doing right then was celebrating all that the empire was and stood for, but I had no choice.

So there were feasts and balls, live plays, and reenactments of some of the greatest moments in imperial history. Every day there were activities scheduled on the palace lawn. Actors were hired to roam the greens dressed as notable historic characters. On my own, I decided I'd dress as Dr. Helmut Schweitzer, one of the earliest members of the IIC and the physicist who had been credited with the invention of FTL technology. I was glad I did. Many children came up to me, chattering their questions, not realizing I was any different from the other strolling historical figures. I enjoyed that very much. It was wonderful, though it made me a little sad, how much I enjoyed those children, so soon after we'd lost yet another pregnancy.

At the official masque, I wasn't allowed to choose my costume. Pete's was chosen by a committee, to make the political statement he wanted. My costume would have to complement his, so the choice was out of my hands.

Pete was fitted up as General Seamus Killearn, the man who founded the empire itself and would become its first emperor.

The implications were clear: the great visionary whose often controversial positions built the empire as we knew it. This cast me in the role of General Ascot Brahn, his second in command. The unintended symbolism wasn't lost on me. General Brahn had been responsible for executing Killearn's plan to eliminate all the religious leaders and the major heads of state, which had ended the war. He died under mysterious circumstances in the first year of Emperor Seamus' reign. The persistent rumor was that Killearn had eliminated him for publicly criticizing some of the new emperor's policies.

Pete listened to my concerns, and offered to change the costumes at the last minute, but I didn't think the offered alternative—with me as Emperor Seamus's wife—was that much better.

When Blaine showed up, he took one look at me and laughed. Clearly the symbolism wasn't lost on him either.

I ignored him. Hera, at least, was as lovely as ever, in every way.

The final day of the celebration involved an endless stream of speeches and award ceremonies, recognizing everything from injured veterans to the nobility. Pete and I, and other important people, rotated in and out of the schedule.

But it frustrated me to no end that for the first of the presentations I would be leading myself—one recognizing the efforts of the higher classes on behalf of the unclass—Blaine would be on the stage with me. I'd wanted Hera, but he had been adamant because of his position as Minister of Social Administration. Hera didn't argue—that I saw—and so I was stuck with him.

Mere minutes before the presentation was to begin, Blaine sent word that he had received an urgent call and would not be able to attend. That was fine with me, even if it did place me on stage alone. But just as the presentation before mine was clearing away, a winded but smiling Hera emerged from the crowd with a giggling Owen on her hip. Her cheeks were red and her eyes bright, but her grin was genuine.

"I thought I would not make it in time," she said.

"For what?" I asked, stupidly.

She waved her hand at the stage, "I have come to support you. I heard that my husband abandoned you, and I have nearly run the width of the lawn carrying this heavy thing," she grinned affectionately at Owen, "to get here before you started."

"I'm so glad you did," I said. "You were the one who helped me, anyway. I wanted you for this from the beginning."

She shook her head. "Enryn was so insistent that he be involved in this and now he cannot even come."

"His loss, my gain," I said.

She beamed. "Indeed. And he does not know I have come so perhaps he will be pleasantly surprised that I represent the family when he cannot."

I personally didn't care if he was glad or not, but I didn't say so.

The coordinator gestured for us to take the stage and I offered Hera my hand, which she accepted with a lovely smile. She stood beside me as the director rearranged the chairs to account for Owen, who was already exploring around our feet. He had recently learned to walk in his funny, lopsided way. I thought the odds of him sitting at all were pretty low.

Maybe I had finally developed a sense of self-preservation, or maybe it was just dumb luck, but suddenly all the hairs on the back of my neck stood up and I *knew* something was wrong.

"Jacob?" Hera asked, but her puzzled voice sounded far away. Something was happening right then and there, or was about to happen, I'd never been so certain of it in my life. I saw it just as I began to register startled gasps and exclamations from the audience.

I looked up to see the decorative sculpture on the wall above us break free and fall straight toward us.

Pure reflex had Owen in my arms before I had a chance to think. I shoved Hera as hard as I could in the opposite direction and then, tucking myself around Owen, I dove off the platform.

The statue fell on the stage with a resounding crash that rattled my teeth even as I hit the ground with a thud. Owen was silent and still in my arms, and I scrambled upright in panic. To my relief, he drew a gasping breath and started to scream. Then there were hands all over us, the rough, competent hands of guards, and someone tried to take Owen from me. I held on to him.

"Hera?"

The bubble of guards and functionaries ebbed and flowed around us, swelling outward as more and more of them were pulled away, merging into a bigger group with their backs to us, flattened against the circle still around me.

"Hera!"

I elbowed my way through the guards, still clutching Owen. They alternately tried to pull me back and open the way for me, and for a time I felt like I was just being shuffled around in the same place, never getting any closer to her.

But suddenly I burst into a clear space. The guards held everyone else back, away from the figure in the center. I wish they'd held me back, too. Then I wouldn't have to take to my grave the image of Hera, her entire torso crushed under the six-foot statue, those incredible eyes dead in her beautiful face, as her son wailed in my arms.

An hour later I was still holding Owen, sitting in one of the private lounges in the nobles' medical building. Owen was hot and sticky against my shoulder and neck, breathing the calm cadence of a child's untroubled sleep. Somehow, in that whole horrible last hour, no one had even looked at me as if they were going to try to take him from me, or even realized I was holding him. It was that, more than anything, that made it real how horribly wrong everything was. Even the trained and competent staff that surrounded us had fallen apart when Hera Blaine died. It felt inevitable and fitting.

Owen had screeched in my ear until he fell asleep, with the poignant sound of a child's grief: unashamed, unaffected, and utterly real. His pure keening was such a perfect accompaniment to that moment that I didn't mind it. I even welcomed it, and the pain in my ear, because it was something to focus on that wasn't the way Hera had looked on the lawn. I absently kissed the damp curls and realized that I'd been doing it for a while. I wished we could just stay there, Owen and me, in that moment, so that neither of us had to face what came next. Owen was almost lucky that he was so young. He wouldn't remember any of this.

But then, I realized that he wouldn't remember her.

Suddenly, that was the most horrible fucking thing I could ever imagine. Impotent rage rushed through me in such a blinding swell that I didn't realize I had tightened my hold on Owen until he fussed and started to squirm.

He opened his eyes and looked at me, his head still heavy on my shoulder.

"Mommy?"

I stroked his hair. "Shhhhh. Go back to sleep."

Nothing will be better when you wake up.

It's my fault," I said to Pete, much later when we were alone in our room.

Pete grabbed my shoulders and turned me to face him.

"No. Don't you ever say that again. It was not your fault."

"I pushed her."

"To get her out of the way."

"And it put her right under it."

"No," Pete said, shaking me once. "It didn't. You pushed her out from under it and off the stage. But it hit hard and fast and rolled off. It was just a horrible coincidence that it rolled in her direction."

I wasn't ready to believe him, but I could tell he wasn't going to accept my version, either.

"How could it happen?"

Pete's sigh was heavy and sad. "It looks like it was just a stupid, horrible accident."

"But how is that possible? There are sensors and integrity fields."

Pete nodded, a slow, ponderous movement. "The erosion around that particular area had affected the sensors and they were sending out false signals, masking the damage, and at the same time, compromising the integrity field. It was all just a ridiculous coincidence."

"Right where the stage was set up? How can you believe that? Our security team is better than that."

"Because all the evidence makes it obvious."

"Exactly."

Pete frowned. It was a lost, sad expression. "Well, at least you know this wasn't Blaine." He stumbled over the name, almost as if saying it reminded him too late who else it belonged to.

Did I? On one hand, he was supposed to have been up on that stage, himself, and even I couldn't believe Blaine would ever put Hera in danger. But on the other hand, he had been called away very conveniently. And it had never been part of the plan for Hera to be there. The uncertainty ate at me. I'd been so sure that Blaine was the driving force behind all the things that threatened me, and that when I found a way to stop him, everything would be OK. It made me sure that all the criticism, all the nonsense the Patriot spouted, all the looks and the whispers and rumors were wrong and that I wasn't to blame, I wasn't the problem, I wasn't at fault.

But now, I doubted everything. Not just who was after me, but whether I might actually deserve it.

"Jake?" Pete's voice brought me out of my thoughts.

"Yes," I said. "I guess you're right."

He watched me, concern etched in his face. "Are you OK?"

I nodded.

He slid his arms around me. "I'm so sorry, sweetheart. I know she was important to you."

"She was important to him, too," I said, hoarse. "But Pete," I said, turning in his arms. "If it's not him, then who is it?"

He looked at me, the puzzled line etching its way between his eyebrows. "What do you mean?" Pete asked.

It occurred to me how little he knew of the whole picture— how he'd never believed any of this was Blaine in the first place. There were all the private harassments Pete didn't know about. He didn't know about the things I *knew* were Blaine's doing. His part in the campaign against me had to be bigger than just nasty pranks. Blaine knew things he shouldn't have known. He had people who fed him information and did favors for him, at the very least. And that sort of networking and scheming didn't happen by accident. If he was already doing it to obtain videos that the officials at Dead End swore didn't exist when I'd been there, the ones that could have proven I was being set up, then it was just a small step up to other nasty meddling and scheming; to creating riots in places that wouldn't have bred trouble without significant encouragement. Or causing explosions that sabotaged my work and killed my friends, whom he had personally maneuvered to be present. Or engineering impossible miscarriages when we tried to have a child.

It was all too damned convenient *not* to be connected. But now that Hera was dead...

"I pulled back, trying to look away, cover my mistake. "Nothing. I don't know what I meant. I was just thinking about her and—"

Pete jerked me back to face him.

"Stop!" he hissed.

I almost pulled away from him in shock.

"Stop," he repeated, a knot of grief in his voice now. "Don't lie to me, please. If you're hiding something, just say you're not going to talk to me about it, but don't lie to me. It kills me when you do that. I hate it that you don't trust me. Tell me to drop it and I will. Just don't lie to me."

I felt the blood in my face drain into a pool of nausea in my gut.

"Pete—"

But what could I say?

"It's not that I don't trust you," I tried, but it was weak.

He sighed and let me go. "I know."

But his body language, expression, tone of voice couldn't have said more clearly that he knew I was lying yet again. I felt like the lowest creature in existence when he gave me a weak smile meant to reassure me, to make peace.

I hated myself.

But I still didn't tell him anything.

Hera's funeral was beautiful. Not the extravagant, costly mess I was sure Blaine would make of it, but a proper Torrea funeral, serious and reserved. I wondered who had arranged it. One look at him made it obvious that he hadn't planned anything at all the last few days. I wouldn't have been surprised if he didn't even realize he'd been dressed and fed and somehow brought to the great chapel. His eyes were half-dead. I felt a stab of pity for him, then anger that I did, then guilt for that.

He was carrying Owen, but he didn't seem aware of it. Owen's eyes were red, his cheeks damp. He squirmed and whined, but Blaine kept his hold somehow, more out of instinctive adjustments for the movement of a package he was carrying than out of any real awareness of the boy—or anything else.

He sat down on the bench beside me, and I don't even think he realized who I was. Owen whimpered and squirreled around, holding out his arms to me. I glanced at Blaine, but he still seemed lost, so I held my hands out toward Owen. I wasn't exactly taking him from his father, but extending the invitation. Owen grabbed me and climbed out of his father's hold into my lap, burying his wet face against my neck. I put my arms around him, murmuring nonsense in his ear, bracing for Blaine to notice and make a scene.

He didn't. His eyes were locked on the urn at the front of the room. Once I let myself look, I couldn't tear my eyes away from it, either. To think that all the beauty and goodness and generosity that had been Hera Blaine could be rendered into something so small and meaningless.

"Mommy?" Owen whined against my shoulder.

I squeezed him tight. "Shhhhhh." I murmured. "It's OK." It was one of the worst lies I'd ever told. Hera would have forgiven me for that, too.

Well into the ceremony, Blaine finally looked over at me. He met my eye and jolted in his seat, as if the realization of who I was hit him like a lightning strike.

"I'm sorry," I whispered, trying to disengage Owen, who had fallen asleep on my shoulder, and hand the boy back. "He got in my lap and I didn't want to disturb you." For the first time I was worried about what Blaine thought of me, and it was a strange feeling. But no more strange than Hera somehow being dead, and Blaine sitting down beside me without even noticing.

He took Owen without a word and with a strange lack of rancor, just a wide-eyed startlement, whether at me or himself or just at what life had done to him in general. Owen settled on Blaine's shoulder with only a half-asleep whimper and I slid closer to Pete on my other side, trying to give Blaine space from me. But though he sat stiffer than he had before, he made no other move and didn't look at me again.

The ceremony was elegant and moving. Hera was praised and her good deeds remembered. It was perfect, and it was perfectly horrible. And watching Blaine leave the chapel with Owen asleep in his arms, I wondered how there was any sense in a universe that would leave Blaine and me alive, but allow Hera to die.

There was no sense to anything anymore.

*The Patriot joins the Blaine family in mourning a truly great woman, a shining example of all that is good and worthy of preserving in our noble families. But what is truly tragic about her death? Not the husband and son deprived of a wife and mother, not those who must now do without her after being privileged enough to have experienced this sweet and caring woman in person, or the countless among the other classes who benefited from her deeds of charity and patriotism who will benefit no longer. The horror of the loss lies in the circumstances of her death, and how preventable it was.*

*The Prince Consort was also in the path of the dislodged statuary. But numerous eyewitnesses saw him push Hera Blaine in his attempt to avoid the falling object.*

*While the palace's official position is that he was trying to move her out of danger, his actions did put her directly in the path of an object that would surely, and did, kill her. Can we be certain that was not exactly what he intended to do? Or was it merely the natural instinct of one not nobly born, to save his own life, no matter the cost to others?*

*What does that mean for the rest of us?*

*Even as we mourn the loss of a Duchess and a truly great woman, it is hard not to find Prince Jacob's role in her death chilling.*

Everything seemed to stop after that. There were no riots, no troubles, no threats, no mails, no nothing, anywhere. It was as if the whole Empire had fallen silent to mourn Hera Blaine.

Blaine himself disappeared into his rooms at the palace and wasn't seen for days. There were enough servants coming and going that I had to accept that Owen was well, though it was like a physical ache, not being able to check and see. It felt like I was letting Hera down somehow.

I kept going to lunch in the aquarium room faithfully, every week. I didn't know if it was some pathetic form of tribute to Hera or a stupid impulse on my part to keep prodding the wound. In any case, I went.

And one day, a few weeks after Hera's death, I entered the room to find Blaine there.

He was sitting at the table, his forearms spread out on its surface, palms down, as if his arms were floating on the water. He stared down between them. When I entered the room he looked up.

His eyes narrowed and his face darkened and twisted with a murderous hatred. I'd been threatened by Blaine many times over the years, and it would have been a lie to say he'd never frightened me. But never before had I been as completely, frankly scared of him as I was just then.

My guards and Jonathan were all between Blaine and me before I could blink. As if they weren't even there, Blaine catapulted from his chair and lunged at me, stopping just before my guards had to touch him. But he leaned between them so that his face was close to mine.

"It's your fault she's dead."

My fists clenched and I sucked breath with effort past the tight fury in my chest. "Don't you dare say that."

"It was supposed to be you," he spat.

"Is that a confession?" I shot back.

He blinked, as if I'd truly surprised him.

"Do you still think I would stoop to that level of crass treason? Why would I? Any idiot can kill someone. You'd be the biggest idiot of all if you think I'd ever have put Hera in danger."

"You didn't know she was going to be there. You were careless and she got in the way."

His face twisted and he lunged at me again, battering against the guards.

"Step back, Your Grace," one of them rumbled.

Blaine didn't acknowledge him but he did step back. He barked a laugh, like a reflex. "She wanted to be part of that presentation from the beginning. You think it didn't occur to me that she might take my place when I was called away? Any half-decent plotter would have anticipated that possibility."

He shook his head, sharp and angry like an accusation. "No, what I did wrong was not step in when she started to become friends with you. You took advantage of her sweet—" his voice cracked on the word and he tipped his head back, blinking furiously. For several long moments he stared up at a shark swimming languidly above him, as if it might have answers for him. "She was in danger every day she was near you, and I was too much of a fool to protect her the way I should have."

He stabbed his finger at me.

"But you knew that, too. And still you cultivated her, encouraged her. You should have been the one to die. She is dead because you aren't." His smile sent a shiver up my back. "No, *Prince* Jacob, you're not in any danger from me. Nothing could be further from the truth. No one will preserve and cherish your life more than I will now. I hope you live a hundred years," he said, with a strange sort of amusement. But all merriment fell off of his face and he pinned me with a cold glare. "I'm going to enjoy watching you suffer through every one of them."

Something pulled at my pant leg and I looked down to see Owen holding his chubby little arms up.

"Ja'ca?"

But before I could react, Blaine bent and snatched Owen up. He shoved his way past my guards and out of the room.

The next morning, I told Pete about the encounter with Blaine. How could I not? This wasn't a game anymore. Something had changed, and though I wasn't quite sure what, it was an ever-present slosh of fear in my gut. Pete just listened, grim and silent, but not surprised. It was only then it occurred to me that he must already know. The guards would have reported it.

Still, when I finished, Pete said, "Thank you for telling me."

I nodded and started to turn away but his face softened and he reached out, laying his hand on my arm.

"No, I mean that," he said. "Thank you for telling me."

I felt myself flushing with shame, but he let me go without having to acknowledge that we both knew what a change that was.

I went to the lab but I was distracted and restless. I felt as if I was waiting for...something. And I didn't want it to come.

The display on my desk suddenly blinked out and was replaced with a flashing alert. I closed my eyes. Not again.

*Imperial Security this afternoon arrested one Edward Dawes, a Reset currently living in Imperial City, for the murder of a co-worker at the refinement plant where he has worked for the past fifteen years.*

The display showed a man being led out of an anonymous apartment complex that could have been in any neighborhood in any city in the empire. When the camera narrowed on the man's face, my stomach fell away.

*The Patriot's sources confirm that this man is the natural father of Prince Consort Jacob Dawes. The Patriot cannot at this time confirm ongoing communication between the two men, both Resets, though the proximity in which the father has been living to the palace makes it doubtful that his son, and indeed, the emperor, were unaware of his existence. The Patriot cannot help but speculate that the father has been working on orders from his highly placed son, and will continue to look into any connection the victim might have to the prince, and what he hoped to gain from eliminating a factory worker. The alternative, that the Prince Consort's father is not only a degenerate, but a common murderer, is distressing, though not difficult, to contemplate.*

The man—my father—was being led to an ISS transport, but suddenly black-and-silver palace security vehicles swooped in.

The screen became a jumble of hovercrafts and moving bodies. A voice screeched in distortion just before the entire feed cut to black, and silence.

Pete came barreling into the room, out of breath, grabbing my hand and holding it so hard I let out a startled "ouch."

There was something wrong with my voice. It sounded wooden, almost unfamiliar. Hollow. Distant. Disconnected. There was a buzzing in my ears, a white noise filling the space in and around me and I suddenly bent double, a spasm of pain and nauseous understanding. It had happened so fast, the face I'd seen twice in the past few years but had no name for. I knew him now.

Edward Dawes. My father.

I saw him looming over me—layered visions, memories of that face—over and over and over again, and always the same, distorted in drunken rage. The back of his head as he closed in on my mother, fist raised. A sick loathing in my gut, holding very still and quiet, biting down hard on tears and whimpers as he hit her, and hit her, and hit her. The startled fury on his face when I hit him from behind with my useless little hands.

Blurred images of fists or belts or things I couldn't even identify hurtling toward me, and the explosions of pain that followed. Carrie crying quietly in the corner, never loud enough to attract his attention, just as I'd taught her. Fear that tasted like blood and smelled like alcohol and piss.

Him passed out in the chair or on the floor. The ever-present fear of him waking. The perverse fear of him never waking again.

I woke in my bed, not quite sure how I'd gotten there. I closed my eyes, hoping that I hadn't fainted like a Victorian maiden. As if things weren't bad enough. My father. A murderer.

Of course he was.

Pete was at my side before the lurch of pain in my gut fully registered.

"Hey," he said, his voice soft and gentle. "You OK?"

I spluttered an incredulous noise. What a ridiculous question that was. Was I OK? Of course not. How many times did we need that proven before we stopped kidding ourselves?

"Jake?"

"Yeah, I'm fine," I croaked.

Pete drew in a breath, but I interrupted. "Did he do it?"

It didn't occur to me to ask if this was a fake too, like the message I was meant to believe was from Carrie. I knew who this man was. I remembered now. The face of the man in the crowd at our engagement parade and again at the premiere of the documentary. The face that was familiar, though I hadn't known why. The sadness in his eyes. Probably that was why I couldn't place him. It was the same face, but missing the contortions of anger and alcohol.

"What?" Pete asked, apparently expecting a different question. Maybe he didn't realize I remembered. This wasn't the matter of a voice made to sound just right. I knew that man.

"Did he do it? Did my—" my throat tightened around the word, "did my father kill that man?"

Pete sighed. "I don't know. We're investigating."

"How long has he been here?"

"In the palace?"

I startled, but after a moment I realized what he meant. "He's here?"

"In the prison, yes. For his own safety."

I snorted, but he let it go.

"I had him brought straight here as soon as I realized what was going on."

"So you didn't have anything to do with this?"

Pete's hand tightened on mine reflexively. "No," his voice was hoarse. "No, Jake, I wouldn't have done this to you."

The question was unfair and unreasonable, but I was beginning to forget what trust felt like. With Pete sitting beside me, the thought gave me a pang of guilt, but it was quickly lost in the bigger pains.

"But you knew he was in the city."

Pete sighed. "Yes. I knew he was there."

"How long have you known?"

Pete wasn't looking at me. "Since I met you."

I shot upright. "What?"

The look he gave me was both pleading and defiant. "Jake, I'm the emperor. Do you think you've gotten this close to me without the most thorough security screening the empire is capable of? Just appointing you to a position at the palace meant that I was presented with reports on any possible security concerns. Of course I knew about your father."

"You mean," the words were sour in my mouth, "you know—" This was going to go all wrong if I wasn't careful. I tried for casual. "What else do you know about me?"

He had the good sense to look chagrinned. "I've respected your privacy as much as I could since then, and I still do. Probably a lot more than I should. And you're my husband now, not an appointee or a noble I need to keep an eye on." He stepped closer. "I want you to feel safe, Jake. That includes your secrets, for whatever reason you keep them. I trust you. I knew about your father but that's all. I promise."

"Why didn't you tell me?" My voice was too loud, ripping itself out of the pressure building in my chest.

"Because you didn't want to know."

I blinked. "What? How would you know?"

"Because you never looked for his data. You found—" he hesitated a moment, "Carrie. You could have found out everything there was to know about your father if you'd wanted to. You didn't. I never hid him from you. But I wasn't about to bring it up, either."

"He was dead."

Pete's brow wrinkled. "What?"

I scrubbed my hand over my forehead, trying to form thoughts that seemed to run and hide from me. Like my brain was flashing error messages. *Don't look here.* "That's why I never looked for

his data. He was dead. I mean, I thought he was. I *knew* he was."
I rubbed harder, as if to force my thoughts into order. "He was...
he was Resettled. He was a drunk with a temper. He wouldn't
survive the camp." I couldn't imagine him surviving Dead End,
though that wasn't exactly the standard Resettlement facility. But
even in the softer camps, he'd have to sober up and not provoke
any other Reset into killing him. It had never occurred to me that
he'd be able to do even one of those things, let alone both.

I paced, restless and angry. Pete watched me. Maybe he didn't
know what to say. Maybe he did, but he knew me too well to say it.

Finally I stopped. "He's here in the prison?"

"Yes."

I nodded once and left the room.

I hurried down the hallway, feeling vaguely like I was running
from myself. Trying to get there before I could talk myself out of
it or lose my nerve. I could feel Pete in my wake, though he made
no effort to catch up. I encountered almost no one. The guards
were moving well ahead of us and clearing the halls. Entering the
prison from the front door felt strange. I'd seen more of the prison
than I cared for, but I'd never been in it this way. I shivered.

The guards bowed as they should, but not one of them met my
eye. None but Sam. It was strangely calming. I'd always known
he didn't like me. Not since I hit his emperor, anyway. Anything
predictable was overwhelmingly comforting just then.

With no more than the respectful "Your Highness" to me and
"Your Excellence" to Pete, Sam led us into the prison itself.

We turned down the hallway. Sam stopped at a door just
around the first corner and I couldn't help but wonder if it
meant something. When I'd been in here, they'd thrown me deep
inside. Was it better or worse that they had put my father in a
more convenient location?

Pete slid his hand into mine and I jumped. I'd already forgotten
he was there.

"Do you want me to come with you?"

I did, in a way. I wanted his strength. "No," I said.

Pete's brows drew down and he examined my face with concern. Apparently OK with whatever he saw there, he gave a slow nod. "I'll be right out here if you want me."

I turned to face the door, cold and impersonal and ominous. Sam gave a nod to another guard and she opened it.

I stepped inside. He was sitting on the bed, his elbows on his knees, his head hanging down over them. He was looking at my shoes, apparently expecting a guard and finding evidence there that he was wrong. His head shot up, quickly followed by the rest of him. He went pale. The descent to his knees looked as much like a fall as a deliberate choice.

"Your Highness," he breathed.

I bit down on a scream. I'd gotten used to being called that, but something about him using the title made my skin crawl. And him on his knees in front of me. I thought of all the times I would have given anything to have him in my power, to have him humbled before me. Afraid. Now it just twisted in my gut and standing there with him, the sensation felt a lot like hunger. Something else I associated with him.

"Get up."

He scrambled to his feet.

"Why are you here?"

He blinked, and I probably did, too. It was a ridiculous question, but it was what had come when I'd opened my mouth.

"Why am I here?" he echoed.

"Did you do it?"

He moved as if he were going to sit down again but stopped himself with a jerk, locking his knees.

"I didn't. I swear it. I didn't even know Jerry that well. I didn't have anything against him. I don't know what happened, but I didn't do it. I swear."

His voice was thick, raw. It hit me like a laser through my brain that the redness in his face and eyes—the redness that I'd taken for the familiar flush of drink—was from weeping. I shook my head hard, but I couldn't shake the last memory I had of him. It rose like a specter inside me: for a moment we weren't there in the cell, but in the apartment. He was towering over me, something in his hand: a broken chair leg. As hard as I'd tried to forget him and everything about his time in my life, I remembered this scene clearly. He'd punched me for some reason and I'd fallen into the only intact kitchen chair we owned. My weight was hardly anything to speak of, but the chair broke under me anyway. He'd gone into a rage, then, snatching up one of the legs and hitting me so hard on the arm that the blow, combined with the shock of the chair shattering, flooded my eyes with tears. Which only made him worse.

"Why?" I choked.

He looked at me, confused and anxious.

"What did we ever do to you to deserve... Ma never did anything to you..."

His face crumpled with agonized comprehension.

"Nothing," he rasped. "You never did anything." His voice was stronger but uneven. He sank to the bed and cradled his head in his hands. "It was never about any of you. I was angry. At myself, at the world. You were just there, and not strong enough to fight back." Bitter contempt seeped from him.

"And that makes it OK?" I shouted.

"No. It's no excuse. It's not even a good explanation. It was so much more than that, and none of it mattered at all. I knew that even then." He looked away. "I never hit Carrie, at least."

"Damn right you didn't. I made sure of that."

He met my eye for a long moment. "Yes. I guess you did." He shook his head and looked away again, his face twisting with some emotion. "You got it the worst," he said. "You got angry, you didn't buy into it. You knew I had no right. You stood up to me. More than that, I knew what you were, and I don't think anything would have spared you, for that reason alone."

"What I was?"

He dropped his head. "I knew you were different. Even so young, it was obvious. I knew what it meant. I didn't need your year eight tests to know what kind of intelligence you had, what it might mean, where it could take you. I hated you for it."

I shook my head, trying to figure out what he was saying.

"You knew about the IIC?" I asked, frowning in confusion.

He barked a bitter laugh. "Oh yes. I knew exactly what the IIC was. Oh yes. I knew."

I stood frozen in disbelief.

"How?"

"I—" he glared at the floor. "It doesn't matter now. It didn't matter then. It just meant you got the worst of it. The worst of me. Even more than your mother and sister."

"They're dead," I snapped. His whole body flinched and then sagged, as if he deflated.

He just nodded weakly.

"Ma died a few years after I left. Carrie—" I wanted to cut him with every word, but the blade was double edged. "Carrie I tried to save, but..."

He looked up at me, his eyes red. "It wasn't your responsibility to save them. You were just a kid."

I shook my head, but couldn't answer past the lump in my throat. I hadn't been a kid when I'd killed Carrie. I could still hear the voice. *Jake?* It didn't matter if the recording was a fake or not. She could have said those words to herself if to no one else. She probably did. It was how life had been for her, before she got desperate enough to end it all so very completely. I'd put her there. I hadn't saved her at all.

"Why didn't you have the decency to die!"

His face snapped up, his eyes going wide.

"You were dead! I believed that. I knew it was true for all these years. It got me through a lot. Why didn't you just die?"

"I thought about it," he said, a small whisper. "But I'm a coward, Your Highness."

"Stop calling me that!"

He pressed his lips together so hard they went white. But it wasn't anger, like it should have been. It was fear.

I stumbled back into the wall, trying to make it look like a casual lean. I needed the support before my knees gave out. I thought of Pete just outside and I wanted him so desperately it was a physical ache. But the thought of him in that room, my father prostrating in front of him, brought such an overwhelming wash of shame it gave me the strength to resist. I thought of how we looked, just the two of us. Of all the billions of people in the empire, only Pete was richer or higher ranking than I was. But on me it was just a veneer, a cracked patina. This was what I really was. This man standing in front of me, the lowest of the low. My father.

"You—" The words crowded together in my throat. "I—" He looked up, watching me.

Whatever he saw on my face, he shuddered, curling into himself, arms clutched around his stomach.

"I hate you," I croaked.

He nodded. "So do I."

I stumbled out of the room as fast as my weak knees would take me.

Pete grabbed me the moment I was out the door.

"Are you all right?" he asked, his eyes flicking back and forth over my face, searching.

I shook my head, though whether or not that was an answer to his question I didn't know. It wasn't anything. A reflex, a knee-jerk. Applied force: reaction.

Pete cast an anxious glance at someone but I was too lost to notice who. Or care. He led me away. His hand in mine was almost too hot, burning into me; a point where I touched reality. Everything else was numb and cold. I shivered.

I do remember Dr. Heinriksen in our room when we got there, but nothing else after that.

# CE 30

I got up before Pete in the morning. I felt different. Empty. As if someone had scooped out everything inside me and thrown it away, like the seeds from a melon.

Somehow there was no place for food, though, and after picking at my breakfast, I stood with a sigh and went to the lab.

I didn't go there to work, but to be alone. Pete would be worried for me, and would want to talk; to help. But I didn't know what I thought or felt yet, and I had no answers for him. Instead I sat down at my desk and pulled up my father's data.

It was all right there, just as Pete had said. Over two decades since he'd been Resettled, and all the data, sealed or otherwise, from his childhood as well. His whole life laid out before me.

I shivered, sitting back, dizzy. He'd been there all this time, just for the asking. Only, I'd never asked. Why had my six-year-old self been so certain he had died? Why had I never questioned that in the almost twenty years since?

I began to read.

I spent the afternoon wandering the halls, my thoughts in a sort of stunned frenzy, while emotions I didn't even recognize tangled in my chest. But I wasn't surprised at all to find that my feet had eventually carried me to the prison door.

The guards fell in behind me as I entered the long central hallway.

I stopped outside the door to his cell, but when the guard moved to open it for me I grabbed his arm.

"Wait. Stop."

He gave me a puzzled look but I just shook my head, releasing him. He stepped back and waited.

Suddenly I was too close to this, to him, to whatever all this meant. I stumbled backward until I hit the wall. My knees let go and I slid to a seat against the wall, staring at the door without seeing it. The guards melted away.

And in the gray haze of the door in front of me, I saw over and over an avalanche of half-glimpsed scenes, jagged shards of memories. My father laughing along with Carrie, bouncing her on his knee while she giggled. A fond smile on his lips when my mother turned away. Him sitting down beside me on the floor. 'Whatcha' got there?' and the sight of my own hands, holding something up eagerly, warmed by the look in his eyes.

I had never seen those memories before, and I wondered if they were real or just stupid dreams I'd forgotten as quickly as I could.

I don't know how long I sat there, only that my knees were stiff when I stood up, gave the door one last look, and walked away.

Pete found me in the reading room, slumped in a chair and staring at the walls of books, wondering what my father's face would look like if he saw this. I scrubbed my face hard with my hands, trying to wash away the thought.

"Jake?"

I looked at him. "Have you read all of it?" I said.

He didn't even ask what I meant.

"Yes."

I looked away. "It doesn't matter. None of it. It's no excuse for what he did to us."

"No. There is no excuse for what he did to you. But maybe it helps, knowing more about him, and maybe how he justified it to himself, or what made him do it."

I shook my head. "I don't want it to help. I don't want it to matter. I hate him. I want to hate him."

Pete knelt in front of me and took my hands in his. "What can I do?"

I laughed a bit at the absurdity of the idea that something might be "done."

"Did he do it?" I asked.

Pete sighed and sank back on his heels. "I don't believe he did."

"And the investigators?"

"Oh they've got a nice, clean case on my desk already. Tied up with a pretty bow. It's the most perfect, flawless case you've ever seen. There's proof of every kind, in every way, that no one but Edward Dawes committed that murder."

"So he was framed."

"By someone very, very good, who clearly underestimates my intelligence."

I sank back into the chair. "What are you going to do?"

"Keep looking," he said. He gathered my hands between his again. "What are you going to do?"

I met his eye. "Nothing. Nothing at all. Do what you want with him. It's nothing to do with me."

Pete frowned but didn't reply.

The next afternoon I found myself entering the prison again. I turned the corner to his cell and stopped short, spluttering a startled laugh. There in front of the door was a chair.

"Just in case you want it, Your Highness," Sam said from behind me. I nodded, not sure whether I was touched or disturbed.

"Bring it in with me," I said, nodding toward the door. With practiced efficiency, the door was opened and the chair was settled inside at a comfortable angle to the bed.

"Thank you," I said, my mouth dry. I entered the cell and nodded for them to close the door.

For the second time in as many days, I was alone with the father I had believed to be dead. In no small part, I'd believed it because I'd wanted it to be true. I sat, so that he wouldn't see me trembling.

He had stood when I entered, but when I sat he dropped back onto the bed, facing me, his back straight and rigid.

"You were Selected for the IIC," I said.

He deflated with a long, hard sigh, his head drooping. With his eyes on the floor, he answered, halting and slow, as if each word had a razor edge. "Yes. I was."

He didn't say any more.

"But your father beat you unconscious and left you in a coma, so they picked another child to go in your place."

He nodded, a slow, ponderous movement of a head too heavy to raise.

"There was brain damage, and you weren't eligible anymore."

He released a shuddering breath.

"Yes." He swiped tears from his cheeks. "They gave me medicine, at the Resettlement camp. It helps with the mood swings and the memory loss." He barked a mirthless laugh. "Best thing that ever happened to me. I should have turned myself in, years earlier."

I blinked. "You turned yourself in?"

"What else could I do? I nearly killed you that night. Do you remember?"

"Yes," I whispered. "The broken chair."

His voice trembled. "I don't remember much of that night, but I remember I hit you in the head, and you were lying on the floor. Well, I went up to the roof, but I was too much of a coward to jump off. So I went back to the apartment and stayed until you came to. Then I went down to the police station and asked them to send me for Resettlement. You know they won't do that just for the asking?"

"I thought you'd died there," I said. "I was sure you would."

"I expected to. It was a coward's suicide."

"That was you at the engagement parade, wasn't it? And the premiere?"

He hung his head. "Yes. I lived in fear for weeks afterward that you'd recognized me."

"I didn't. You were familiar, but I couldn't figure out why. I never even considered that it might have been you."

"I'm glad."

Was I? I looked at him. He looked so different than the man I'd known as a father, the sickly, half-starved man drinking himself to death. Now he was sober, clean, healthy.

There were laugh lines around his eyes.

I stood so quickly my chair fell over with a crash. The door flew open and two guards filled the doorway, weapons leveled at my father.

I bullied my way through them and out of there.

Two days passed. Three. Five. And somehow, at some point in every day, I found myself standing in front of the door to my father's cell as they opened it for me, set up my chair, and left us alone together.

I don't remember most of what we said. Or even that we talked much. There were long periods of silence, with too much pain on either side to break it, and yet I couldn't bring myself to leave.

"Pete doesn't think you did it," I said, on one of my visits.

Deep lines formed in his brow, the furrows of age and hard work. "Pete?"

"Pete. My husband."

His eyes widened. "The emperor?"

I nodded.

"But he doesn't know for sure?"

"He can't find proof that you didn't do it. And there's a whole lot of proof that you did."

He sighed, looking off into the distance, through the door. "So it would be problematic if he didn't execute me."

"I didn't say that."

He gave me a look of mild reproof, as if I should have known better than to think he didn't understand the complexities of the situation. Which I suppose he did, having spent the past seven or eight years trying to hide any connection he might have to the man at the emperor's side.

"I'm a liability, Jacob."

That was either a simplistic way of looking at things, or a horribly a profound truth.

Probably both.

A week passed.

When the guard opened the cell door, I saw my father look straight at the guard and quickly look away. I glanced at the man but his head was down. Probably nothing.

"It can't be good for you," my father said once I was seated, "that I'm in here, when the whole empire saw my arrest."

"That's not your problem."

"It's yours?"

I didn't answer.

"I've seen the broadcasts, Jacob." His voice was oddly gentle, understanding. "I'm making it worse for you."

"No worse than it was already."

"Your Pete still can't find proof?"

"I said it's not your problem," I snapped. Which I suppose was ridiculous, as it was his life at stake even more than mine.

"And what happens if I'm not publicly exonerated, or executed?" he asked, with a quiet authority, a grown-up to a child. "The emperor lets me go? An unclass murderer pardoned because it's his unclass husband's father."

"Stop!" I took a deep breath. "Drop it," I said. "Pete's working on it."

He sighed and said nothing more about it. That day.

The next afternoon, he was standing when I entered, a strange, solemn formality about him. I shivered.

The door closed behind me.

"What's this all about?" I asked.

He inched forward and fell to his knees awkwardly, in front of me.

"Kill me."

My heart stopped with a painful thump, then pounded like thunder in my ears.

"What?"

He took my hands and put them around his throat. "Kill me, please. Do it now. Make me go away. I can't hurt you anymore if I don't exist at all. Kill me, Jacob. Please."

I snatched my hands back as if scalded. I couldn't catch my breath.

"You said you didn't do it," I gasped, desperate to make this stop.

"I didn't. But that doesn't matter. There's no way out of this that doesn't damage you or the emperor. Except this one. Kill me."

"Stop it," I said. "Stop..." It trailed off like a plea.

He held my gaze, imploring.

I catapulted out of my seat, pounding on the door as if wild animals were after me, and when it opened, I threw myself out into the hallway. And ran.

I thought I heard someone call my name, but I ignored it. I heard orders shouted and the pounding of footsteps behind me but I just ran harder. Ran from this, ran from him, ran from me.

I passed a set of guards in the hallway and with only a glance between them, they fell into formation, flanking me. I was already running as fast as I could. I wondered briefly if they were attempting to protect me or apprehend me. My whole life had turned upside down and I wouldn't have been surprised if they had been trying to take me. But they stayed just behind, and so I ignored them. Rounding a corner I slammed full-on into someone, shoved them out of my way and kept running.

"Make way!" One of the guards shouted. "Make way for the Prince!"

I tried to close my ears, not hear. I would have ordered them to shut up, but I had no breath to protest. I ran. My lungs burned, but so did my eyes. My legs felt like they were on fire and I wished they were. I wished something, anything, would make it all go away quickly and permanently. Jacob Dawes burning up and away. Ash and energy. Problem solved.

It was probably half a mile from the prison in the southern corner of the palace to the private strip of beach reserved for the Imperial Family. I took a couple of wrong turns—I wasn't often in that part of the palace—but eventually I burst out onto the strand, sand flying behind me. My sprint slowed to a jog from a lessening not of urgency, but ability.

The guards dropped back. Alone, I trudged to the edge of the water, finally stopping, slumping over, my hands on my knees, gasping.

I really hadn't been there long when Pete came up beside me, standing close but not touching. I glanced at him. He wasn't looking at me, but out over the ocean, his expression closed. I felt a stab of fear and the answering wash of guilt. Would time and experience ever replace the knee-jerk distrust for what I already knew: that Pete would never reject me? The worst mistakes of my life had been born of not trusting him.

But there were just as many, and more powerful, reasons I'd learned not to trust anyone but myself. One of them sat in a cell in the palace prisons.

For a long time we just stood there.

"He asked me to kill him."

Pete's lips drew together but he didn't answer or move.

"I should do it. I should *want* to do it."

Pete looked over at me, his brow furrowed. "Did he confess to the murder?"

"What difference does it make?" I barked a laugh tinged with hysteria. "He said that. It doesn't matter."

"It should matter. It does to me. What justice would there be in killing an innocent man?"

"Who said he's innocent? He may not have killed that man, but he isn't innocent. Never. Not after all he did to Ma and Carrie."

"To you."

"Doesn't matter."

"It matters what he did to your mother and sister, but not what he did to you?"

"Yes."

"Why?"

I looked away. "It just does."

Pete didn't reply.

"I've always hated him. I should hate him."

Pete let it drop, not saying anything. Before long, his slipped his hand into mine and we stood like that until finally I turned away. He came with me.

Another week passed in which Pete's handpicked team of ISS investigators dug into the murder. I stayed away from my father. No matter how many times I found myself at the prison, I always managed to stop before I let them open the cell door. But I couldn't forget for even one waking moment that my father was in there. I dreamed of him. Confusing mosaics of him screaming, drunk, furious, and flashes of times when he wasn't, when he smiled and was happy, and we laughed together, all of us, Ma and Carrie and Pete. Sometimes the scenes were so vivid that I woke disoriented, uncertain anymore which version was real.

I went to the prison. Sam led me, without a word, to my father's cell and opened the door. I held out my hand to Sam.

"Give me your gun."

His eyebrows shot up. After only a brief hesitation, he pulled the weapon from his belt and handed it to me.

"Show me how it works."

He took my hand, with the gun, and held it up in front of me.

"Handle," he pointed to it as he spoke. "Barrel. Trigger. Setting." This last was a slider. "This," he said, pushing it all the way forward, "will kill from 5000 meters, assuming you can still see the target *and* hit it." His mouth hitched in a brief smile but then he sobered. "This," he pushed it all the way back, "is the lowest setting. Even at point blank range it's no more than you could do with a good punch." He studied my face. "What do you need it for?"

"Don't come in there, no matter what you hear, unless I call you," I said. He gave me a long look before he nodded.

"Yes, Your Highness."

I went inside. My father's eyes landed on the gun and widened. Then his face closed, his expression stiff and hard. He sighed, and it sounded like nothing less than profound relief. He stood and knelt in front of me, closing his eyes.

"Are you sure this is what you want?" I croaked.

"Yes," he whispered.

I pulled the trigger.

It was much louder than I expected and I jumped. He fell to the floor, but his eyes flew open and he looked up at me, his hand on his forehead.

"What was that?"

"The lowest setting," I said.

He levered himself to sit up.

"I know you don't really want to die."

His expression fell. "Do you think I have anything left to live for after this? What is the point of my life now, Jacob? How many times over have I earned this? How many times have I earned it from *you*? This is the only way that doesn't hurt anyone but me."

"How can you think that?" My throat was so tight that I couldn't force out more than a whisper.

He looked at me with something like pity on his face. "It's an illusion, Jacob, this thing you think we've built in here. You'll remember to hate me soon enough."

Didn't I still hate him? I couldn't think. I couldn't make sense of anything anymore.

"Stop it," I said, but I couldn't move as he stood and came forward.

As I watched, his expression morphed into a sneer. "You're not just stupid, you're a coward."

I shook my head, backing up. "No."

He advanced on me. "Stupid, worthless, sniveling coward. You always have been." He was so close I could smell his breath. Disoriented and stunned, I was surprised it didn't smell like gutter alcohol.

"Stop this." The protest was so weak it sounded like a plea.

He slapped me, an openhanded, ringing blow. "What good have you ever been to anyone!" He yelled. "I should have killed you! Broken your stupid little neck back in Abenez, where you belonged." Spittle peppered my face as he flung the words at me. "Everyone hates you. We always hated you. Even your mother hated you, she was just too stupid to say it."

Rage washed red across my vision and my fists tightened, the handle of the gun pressing painfully into the palm of my hand.

I slammed it into the side of his head and he fell to the ground with a thud.

I threw the gun across the room and grabbed him with both hands, hauling him upright. He grabbed the front of my shirt, jerking me closer. I tried to pull away but he wouldn't let go. I punched him. Again. Again. I braced myself for his blows but he didn't let go of my shirt, both fists gripping it so hard it became a painful vise on my torso.

"Hit me now, you son of a bitch!" I screamed.

I punched him again and his knees buckled. When he let go of me without warning, I almost fell backward. He dove across the room, his hand closing on the gun. I threw myself back against the door, drawing in breath to yell for help. Before I could, he turned to face me and met my eyes, his own dark and heavy with tears.

He put the barrel in his mouth and pulled the trigger.

The door flew open and bodies rushed into the room. The thought flitted across my mind that I'd told them not to come in, but I couldn't stop staring at my father, fallen in a tidy slump on the floor.

I was grabbed by the arms and spun to face Sam, his face pinched tight as his eyes scanned me.

"Are you all right, Your Highness?"

There wasn't even any blood. The beam would have cauterized

the surrounding tissue as it punched through my father's spinal cord. Just a different type of laser than the one I was known for, really. I wondered if my father had heard about that.

Sam frowned harder and pushed me out of the room with an oddly gentle touch. I almost asked him where we were going and why. We were halfway down the hallway when the fog cleared and the realization of what had just happened punched through my gut like the energy blast through my father's brain. My knees gave out and I vomited, retching in great heaves as if I could purge myself of what I'd just seen.

# *CE 31

T he next few days passed in a haze. I remember that I spent a lot of time in Pete's office, but I contributed about as much as the chair did. Jonathan put a tablet in my hand, I suppose to make it appear to all those coming and going that I was actually doing something.

I never turned it on.

I wasn't even sure why I was there. Was I trying to keep abreast of developments in the investigation? But hadn't that dead ended days ago? Hadn't that been my father's point?

I think, more than anything, I didn't want to be alone with my own thoughts. Or memories.

So I was there when Lord Laudley was brought before Pete.

I blinked, vaguely aware that I'd heard his name mentioned earlier in the day. Also that I'd tried to tune it out, because he was another bruise on my memory that I didn't need to prod.

Pete went very quiet, watching Lord Laudley approach his desk, flanked by two guards. Laudley stopped there but didn't bow, and no one said anything. No one looked at me.

Finally Pete broke the silence.

"Why?"

Why what?

"Because it needed to be done," Laudley answered. "And because I was in a position to do it. I have lived my life in service to the empire and all it stands for. I have always been willing to give everything, even my life, to protect its interests."

Pete's face had gone hard.

"Wait," I said, touching Pete's arm. "What are we talking about?"

Pete cast me a worried look, but then with a swipe of his finger and a nod of his head, he sent the info to the tablet in my hands.

I did. My hands grew cold and started to tremble as the conclusion became clear. I looked up at Laudley.

"You framed my father for murder."

He condescended to look at me. "I did."

It occurred to me I should have been angry, but mostly I felt sick.

"You tampered with the documentary?" The horrors of the last months tumbled over me. "The explosion in Tonga? The poisoned food? The riots?" Laudley nodded along with my list. I closed my eyes. "The miscarriages," I whispered.

"Of course."

"The assassination attempts?"

Pete gave a weary nod.

"I am responsible for all of it. It was all my doing," Laudley said, as if claiming a prize.

I looked at Pete. "He's the Patriot?"

"I am," Laudley answered, as if eager to make this clear, to make sure I understood.

"It's been *you*?"

Laudley gave me a condescending smile. "Have you enjoyed my efforts to remove you, *Your Highness*?

He smirked at me.

"You've succeeded in giving your life, Lord Laudley," Pete said, "but you'll die a traitor. You can redeem your honor and do your lawful duty to the empire by telling me who else was involved."

"I will not tell you anything. I will go to my death loyal to *the empire* and those who have helped me defend her. It is you who have betrayed us, Your Excellence. That man," he nodded in my direction, "is a criminal and an *unclass*. His presence here is a betrayal of all we are and all this empire stands for. It is you who put him there. Out of loyalty to the Empire, *I* have done my best to remove that stain on all of us. I can only hope that someone will take up the cause and carry on my work when I am gone. I will go to my death with the fervent hope that they succeed where I failed."

And so he did.

On a cloudy morning, Laudley was executed in the public square where I had once been beaten and exiled. He was dressed in his finest, with only an invisible force field restraining his hands and hobbling his movement. There was also a tiny field generator on the back of his neck that prevented him from opening his mouth or making any sounds. We had already heard his last words and Pete was taking no chance he'd repeat them publicly.

On the platform, Sam shoved him to his knees and grabbed a fistful of his hair, jerking him into position for the executioner's axe. I had a feeling Laudley would have positioned himself, but he wasn't allowed that dignity. There was no sound other than the slight thump when the blade fell and the louder one when Lord Laudley's head hit the platform, rolling once, twice, and finally settling. It was facing away from us, as if even in death he couldn't bear to look at me. The feeling was mutual.

From what the ISS teams dug out of Laudley's personal correspondence and activities, nearly a dozen men and women— not as many as Pete expected or hoped—were identified as co-conspirators. One by one, they were paraded before the crowds and into the incinerators.

I should have felt relief, satisfaction, vindication. He had been caught, justice had been done, the Patriot was dead. It was *over.*

But my father was dead, too. And I'd been the one to kill him, after all.

# CE 32

The annual celebration of the founding of the Duchy of Mexico was in a week.

"We don't have to go," Pete said to me as we lay in bed.

"Go where?" I asked. My mind still felt thick and slow. As if a frost had been settling over me since the day we were married, but so gradually that I hadn't noticed until I was locked in ice and couldn't get out.

"Mexico City."

"Oh."

"We can visit Puerto Vallarta instead. Or just not go. We don't even have to give a reason."

As if people couldn't guess.

"It's fine," I said.

We lay there a while longer, but I know he didn't sleep any more than I did. I had nothing else to say. And I suppose he'd figured out that nothing he could say would help.

We traveled to Mexico City on a bright blue spring day. I had gone ahead with the plan to make Mexico City the duchy's capital again, and the whole city had been repaired, upgraded, and decorated in preparation. I knew exactly how much they'd done because I'd seen the expense reports. And I'd glared at the grumblers when I diverted a quarter of the celebration-preparation budget to Abenez—and half of that to the vital services that they needed more than paint and light-streamers.

But that had been months ago. When I cared about such things.

Even numb as I felt, I could see the changes, and the pride on people's faces. Everything and everyone was bright and beautiful. It made me ache.

The mayor of the city was Lord Helios. He was a bland, uninteresting sort and I was very grateful for that. I didn't need jolly people around me that I had to make an effort to tune out. Kagawa was also his guest for the celebration and something about seeing him was reassuring.

There was the obligatory welcome feast and ball, and I did my best to be what I was supposed to be. But I had always been bad at this game, and I had no heart for it anymore. When Pete came to claim me for the opening dance, he gave me a long look and then said, "Would you mind if I asked Lady Helios to dance with me instead?"

He knew I didn't mind and I nodded, hoping he also knew I was grateful, even if I wasn't capable of showing it.

I hid in the garden reserved for us, which did nothing to protect me, in the end. My guards and Jonathan all got the most important alerts on their port-vids. It was under a beautiful night sky that I once again heard the dreaded tones of the Patriot, who should have been dead.

And heard, for the first time, about Revan.

*The brutal and unexplained murder this weekend of a high class Seattle couple, and the kidnapping of their daughter, has led to shocking discoveries pertaining to Prince Consort Jacob Dawes. The couple, identified as Bradley and Elizabeth Shaw, were stabbed to death this weekend in their home. Their daughter, Revan, a five-year-old they adopted at birth, was kidnapped by the murderer.*

*The man, who took his own life as authorities closed in, has been identified as a long-time palace employee, Tali Olin. The motivations for the murder might seem inexplicable, but the Patriot has learned that the girl—who is now safely in the hands of ISS officials—is the natural daughter of Prince Consort Jacob Dawes by this woman, now known only as K52, a Reset in a secret labor camp where she has been an inmate for seven years. The Patriot has confirmed that the Prince Consort spent six months at the same labor camp during his Resettlement.*

*The Patriot cannot help but speculate that the murder of an innocent high class couple and needless loss of life of what may well have been simply a loyal palace employee acting on orders, were all the carnage left in the wake of the former Reset, Prince Jacob, presumably to conceal these facts and persons from the emperor himself. The Patriot isn't sure which would be worse: that the emperor was aware of and condoned this action, or that he did not know his husband already had a child.*

*This certainly casts a new light on the emperor's ongoing difficulties bringing to birth an imperial heir. Has the prince been deliberately sabotaged their efforts in order to make way for his own—illegitimate—child?*

I didn't run, or even walk that fast, back to our rooms in the mansion. I was dimly aware of the guards around me, that the hallways were cleared ahead of my arrival and that I encountered no one. The whole thing had a feeling of déjà vu about it; an air of inevitability, defeat. They'd stabbed me in the heart so many times now that it was with a distant sense of curiosity that I watched my lifeblood flow red and terrible across the public datastreams, draining away life and all the mess that went with it. Cleansing. Freeing.

A child?

Kafe.

The thought sent a shiver down my spine, dispelling some of the numbness for the first time in days. She'd borne my child? Nausea washed over me, but it was as if it were happening to someone else. I wondered in a detached, incurious way if I was going to throw up again.

I stepped into a swarm of activity before I was even in the room. Functionaries and ISS officers and guards and servants boiled from the outer room like ants from a kicked anthill. Pete stood by a desk in the room set aside for his office, straight and sure. Calm. Commanding. He directed the storm with his usual capable assurance. Pete didn't deserve any of this.

He looked up and caught sight of me.

"Out."

His command was not loud, but clear, and my stomach clenched with despair. Of course. This would happen now, too.

But I realized that people around us were bowing and retreating like a well choreographed dance. He hadn't meant me. Relief made me light-headed.

Before two minutes had passed, the room was clear of everyone but us. The sudden silence was loud in my ears, somehow merging with the constant rushing that had filled it since that picture of a little girl had filled the screen, and Kafe.

The picture they'd chosen of Kafe had been masterful. It was of her on Dead End, moving among the inmates. It highlighted all of her good qualities, the one or two she had—purely physical— and made her look attractive even while painting her clearly as a criminal. An unclass and a criminal.

Pete crossed the room to me and took me in his arms, pressing my head to his shoulder.

"Are you all right?" he whispered.

For a moment I just stood there, stiff and unresponsive, numb and confused, still recovering from the fear that Pete had finally had enough and was done with me.

"Jake?"

I clutched him like a life preserver in a storm. Burying my face against his neck, wanting comfort, wanting to hide. Wanting him to make it all go away.

"I'm sorry," I whispered.

He pressed a kiss to my cheek but he was quiet before, almost reluctantly, he said, "Did you know?"

I tried to rear back but he held on tight, his hand behind my head, fighting to keep it on his shoulder.

"I'm sorry," he said.

"Pete..." He didn't move or alter his hold on me one bit. "There are things you should know."

He nodded, and I wondered what that meant. That he knew already; that he knew I was keeping secrets from him; that none of this surprised him...

But what he actually said was, "Let's sit down."

"I didn't know about the child." That felt like a very important point.

"I believe you," he replied.

For some reason, I laughed. "You probably shouldn't make a habit of that."

He took my hand. "I'll always believe you. I love you."

He said it so sincerely, as if it was somehow logical and explained everything.

I shook my head, looking down at our hands. I didn't deserve his trust. At the moment, it felt like a weight, a punishment for all my lies.

I started again. "I didn't know about the child. But there are other things I haven't told you, that I should have told you a long time ago. That I should have been telling you all along."

He squeezed my hand. "No blame or guilt or self-recriminations. Just talk to me. Tell me what I need to know. I'm not angry at you, or judging you. Not for any of it, OK?"

I just stared at him, trying to figure out how the depth of his generosity and kindness could still surprise me after all these years.

I sighed. The fortress of lies I'd built around myself was such a familiar obstacle that I had a hard time remembering which stone was the foundation of this particular wall.

"At our wedding," I started, quiet. "At the reception, I told Blaine I wanted to make peace, and he insinuated it wasn't necessary because he could get rid of me again."

Pete watched me patiently.

"He'd threatened me before, and I didn't think it was any more than that. But he knew about—" panic trapped the name in my throat. "He knew about things he shouldn't have, things that had happened to me on Dead End."

Pete closed his eyes, squeezing them shut against a private pain. "Dead End." There was no question in his voice. It was a statement laced with dread. "They sent you to Dead End."

I clutched his hand, he looked green.

"Oh Jake," he whispered. "I'm so sorry. I didn't know."

"I know you didn't."

He squeezed my hand. "Blaine knew you'd been there?"

"Yes, and he knew...things that had happened. Names of people. He made it pretty clear that he wanted me to know he had gotten to me before and could again."

"I don't understand," Pete said. "That was before we were married. It was such a different situation. It can't have been hard for him to get to you out there—I was deliberately ignorant of where you were and what was happening to you. But after our wedding? He brought it up as if it meant he could hurt you again? How could he think that, when I'd already done a great deal to make you safe? He had to know I wouldn't let anything happen to you."

"I know," I said. "In hindsight it doesn't make much sense, but at the time, well, it shook me, because the things he made me remember were—"

Even sidestepping *her*, it was still hard to get out.

"What happened, Jake? What did they do to you?"

I shook my head. "They didn't *do* anything, so much as set me up to earn punishments."

He closed his eyes again, his hand squeezing mine. "How many days were you out there?"

When I didn't answer right away, surprised that he already knew what I meant, he opened his eyes and focused on me.

"Every imperial world has its version of Dead End. The official punishment is the same on all of them. I've seen the psych reports on the effects. People have had complete psychotic breaks from one day of solitary work detail on an asteroid like that. The number of people who have served more than four days is infinitesimal, considering how long they're there."

He watched me, intense.

"How many days?"

"The last time?"

He flinched.

"My last eight days there were on solitary."

Pete's eyes filled with tears. "Oh Jake," he whispered. "It starts out at one or two days and compounds after that, doesn't it? If you were up to eight days at a stretch... You spent fifteen days on solitary in just six months?"

"Twenty." My throat thickened with tears of my own, but I was not going to do that again. I wasn't scared of Dead End anymore. I wouldn't be. "I survived."

He took my head in his hands and kissed me, fierce and hungry, as if this was our first reunion after all those days I'd spent alone on the surface of a barren asteroid.

He kissed me breathless and when he pulled away, both of us panting, he put his forehead to mine.

"I'm so, so sorry. I left you out there alone because I didn't want to torture myself, and I ended up letting them torture you. I'm sorry, Jake. I'll make it up to you somehow, I promise."

I leaned into him, soaking up the intensity of emotion. "It's not your fault," I said. "You thought you were making the right decision and you did it for a good reason. It's over now. Let it go. I'd forgive you if there was anything to forgive. But please, let me leave it in the past."

Pete took a huge, shuddering breath, nodding our heads together.

"You're right. I'll do whatever you want. Thank you for telling me. Now I understand why you were keeping things from me. I admit, it hurt me, but I should have trusted you had a good reason. Forgive me for not trusting you, at least."

We were getting too far off track, and he was wrong about that, anyway.

"Of course. Anyway, that's not even what I really need to tell you. Only, you need to know the circumstances to understand the rest."

Pete straightened and gave me his full attention again, wiping all concern for himself off his face.

I dropped his gaze. Why did he have to do that?

"The important point is that Blaine threatened me at the wedding ball and made sure I knew he'd been involved in making my stay at Dead End as miserable as possible. Only a few months ago, when you gave him Social Administration, he reminded me of that conversation, and said that he still meant it."

Pete's expression hardened.

"Not long after that, there was a mail for me, a video straight from the security feed on Dead End, of the last time I was set up, the time that got me eight days outside."

Pete's jaw tightened. I bowled ahead before he could make me talk about it.

"And it happened another time, a few weeks after the message from Carrie."

"The same video?"

Even talking about a video of the event made my palms sweat. I could almost *smell* her.

"Similar."

Pete's hand had been tightening slowly on mine. It was cutting off my circulation and I hadn't even noticed. I didn't want him to stop.

"So Blaine's been harassing you, torturing you, for months, and you didn't want to tell me?"

"I did want to," I said, because that was true.

"Why didn't you?" Pete sounded genuinely puzzled, as if he didn't suspect there was still so much he didn't know.

"I—" I attempted a chuckle. "I didn't want to be a baby about it. I didn't want to go crying to you over a bully. And you had enough to worry about with the real problems around the Empire, and the Patriot."

Pete's hand jerked in mine. "Do you think any or all of those things are more important to me than you are?" His tone wasn't angry, only sad; regretful. Not nearly enough blame in it. None at all, really.

"Pete, you're the emperor."

He took both my hands, pulled me to face him straight on. "Jake, you're my husband."

I hid my face in his hands. "I'm sorry."

"No more, Jake. Promise me? No more hiding. We do this together. Please?"

I nodded. As much as I can, Pete.

"It's OK, you know," he said.

I blinked, not sure what we were talking about now. "What is?"

"That you have a daughter."

And, stupidly, it was only then I realized what that meant to him. Not just that I had a daughter we hadn't known about—a complication now—but the Patriot's last, cutting words. I had a daughter already, but he didn't.

I grabbed him. "You're not buying that idiot's bullshit, are you?"

"No," he said. He was completely unconvincing. "Of course not. Laudley confessed to—"

"Laudley lied about other things. Like being the Patriot, for example."

"It doesn't matter. I know you're not the problem. I just..." he sighed. "Well I *know* that's not the problem, but it still feels..."

I squeezed his hand. "I know. I'm sorry. I'm so sorry."

"None of this is your fault, Jake."

I wished I believed him.

I'm ashamed of the fact that I was thinking of Kafe and not the girl when Pete said, "I should have another report on her by now."

"What?"

"Your daughter," he said, with only a slight hesitation on the phrase.

"Oh, right. Of course."

Of course.

It wasn't until I found myself rubbing my hands on my pants that I realized my palms were sweating.

# CE 33

Pete went back to his reports and functionaries, inviting me to sit with him, to be a part of it all. There wasn't anything I wanted less. The fog that had clung to me for weeks had suddenly become a pounding, choking, thunderstorm. I needed to move.

I paced out on the balcony with Jonathan, who stood in the shadows and watched; he was my ever-present, worried shadow. His concern was easier to bear than Pete's. I didn't feel guilty that I didn't pretend for Jonathan. Maybe it was the consequence of him withholding the name of friendship from our relationship all those years. It freed me of the obligation to feel responsible for how I made him feel.

At some point, the nervous energy left me all in a rush. The blanket of depression descended again as the enormity of it all hit me.

I had a daughter.

Kafe.

I stood on the balcony of our room, looking out over the sparkling city under a flawless night sky.

Pockets of bright celebration were lit up all over; color and light and the ebb and flow of music and laughter all around me. I felt out of place, dirty and discarded.

I was just turning away from the city when something about the lights to the north caught my eye. They were brighter than the others, though indistinct. I watched the flickering red, yellow, orange dance of them, wondering why they seemed wrong somehow.

I sucked in a breath but the word came out as barely a whisper. "Jonathan."

He didn't waste time answering me. What he said was to others: calm but urgent orders and directions. I felt the movement of people in the room behind me swell and recede with frenetic activity and every one of them ignored me.

It was Pete who slid in beside me, taking my hand.

We stood there together and watched Abenez burn.

I didn't leave the balcony all night. The fire caught and spread as if Abenez had been assembled for this very purpose, and the wall of dominoes toppled at last. It was breathtaking, precise, and efficient destruction. A devastating cascade effect, as each crumbling building caught five others alight with flaming debris. The explosions, when they happened, where no explosive materials should have been, didn't even surprise me anymore. More than nineteen million people died that night. They were "only unclass," but the scale of destruction was enough to make even the other classes notice and shake their heads.

I wondered, with a half-hysterical chuckle, if Pete would levy fines against the duchy this year; we'd more than exceeded the acceptable percentage of unclass lives lost per annum. Pete looked at me, concern etched in his brow. I just shook my head.

Fire protection fields sprang up between Abenez and the low class districts, but unlike any other area with a concentrated group of people, slums didn't have periodic fire-break force fields to keep the flames contained. The size and fury of the blaze kept even the fire suppression aircraft at bay; they could do little more than harass the fire within the slum itself, where it drank, long and deeply, of the lives of those that no one cared about. Not even me, anymore. Caring about things hurt too much.

Pete came and went, alternately taking reports and waving people off so he could stand alone with me. I was dimly aware of his presence, only sometimes noticing him with the sense that he'd been there awhile, or suddenly realizing he was gone and not knowing how long ago he had left.

At last, when the morning's own display of red and orange lit the eastern sky, washing out the remains of the blaze that had burned high and fast, Pete tugged on my hand.

"Come to bed," he said gently.

I stayed where I was.

"Jake?"

"It's probably better this way, don't you think?"

"No," he said, firm and sure.

"No one wanted them there. They weren't even happy themselves. Everybody wins."

"You don't believe that."

"Don't I?"

"Jake..." There was a tone of entreaty in his voice, but I don't think he knew what he was asking any more than I did. For me to not feel so horrible? I wanted it as much as he did. Or maybe that wasn't true. I wasn't sure I wanted much of anything anymore.

"I'm sorry," I said quietly. I was. I should be.

He wrapped his arms around me from behind, laying his head on my shoulder.

"Come to bed."

He made love to me, and I think he felt better because of it. I didn't feel anything at all.

# CE 34

I woke up that afternoon with a sensation of surprise, as if I hadn't expected to wake at all. As if now that Abenez was gone, I would just cease to exist. Pete was already up, sitting out on the balcony, staring out over the smoking ruin. The day was crisp and clear, beautiful; the curls of smoke painting a complex, abstract work of art in the sky above the ashes and the dead.

Only once I was sitting beside him with a cup of tea he'd gotten for me, did I realize we weren't alone. Pete moved to the chair beside me, facing our visitor. He slid his hand into mine and held it firmly.

"Go ahead, Lord Weyler," he said.

"The DNA is a match," he said.

It took me a minute to realize what we were talking about.

"She's mine?" I croaked.

Pete nodded slowly.

"Dr. Heinriksen will have to do the tests again to make sure," I said to Pete.

"Of course," he answered, squeezing my hand in reassurance.

"Does she know what happened to her parents?" Pete asked, absurdly calm in light of the topic.

"No, Your Excellence," Lord Weyler said. "According to the reports, the girl was with a family friend that day. The parents were killed in their home. The friend was returning the child to her apartment but they were accosted in the hallway. The friend was knocked unconscious and when she came to, the girl was gone. There is no indication that the kidnapper took her back into the apartment. It appears he took her directly from the hallway to his transport."

"Maybe he took her in there to show her. We don't even know what his objective was or why he killed them," I said.

Lord Weyler replied, "All the evidence indicates that the perpetrator was acting from a plan, no doubt on someone's orders. We can find no link between him and the parents. The pattern of his actions suggests that his intent was indeed to murder the parents and abduct the child. He left no ransom note, which suggests he was obtaining the child for himself or someone else. It's only speculation at this point, but I think he was set up. The ISS officials were operating on an anonymous tip they'd received. When they showed up at his hideout, they reported that he was alive. I don't believe he intended to or even did kill himself."

Pete frowned. "Why is that? And who would have killed him? Wasn't he alone with the girl?"

"The cause of death was a poison released from a device inserted under his skin."

"Like all the others," Pete said.

"Yes," Weyler answered, "but this specific device had the ability to be triggered remotely, as well. And it was."

Pete pursed his lips. "So someone sent him to murder the parents and abduct the child, set him up to get caught with her, and then killed him off before he could be interrogated."

"Precisely."

"But *why*?" I asked. "If they targeted her, they must have already known who she was. Why not just expose her parentage without killing anyone?"

"Perhaps they wanted to make it look as if the discovery was accidental? The damning piece of information, in my opinion, is that the girl's DNA was never examined for parentage, according to any official records. Yet whoever orchestrated the kidnapping was confident of it."

"Where is she now?" I asked.

"In an ISS facility in Seattle. She was sent there for medical assessment and to be held until we received further instructions."

"She's being held in some *facility*?"

Pete laid his hand on my arm.

"It's not a jail, Your Highness," Weyler said. "It's a very nice apartment, from what I'm told. And the family friend is staying with her." He shot a quick glance at Pete. "We wouldn't treat her with any disrespect," he said. "We do know who she is."

I sat back, stunned. Right. She was the Prince Consort's bastard child.

"As for the natural mother," Weyler continued, "her name is Katherina Asturias."

They both looked at me as if for confirmation. It took me a minute to process the change, and when I realized what we were talking about, my stomach seized. "That's not the name I knew her by." I was relieved to hear that my voice didn't shake.

"No, you wouldn't," Lord Weyler said. "Katherina Asturias officially ceased to exist when she was sent to the permanent Settlement 14R2. She's known by the designation K52 now."

"Kafe."

They looked at me.

"It's the name she goes by. K52. Kafe."

"How did a Set carry a baby to term?" Pete asked Lord Weyler.

"She successfully hid the pregnancy for over six months. By the time the authorities became aware of it, it was too late to do anything but make arrangements for an adoptive family."

"She hid it well," I said. "I didn't know. I was there a full six months and it was the first night, when— It was only the one time."

Pete was watching me. His brow wrinkled when I didn't complete the sentence.

I looked at Lord Weyler. "Who did she claim the father was before this?"

"She didn't," he answered. "And it didn't matter, so there was no effort made to determine paternity. The baby would have been taken from her anyway. The same with the potential pool of fathers. No other Set had rights to the child, and the guards had no business being with the inmates. She volunteered no father's name, and no one asked."

"So the girl was adopted?"

"Yes. K52 was brought to Earth to deliver the baby, and Bradley and Elizabeth Shaw were waiting for her." He looked up from his notes. "Newborns are easy to place."

"I want you to bring the woman here," Pete said. "I want all the information we have on her. Also on Revan and her adoptive parents."

I stared at Pete as he calmly set in place the events I'd tried so hard to avoid. An almost welcome surge of anger swelled in my chest and I clung to it. It was something to feel. It was somewhere to hide.

"Bring the woman here, Your Excellence?" Weyler asked. "Not the palace?"

"The palace," Pete said. "We're leaving here this morning."

"Here," I said.

They both looked at me.

"Here. Not the palace." Not that I didn't have plenty of horrible memories associated with the palace already, but I didn't have to come back here ever again. If Kafe was going to walk into my life, it was going to be somewhere that could burn to the ground when she was gone if I wanted it to. Or maybe while she was still in it.

Pete was watching me. He looked back at Weyler.

"Have her brought here."

"You could have asked me first," I said, keeping my voice steady with effort.

"About what?"

"Bringing her to you."

His eyebrows crinkled in confusion. "The mother?"

"Yes."

He hesitated. "I'm sorry. But I do need to speak to her. I can't go to her."

"That's what vids are for," I spat. Pete's eyebrows shot up and I looked away, breathing deliberately to get my voice back under control.

"You OK?" He stood and came over to me, laying a gentle hand on my arm.

I jerked a curt nod without looking at him.

He stared at me for a moment before he continued. "I didn't realize you hated her. I assumed there was some...well, you did sleep with her."

I took a deep breath before I managed to answer. "It wasn't like that. It was a mistake, that's all. It only happened once, and then I did my best to avoid her for six months."

"OK," he said, though he looked puzzled. "If you don't want to see her, I don't see why you have to."

I would have given a lot to never see or hear of Kafe again. But there was no way I was going to leave her alone with Pete.

"I'm not afraid of her," I said, then almost bit my tongue when I realized he'd never said anything about being afraid. "I just don't want to see her. It doesn't matter."

It did matter, but I couldn't tell him why.

Kafe was in the city the next morning.

She was waiting for us in a plush lounge lined with windows, sitting in an overstuffed chair, flanked by two guards. Her hands were shackled in front of her and she wore leg restraints, the kind that simulated real iron chains. When we entered, one of the guards hauled her to standing with a handful of the back of her shirt. Judging from the ungentle treatment, I guessed she'd already used her charms on them.

A frown line appeared between Pete's eyes, but he said nothing. Kafe bent into what, even handicapped by the restraints, was recognizable as a curtsy. She held my gaze the entire time. Pete made no comment, and I wondered if he realized the gesture was meant as a mockery of me, rather than a show of respect for him.

"You may be seated, Ms. Asturias," Pete said.

She cocked one eyebrow as she sank into the chair. "There's a name I haven't heard in a while. Are you giving it back to me, Emperor?"

"You address the Emperor as Your Excellence," one of the guards barked.

"I'm sorry," she said. With a smarmy smile in my direction she added, "And what do I call the other one? Your Highness?"

"That's right," he answered, oblivious to the barb in that for me. And of the way the predatory gleam in her eyes made my palms sweat. I realized my jaw was clenched, and made myself relax.

I couldn't possibly be afraid of her anymore.

Pete ignored the byplay. "I'm doing nothing at this point but asking you some questions," he said. "Your cooperation could go a long way toward improving your situation."

I shot Pete a look. We weren't going to improve her situation!

But he didn't know. He didn't understand, because I hadn't told him.

Kafe saw my reaction and grinned at me.

"It's lovely to see you again, Your Highness. The Abenez brats really are moving up in the world, aren't we? I've never seen a room like this—"

"Why did you do it?" I interrupted.

Her eyes widened artfully. "Why did I do what?"

The feigned innocence didn't work for her now. She hadn't aged well, and looked older than the years could account for. There were wrinkles around her eyes and mouth that weren't laugh lines. She was still very attractive, but it was no longer the girlish prettiness she'd wielded like a weapon when I first knew her.

"Why did you hide her?" I said, forcing the calm, patient tone.

"Revan? They kept the name I gave her? She was a pretty baby." She shrugged. "What I got to see of her, anyway."

"Answer the question."

She lifted and dropped one shoulder. "I wasn't sure what he would do." She nodded toward Pete.

"What I would do?" Pete asked. "What do you mean?"

She held her palms up, in another attempt to appear naive. But she answered me, not him. "You hear things about powerful people and the ones who get in their way. I mean, look what happened to our home, Your Highness." She gestured absently in the direction of Abenez.

Pete was looking at her with an expression of absolute astonishment. "You think I would harm a child?"

She gave him a fake smile. "We unclass kids don't presume to know about you important people."

"Stop that," I snapped.

She turned wide eyes back to me. "Stop what?"

"Stop pretending like you don't know exactly what you're doing."

She raised a shoulder and said nothing.

"Why did you conceal the pregnancy?" I asked. "You never struck me as the maternal type."

"Why not? I got a trip back to Earth out of it, not once but twice. Who knows what else might happen? A girl like me can't just throw away opportunities like that."

"Do you even care anything about her?"

"Do you?" she countered. She cut a quick look at Pete. "Anyway, of course I'd care about her. But that's not one of the privileges Sets on Dead End get."

"Would you like to see her?" Pete asked.

I shot out of my seat, trembling from the rush of adrenaline. "No!" They both looked at me. "No. She's done enough to that kid. No way is she going to see her."

Pete watched me, his eyes wide with surprise.

Kafe giggled. "He doesn't know how much you hate me, does he? You didn't tell him?"

"Shut your mouth," I ground out through my teeth.

She threw her head back and laughed. "What's the matter? Too scared?"

"You're already a lifer on Dead End," I growled. "I wouldn't be advertising other crimes in front of the emperor if I were you."

"What crimes?" Pete said.

"Why?" Kafe countered, ignoring Pete. "Things could get worse for me? Are you going to cry to your husband and ask him to kill your daughter's mother? I don't suppose that's the sort of thing you tell a child as a bedtime story."

I yanked her up by the front of her shirt. She grabbed my arm to steady herself but otherwise did nothing. She smirked at me.

"Jake!" Pete said.

"Aren't you scary?" she purred. "I'm shaking in my leg-irons."

I threw her back into the chair. Pete grabbed my arm. "What's wrong? Do you need to take a break?"

I jerked my arm away. "I'm fine. Did you have questions for her, or not?"

He gave me a long, considering look. Finally he turned back to Kafe.

"You will stop needling him," he said.

"Will I?" She gave him her one-shoulder shrug. "I might. But I'm not so keen to return to Dead End. You see that? That's real sunlight. An execution here can't be much worse than wasting away on that lifeless rock."

"I don't execute anyone without good reason, Ms. Asturias."

Her smile made my teeth hurt. "But he didn't tell you what I did, yet."

Pete didn't take the bait. "You weren't even a legal adult when you were sent to Dead End, were you?"

She settled back into the chair, making herself comfortable. "I had my birthday on the transport. I was eighteen when I got there."

"Why'd you get sent there, anyway?" I asked. Pete gave me a *you-didn't-read-her-data?* look but didn't say anything. It was true, I hadn't read it. Even her file was closer to her than I wanted to be, if I could help it.

"My brother and I led an attack on a rival gang. We killed eight of them."

"And you didn't get an execution out of that?" I asked.

"I wasn't there when it went down. And, as Mr. Emperor here already knows, I was only seventeen. Between kiddie jail and the incinerators, they compromised and sent me to Dead End."

"What about your brother?"

"They cooked him. He was nineteen. I think you knew him. Percival Asturias?"

I did, actually. It's hard to forget a name like Percival in Abenez. I didn't answer her, though.

"But look at me now," she said. "My daughter is the bastard child of the Prince Consort. See how I've come up in the world? You were right, Your Highness: classing-up isn't that hard, after all. A little brains and ambition, a dose of street smarts, and just like that." She snapped her fingers. "We should write to our friends in Abenez and let them know. Oh, wait, I guess we can't—"

"Stop it!"

The guards beside her fidgeted, casting looks at me and Pete as if they weren't sure if they should do anything to her or not.

She looked at Pete. "He's scared of me, you see. He didn't tell you about it, did he? I've laughed a lot over the years about how quickly he—"

I hauled her out of the chair again but she kept going.

"Gave in. And he liked it too." She looked at me now. "Didn't you? That's what you're so mad about. Not that you got raped by a girl, but that you liked it."

A thick silence fell over the room. I still held her on her tip-toes, breathing hard. She smirked.

I threw her into the chair and stormed out of the room.

# CE 35

I was standing on our balcony, looking out over what used to be Abenez, when Pete found me. He stepped up to the rail beside me but didn't say anything. Waiting.

"Why didn't you tell me?" he asked finally, his voice soft, gentle.

"Because I wanted to make sure no one ever found out about it. That's why. Telling you would have completely missed the point."

"You didn't think I'd understand?"

"I thought that no one was ever going to know, that's what I thought. I wasn't going to tell *anyone*. Not even you. Especially not you."

"Especially not me? Why?"

"Because of this!" I threw my arms up in the air. "Because now we're talking about it! I don't want to talk about it. I don't want it to have happened. Not one minute of it. I can't make that happen, but at least I can fucking *not talk about it*!"

"It wasn't your fault, Jake."

"What wasn't my fault, Pete? Huh? The fact that she—" I choked on the word. "The fact that I was there? That she made my life as miserable as possible for six months? The fights that she set up and had blamed on me? The twenty fucking days I spent on solitary? All the nights I hid in my cell hoping to avoid getting any more, and it didn't matter for shit? Which part wasn't my fault, Pete? And how does that even fucking matter?"

He stepped toward me and put his hand on my arm, but I jerked away. "You weren't supposed to know. And now, on top of all the fun of talking about it and knowing you know about everything I've tried so hard to forget, now I get to live with knowing you feel guilty about it."

He nodded. "I do feel guilty."

I threw up my hands in a "see?" gesture.

"I can't help how I feel, Jake. Neither can you."

"I can. I can not make it worse."

He sighed. "I'm sorry."

"I'd like to be left alone, please."

"Jake—"

When I rounded on him, he nodded slowly. "OK. If that's what you want."

I didn't say anything more. After a moment, he left.

I had been brooding alone for almost an hour when Jonathan came up to me. His expressions and body language were always subtle, his thoughts well masked. But there was an exaggerated blankness in his face and tone, as if it were taking more effort. I looked away and tried to ignore him.

"His Excellence instructed me to make arrangements for you to leave for a few days, if that's what you would like."

My head shot up. "He's sending me away?"

"That's wasn't the impression I got, no. He seemed to think this was something you wanted."

"Fine," I snapped. "Yes, I want to get out of here."

"Any destination in particular?"

"I don't care. So long as it's isolated and as far from anyone as it's possible to be on this overpopulated, nosy asshole of a planet."

His eyebrows went up, but he turned to leave.

"What's wrong with you?" I said.

He was slow to turn around. When he did, there was nothing out of the ordinary or telling about his face or his posture. Still, something was off.

"It bother you?" I pressed. "That I slept with someone else

a week after I left him behind, grieving over me? That I'm a complete bastard who screws over everyone who is stupid enough to love him?"

"No."

"Yeah, I can tell. You're not treating me any different than you usually do, you're not patronizing me at all."

"You don't usually act this much like a petulant child."

"Oh go fuck yourself."

"Shall I make arrangements for that as well?"

I wanted to punch him, wanted to hurt him so much it ached inside me along with all the other festering, unclean, rot of who and what I was. Horrible husband, horrible brother and son and father, horrible friend or employer or whatever Jonathan saw me as. Horrible person.

"Get out!" I screamed. "Get out!" He left without even acknowledging me.

Pete wasn't alone when I found him in his temporary office, but when he looked up and saw me, he sent everyone away. When we were alone we stood there for a moment, just looking at each other.

"Jonathan told me you didn't to get away and have some time by yourself."

I blinked, searching my memory of the conversation. I was pretty sure I'd said the opposite. As usual, Jonathan knew better than I did what I really meant. I felt even worse.

"I'm sorry for what I said to you."

His smile was sad, and half-hearted. "It's all right."

"No, it's not. You're just uncommonly bad at holding grudges."

He huffed in amusement, looking down. "That's probably true. But, Jake, it's OK, I forgive you." He looked back up at me, his expression tired, heavy. "In any case, there's something else we have to talk about right now."

"Revan's gone?"

Pete sighed. "She was abducted."

I stared at him.

"Again?"

"Yes. From us. She disappeared from the facility about an hour ago."

"I—"

I what? My mind was blank, my life was— I didn't know what it was. Everything I'd ever had was being chipped away, one by one. Even the things I thought I hadn't wanted. Even the things I hadn't known I'd had until it was too late. I looked up at Pete, a stab of panic in my chest. Was he next?

I catapulted out of my chair. "We have to leave."

He nodded. "Yes, we're going now. We'll go home and sort this out. And I'll find her, Jake, I promise."

That wasn't what I'd meant at all. I slumped back in my chair, my complete and utter powerlessness hitting me like an asteroid.

"Right. Home. Of course. I know you will." A rush of anger tightened my chest. "Have you asked Blaine where she is?"

Pete looked down at his desk. "Blaine left the palace a month ago and hasn't been seen since."

I blinked, staring at him in shock.

"I had him under surveillance, but ISS lost him two days out from Earth." He looked up at me, wincing. "I didn't tell you because I thought...I don't know. I didn't want to tell you."

I just nodded dumbly. It was OK. I didn't want him to tell me either.

We rode home, Pete in a constant state of activity: receiving reports, issuing orders, planning in silence. I sat alone, wrapped in my own thoughts.

A sudden thought shot me out of my seat.

"Where's Kafe?"

Pete looked up at me. His mouth twisted in a funny way. He

cocked his head toward the front of the transport. "Up there."

My knees went out from under me and I plunked back into the chair.

"What?"

His mouth lifted into a hint of a wry smile. "After our little... argument at the IIC, I had a brig installed on my personal transport."

I gaped at him for a long, stunned moment.

"You did not."

He chuckled. "Actually I did."

The giggle ripped out of me without permission, and suddenly I was laughing. Hard and unstoppable and desperate. I laughed and laughed as if it could drive away everything else. As if I'd never laugh again.

When I finally stopped laughing I felt empty, scrubbed clean and raw. I soon found myself leaning against the wall in front of an otherwise nondescript door in the front of the transport. I hadn't asked, but the two guards standing on each side of the door made it obvious this was the brig. I had no desire to go in, to see her. But for some reason I couldn't leave, either. I wondered if there was a window in the room; if she was sitting there watching the scenery fly by. What an incredible thing that would be after years on Dead End.

I hated her. But I didn't have the strength to do it properly anymore.

At some point I became aware of Jonathan standing just the perfect distance down the hall; the point at which his presence was not obtrusive, but he was still accessible. That wrung the last remaining chuckle from me.

"For fuck's sake, Jonathan," I said. "Don't you think it's about time you stop pretending you're just some robot programmed to see to my comfort, and act like a real person? You know, you're probably one of the best human beings I know. You're a lot better than me, that's for sure."

"Jacob Dawes," he said, low and intense, his voice hot with anger. My head shot up in shock and I stared at him. He was looking at me, his glare burning through me with such intensity that I shivered. "You have never been more wrong in your entire life."

And, with that, he turned his back on me and walked away.

It was a long time before I did anything at all. I had no idea what the hell that could have been about—he'd actually called me by name, and yet, what he'd said...I didn't know what was going on, but it still hurt. A lot. Something else I'd screwed up, ruined, and I didn't even know how or why.

When at last we made it back to the palace, Pete and I left the transport together, entering the palace privately and alone. Pete was preoccupied, focused and intense.

I looked around.

"Where's Jonathan?"

Pete's expression hardened. "He's working on something for me right now."

Something about the way he said it made me shut up.

I didn't see Jonathan at all for the next two days—two days I spent lost in the midst of the teams of investigators that ebbed and flowed around Pete, pretending like I was of some use as other people worked on finding my daughter, and Blaine, and probably fixing a million other things that were falling apart that Pete was kind enough to just not tell me about.

Pete woke me in the early morning hours of the third day.

"We found her," he said. I sat up, trying to scrub the remainder of a dream from my mind.

"Is she all right?"

He smiled. "Yes. Come with me. You can see her."

He led me to a grand bedroom within the Imperial area. One of the family bedrooms. And there, sleeping alone in the big bed, was one tiny little girl. Even in the dim light I could see the coppery tint to her brown curls, the creamed-coffee color of her skin. I wondered what her eyes would look like when she woke up. Would they be dark brown like mine, or would they be amber, or hazel?

I stood there for a long time, just looking at her, with Pete at my side, his hand warm in mine.

"Is this what Jonathan's been helping you with?" I asked. "Did he find her?"

Pete stiffened, his hand jerking within mine. I looked at him. His expression was stony.

"Something like that," he clipped off the words, as if to be rid of them.

I backed up a step, almost stumbling. He reached for me.

"No," I said. "Don't. I need... Please. Just tell me. What's wrong? Did something happen to Jonathan?" I grabbed Pete's hands with both of mine. "Please. I need to know."

Stark pain crossed Pete's face, chased away by that same, terrible anger.

He dropped my hands and looked back at Revan sleeping on the bed, his arms crossed as if he needed to keep them under control.

"Jonathan helped," he spat, "by confessing to his role in spying on you for the past ten years. And offering up everything he knew about Blaine's plans, and the names of everyone else he knew of in Blaine's network." He looked back at me, his posture softening with defeat and sadness.

"He didn't have to find her, Jake. He already knew where she was."

I entered the cell.

He was lying on the bed, an arm thrown over his eyes. He didn't move or give any indication he knew anyone was there, though he must have heard me. I gestured to Sam that he should shut the door and after a long frown at me, he did so. I stood facing Jonathan, who still hadn't moved.

"So, none of it matters anymore?" I croaked. "What if I'd been Pete? You didn't even look to see who you weren't showing the proper respect to."

"His Excellence wouldn't have come in here to see me," he said, his voice hard and bitter. "You're the only one who does things like that."

I swallowed hard but my throat was still too tight. "And what I think doesn't matter."

"Obviously," he drawled. There was so much hatred in his voice.

"Why did you do it?" I gasped.

He was silent so long I thought he was ignoring me, but then he blew out a long breath. "I didn't really know you when it started," he said. "Blaine asked me for what seemed like harmless, unimportant information on the new palace appointee I was assigned to, and I gave it to him. He was a powerful duke. Who was I to tell him no?"

"So it was because I was an unclass. You, too."

He grunted. "Maybe. Though I didn't think about it like that. But you're probably right. He was important and you weren't."

Any further questions got trapped behind the grief in my throat. It took several painful minutes to find my voice again. "But you didn't stop."

"No. By the time I had reason to want to, I was in too deep."

My mouth was dry and I wondered if the words would come out of it.

"Pete told me you have a daughter." For some reason, that bothered me more than many of the outright lies and betrayals. That he had a daughter and I'd never known.

He stared at the floor. "Yes."

"Where?"

"Her mother works for Blaine. Somewhere I'm not allowed to know. They let me see her, from time to time."

"You never thought that you could come to me for help?"

He rose up on an elbow with a sardonic lift to one eyebrow.

"How would that conversation have gone? 'I've been betraying you and spying on you for years and I'd like to stop, so would you please protect me and my family?'" He chuckled, a miserable sound, and thumped back down on the bed. "Even you're not that gullible."

I wanted to argue with him, but I wasn't sure which point I wanted to protest.

"I trusted you," I said.

"Yes," he said, hollow and bitter. "Now you know better." He turned his face to the wall. "Go away, Jacob."

Pete was waiting outside the cell, propped up against the wall, glaring at the door. He took my face gently in his hands.

"Are you all right?"

I shook my head between his palms. "I don't know."

He just gave me a long, searching look. So much pain in his eyes. "It's not your fault," he said softly. "None of us suspected him."

"But I knew him better than anyone," I said, and then stopped myself with an awful laugh. "No," I said. "That's not true. I guess I didn't know him. I never knew him at all."

We left the prison together, holding hands, walking in silence. Eventually I realized we were entering the Imperial area and I stopped.

"Revan."

Pete squeezed my hand. "She's fine. She woke up about an hour ago. The servants were going to get her dressed, fed, and all of that. But I thought you'd want to be the first one to talk to her about what's going on."

I gaped at him as all the blood rushed from my face. "Me? What in the world am I supposed to say to her? I can't be the one to tell her—" My breath caught in horror just thinking about it.

"No," Pete said. "No. I don't mean that. I've been talking to specialists about how to tell her about her parents and about who she is to us. I mean, I thought you'd want to introduce yourself, before all the rest of it."

I took a deep breath.

"What does she know?"

"Only what she went through herself, and where she is now. And from what I can tell, when Blaine's people had her, they only told her they were taking her somewhere safe. So I don't think she even knows any of that wasn't supposed to happen."

I searched his face. For answers, maybe. Imperial intervention.

"I don't know if I can do this," I said.

"Do you want me to go with you?"

Did I? Of course I did. And yet...

I shook my head slowly. Reluctantly. "No. I should do this alone."

Pete gave me a solemn nod, and I knew he understood.

I wished I did.

I met her in a sunny playroom with an expansive view of the ocean. I was waiting for her there, but when she first entered, the window wall facing the ocean held her attention and she didn't notice me.

She was a lovely little thing. Children older than Owen meshed into a long "kid" age in my head, but I knew how old Revan was. Almost six. So this was what that looked like.

Her hair, in the sunlight, looked almost red. Her eyes were closer to peat, with the faintest tint of amber, like a patina. She only gave in to the view for a few moments before she looked around. When she saw me standing there, watching her, she gasped.

"Hello," I said quietly. "Are you Revan?"

She nodded.

"It's nice to meet you, Revan, I'm Jacob."

She examined me with a child's frank curiosity. "You're the prince."

It startled me, though I didn't know why it should have. "I am now." When she didn't say anything more I added, "I wasn't always."

She shrugged as if that didn't matter, and looked at me, quiet and intense. "I learned about you in school."

Not surprising, but it was disconcerting nonetheless. "Oh? What did you learn?"

"You're the Prince Consort. You're married to Emperor Rikhart IV."

I felt my heart sink a little. I hated that these were the things she knew. I cleared my throat and looked away, looked for something else to talk about.

"Have you seen the ocean before?" I said.

"We went to the beach one summer. But it was different."

"The ocean's very big."

"It's 75% of the earth's surface," she said.

I blinked but couldn't help but smile. "Does that sort of thing interest you?"

She shrugged, looking out the window again. "I guess."

I moved over and sank down beside her. "Are you...are you all right?" Was that how you asked a child how she was coping with being abducted from her parents, rescued from her dead kidnapper, abducted from the rescuers, and then re-rescued in the space of a few days?

"Do you know where my mommy and daddy are?" she asked, her voice quiet, small. Like her.

"They're...they're sick right now." I tried not to groan out loud. I really was a terrible liar. Even I wouldn't believe me.

I heard her sniffle. Her soft little hand slid into mine. "Can you make them better? Can you bring them here too and ask the emperor to make them better? Please?"

"I—" I had never felt more powerless than I did in that moment. "I'll try."

Her arms slid around my neck and she climbed into my lap, burying her face in my shoulder.

"Thank you," she whispered.

Just then, I don't think anyone in the empire hated me more than I did.

I gestured frantically to the servant, and, thankfully, she got enough out of that to bring Pete. I made faces and mouthed words at him, hoping he'd understand that things weren't going well at all.

Without missing a beat, he sank to his knees in front of us.

Revan turned to look at him.

"Hi there," he said.

Over the course of the next half hour, Pete patiently and clearly explained everything she needed to know. Who we were to her, the highlights of how we had learned about her, why she was here. She started to cry when he told her, very gently, that her parents were dead. He held his hand out to stroke her hair and she reached for him, climbing into his lap and burying her face in his shirt. He looked down at her in wonderment for a moment before he put his arms around her, rocking gently as he held her.

# CE37

W hat Jonathan knew was enough for the ISS to make a crack in Blaine's defenses, and things snowballed from there. In all, over two hundred people were arrested over the course of the next week. They included guards at Dead End, ISS officers, an entire palace tech team, servants, guards, and the med tech who had administered the injections that terminated each pregnancy and then falsified the lab results to cover her tracks. And there was Jonathan, of course.

Owen was recovered from a noble family who had been helping Blaine recruit and place his agents and spies. Pete had him brought to the palace and I insisted he be housed in the Imperial area with us. He was given the bedroom beside Revan's. Both rooms opened up into a shared playroom for the children.

The ISS caught up with Blaine on a dinky old transport almost at our border with Zeltia. He was disguised in the clothing of a poor laborer, in a cargo space with the other low class travelers. I wished I could have seen it.

I was waiting for him on the platform when the ISS brought him the palace. Pete had asked how I wanted it to be, and seemed to understand when I said I wanted to go alone.

I wasn't entirely alone, of course. Sam and a full contingent of the guard waited with me. I thought it was too much of an honor for Blaine to be allowed to look like that much of a threat, but I didn't argue it, either. Physical threat he may not have been, but he had managed to nearly destroy my life, and eviscerate me as part of the bargain, in the space of just a few years.

I watched him disembark, escorted by guards, with savage satisfaction. Force of habit almost made me turn and make a comment to Jonathan, but then I remembered he wasn't there. Another thing Blaine had taken from me.

They brought him to a stop in front of me. He was dirty and unkempt. I'd never seen him that way before, and it somehow lessened my satisfaction. This wasn't right, this wasn't him.

He hadn't lost any of his self-righteous contempt, though, if the sneer on his face meant anything. I was proud that I only thought briefly of hitting him. I was the better man this time; I always had been, even at my worst. He'd made me doubt that more often that I wanted to admit.

"So," he said. The guard at his side punched him in the stomach and he doubled over, gagging.

"You say 'Your Highness,' and you wait until you're given permission to speak."

I waved away the guard's objection, even as I marveled at it. Did he defend me for Pete's sake? Did he really dislike Blaine so much in his own right? Did he really not agree with everything Blaine had made people believe about me?

"Thank you, guardsman," I said, still a bit astonished, "but I don't need the prisoner to lick my boots just yet."

Blaine's eyes widened only slightly and I allowed myself to enjoy having scared him a bit. I led the guards and their charge to the prison by the longest, most public route possible. It was a gamble, but I was shocked at how it paid off.

They booed him.

Lost in the shock of it, I didn't realize we had come to the prison until Sam approached me.

"Your Highness?" he said.

I waited.

"Shall we take him in now and get him settled before you come in?"

I gave him a long look. "You mean, beat him to a pulp before you put him in his cell?"

Sam didn't even flinch. "Yes." There was no apology or hesitation.

"Pete hasn't agreed to it. You'd probably be punished."

Sam shrugged casually. "I know I speak for all of us when I say that it would be worth it."

I examined his face. "Is that how it was with me?"

He had the grace to look embarrassed. "Well, you were our first prisoner under this emperor who had earned himself a beating. It's against the rules, sure, but most emperors look the other way. His father did. We didn't know he would do anything about it. If I'd known I'd be punished for it, I still would have done it."

"I punched the emperor," I said. "In your place, I probably would have done the same thing." I glanced at Blaine. "But I'm not sure I can—"

"Your Highness," Sam interrupted. "Forgive me, but I'm not asking you to give permission or authorize it. Just...just give us some time to lock him up without an audience."

"Willful ignorance would be the same as tacit permission."

He shrugged. "I can't tell you how to see it, Your Highness. But I think you should know, it's important to all of us."

I looked around at them again, all of them holding my gaze now.

I turned back to the captain. "No," I said, not without some regret. "The emperor decides his fate, not us. You're talking about revenge, not justice. We can't sink to his level. We're better than that."

Sam stared at me for a long time, then he gave me a deep, meaningful bow.

"You're right, Your Highness" He looked around at his men. "We are better than that." He faced me. "Thank you for reminding me."

I blinked. "When did you and I become allies, Sam?"

There was no hesitation, no thought. "When you became my prince, Your Highness."

Even doing it the proper way, it took time to process a new prisoner. But two hours later, I stood in the prison's observation room, watching Blaine in his cell. It was a bit anachronistic, as if proximity was required for observation or a secure data feed. The room was fitted with all the luxuries a high official would want, with vids on the walls so that any or all prisoners could be observed in comfort. The irony of me inside the prison, in such a room, was not lost on me.

I hadn't come to the prison to sit in the observation room. I'd come to see Blaine, confront him, something. And in the end I'd chickened out. I wouldn't have admitted as much to anyone, but it was the truth. I was afraid. Of Blaine probably, of myself definitely, of my past in a more obscure, shadowy way. He was too effective at digging out the things I tried to hide from.

He was sitting on the bed-shelf. It had been stripped of its comforts, just as it had been when I was there. He shivered his arms clutched around him for warmth. So maybe they hadn't beat him, but they weren't going to let him be comfortable, either. I discovered I didn't mind that at all. There was still an arrogance about him that made me grit my teeth.

Maybe I was imagining it. Yet I knew I hadn't projected such a confident air when it had been me. Maybe it was just that when I'd been put in there, I was no one, with nothing but the love of the emperor I'd just driven away. Blaine had never known that kind of desperation, the shadows of hopelessness and despair that had punctuated my whole life. He didn't know how to live with it.

I intended he find out.

Pete entered the room, coming to stand beside me and sliding an arm behind my back.

"You OK?"

I stared at the vid, wondering. Was I? The automatic "yes" was on my lips, but hadn't I learned to stop lying to him yet?

"I don't know."

He didn't say anything, though his grip on me tightened for a moment.

"Are you going in there?" he asked.

I thought about it. I wanted to, and I didn't. I was afraid.

But Pete made me brave.

"You're coming with me?"

The way he smiled made me sorry I'd kept things from him for so long, and happy that I wasn't hiding from him any longer.

The guards didn't take any chances. When they opened the door to Blaine's cell, three guards rushed in. One activated restraints on Blaine—the ones that simulated obvious, heavy chains—and the other two took positions inside the room. Two more flanked us. They didn't move into the room, but stayed just outside the door, their weapons pointed at Blaine.

He was watching us, as if considering how to handle this situation since Pete and I were both there. I'd had plenty of encounters with him on my own, but this was the first time I'd confronted him when I had nothing left to hide from Pete.

He nodded slightly at Pete. "Your Excellency," he said. He ignored me.

I snorted. He turned a lazy gaze on me.

"Why pretend to respect him but not me?" I said.

He shrugged. "Force of habit."

Pete slid his hand into mine. I got the feeling he didn't realize he'd done it.

"So it was really you all along," I said. "The Patriot, the messages, the riots, the miscarriages, all of it."

He didn't look at me. "Of course."

"And Laudley just took the fall for you?"

"He did what he thought best, but I am responsible for all of it. It was my doing."

I blinked. Why did that sound so familiar?

"Was it worth it?" Pete said.

Blaine slowly turned his face to him. "I don't know yet."

"If you think you're going to find some way to convince me not to execute you, then you're clearly not as clever as you imagine."

"You'll let me plan it, won't you?" I said to Pete, casually, as if Blaine wasn't there. "I can think of some things I'd love for him to experience, in public, before he hangs."

Blaine moved as if he was going to stand and one of the guards shoved him back down, planting his weapon in Blaine's gut. "Don't move," he growled.

Pete waved him off and the man backed up, glaring at Blaine.

Blaine was winded, but after a moment he recovered breath to speak.

"I'm entitled to an honorable and dignified beheading. Scum like you gets public floggings and labor camps. You can't scare me with your pathetic threats. I'm better than you, and everyone knows it." He nodded in Pete's direction. "Even him."

I looked at Pete. He was glaring at Blaine with such anger that I shivered.

"You are a profoundly stupid man," he said, quiet and intense. He tugged lightly on my hand. "I'm finished here."

# CE38

Even with Kafe and Blaine in the prison, my sudden daughter and Hera's son both down the hall, and the aftershocks from my father's death and Abenez's destruction still rippling through me, the one thing I couldn't get off my mind was Jonathan. I walked the halls for hours, unable to sleep, unable to think or do anything but pace and brood.

The whole past decade of my life no longer made sense.

Had I imagined it? I had been so sure of him, so certain that he really did care and was just too stubborn to admit it. There were so many times I could have sworn he was saying, in his Jonathan way, that he really was my friend. Had I made them all up?

I found myself in front of his cell again.

I went in, and leaned back against the door when it shut behind me. I needed the support. Jonathan was sitting on the bed, head down, looking at the floor between his feet. He looked up when I came in, but dropped his head again.

"You tried to warn me," I said.

"Many times."

"When I was sent into Resettlement, and you told me you were glad I was leaving?"

"I don't know if that was a warning or just my guilty conscience. I didn't think you were coming back."

"And when I did come back, and you said you weren't happy I was here."

He shrugged. "I don't think I put it quite like that."

"And a dozen times since the wedding. But I was too stupid to understand."

"No. I was too much of a coward to tell you outright. I couldn't stop it and I couldn't tell you and yet I was desperate for you to figure it out for yourself and just end it all for me. I rationalized it in many different ways over the years. I even told myself that it was better that it was me than someone else. If I was gone, Blaine would get someone who wouldn't care how he hurt you, who wouldn't try to mitigate the damage as I did. I told myself that I was protecting you by putting myself in a position to better anticipate his moves and shield you. Believe me, I came up with as many reasons as I could to convince myself that I wasn't just being a coward."

"I thought we were friends."

"I told you not to think so."

That seemed to leave us both speechless for a while.

"It used to make me almost sick sometimes," he said eventually, "the way you wouldn't trust him but you trusted me so completely. I could never understand it."

I shrugged, flushing. I didn't understand it either.

"So you've known all this time," I said. "About Revan, about—" I *could* say this, "about Kafe. Did you help him with that?"

He shook his head. "You have to understand, Blaine never trusted me. He used me, but I only ever knew what he absolutely needed me to know. For the most part, that wasn't anything at all. I was never a part of any of his active efforts. My main role was to pass him information."

My eyes burned. I wished he'd said he'd planted the bomb, or was the Patriot, or anything else but that. After all I'd done to keep my secrets, and all I'd lost, or damaged, or destroyed because of it, the one person I trusted most was telling them to my enemy all along.

"You knew where Revan was."

"No. But I knew enough that the ISS was able to figure it out. I 'knew' very little. There were a lot of things I guessed over time, some of which turned out to be right."

"But you knew Blaine was the Patriot?"

"I don't even know that now. I asked him once and he denied it."

"He could have been lying."

"Of course. Maybe he was. I had no way of knowing. I wasn't important in Blaine's schemes. Just convenient. He didn't confide in me or even use me very much. He knew I didn't want to be helping him at all."

"But you did anyway."

He nodded. "Yes."

I turned away, swallowing hard on tears I refused to shed. I was so tired of grief. I'd lost too much over the past months—things that were real, and things that had been all in my head. I knocked on the door, which the guards opened for me. I stepped into the hallway and looked back at Jonathan.

"Get out."

He raised his head, eyebrows high, his face no longer blank but some muddle of confusion, pain, anger, and self-loathing.

"Get out," I said.

Jonathan moved slowly out into the hallway, watching me, and then waited.

"Get out."

Jonathan looked around, puzzled. "Get out of where?"

"Get out of here. Get out of the palace, the city. Get out of the empire. Get out now before I change my mind."

He gaped. "But His Excellence—"

"Get. Out."

He took one long look at me, then glanced at the guards, who were conspicuously not hearing anything.

"Put him on a ship leaving the planet," I said to Sam.

"I'll take care of it," he said.

I nodded. "His daughter, and the mother too."

"Of course, Your Highness."

I left the prison, silently vowing to have no reason to enter that building ever again.

Everyone involved in Blaine's schemes was executed, taken publicly to the justice building in Imperial City, led through the frothing crowds before they were taken inside and down to the incinerators.

Blaine's beheading was held in private and the recording broadcast to the entire empire. It was necessary, Pete said in the official statement, for security reasons. But the traitor had paid the price for his crimes against the empire. We were all safe again.

May the emperor live forever.

But what you see on the vids and what actually happens are rarely the same thing.

I went alone to see Blaine in his cell.

I didn't argue with the guards about coming in with me. In fact, I would have asked them to. I fully intended to make Blaine want to strangle me. It was my turn, and a long time coming.

I entered his cell in the wake of the guards. He was lying on the bed. One of the guards hauled him upright with a fistful of his shirt. When he was on his feet, the guard didn't wait to see whether Blaine would bow of his own volition, he simply punched him so that he doubled over. He was pale when he straightened, glaring at me.

I leaned back against the wall, propping my shoulders against it, crossing my arms casually across my chest as I examined him. For a long time we just stood there; him doing his best to murder me with looks and intentions, me doing my best at not seeming very impressed.

In truth, he looked so strange, so different. They hadn't allowed him a change of clothes or a shower, this unkempt and bedraggled man was nothing like the immaculate, polished Blaine.

I almost felt sorry for him. If he hadn't been projecting pure hatred at me, I might have pitied him.

Finally, with a deliberately absent-minded gesture I said, "You can sit down."

His expression darkened further but he sank back down to the bed.

"It's all over," I said. "They've found all your little compatriots and they've been marched off to the incinerators, or will be soon."

"I highly doubt that," he said.

I shrugged. "You're right. I doubt they've gotten all of them already. But they will. Some of them have been surprisingly willing, even eager, to tell us everything they know. Not that it's helped them, unfortunately."

He didn't react, and I had to give him credit for that. Or maybe he really didn't care.

"Oh," I said, as if an afterthought, "I have your son, too."

He twitched, his face spasming into pain before he got his expression back under control.

"Don't worry," I said, "I'd never hurt Hera's son. He'll be well taken care of. Pete's already arranged the official guardianship. Mine, not Pete's. You understand, I'm sure, the politics of it. Can't have any confusion in the succession. After all, we found your lab tech, the one who murdered our children. So with that taken care of, Pete will have an heir soon. But I won't let Owen feel neglected. I'll be a good father to him."

Blaine had only risen halfway, fists clenched, eyes telegraphing pure murder. The guard rammed his gun into Blaine's chest and he fell with a pained yelp back onto the bunk.

"I think it's best, too, that he never find out what really happened to you. It'll be easier all around if he believes you were executed for your treason. However painful that knowledge is, at least it's wrapped up and final. I wouldn't want him to feel conflicted."

He didn't want to ask, I could see it in his face.

With another glare at me he gave in. "What really happened to me?"

"You're going to Dead End."

He shot up again, with the same result as before. He huddled on the bed, clutching his chest in pain, panting.

"You can't do that," he gasped at me.

"It's already done. And we found your friends on Dead End, too. They've been taken care of. So, I'd watch my back if I were you."

I moved closer to him. "Think of how much you'll enjoy your first time on solitary work detail. Don't fool yourself that you won't get any. We all know how good you are at making friends with the unclass." I stepped away. "You'll have a long, miserable life in a labor camp. No one will even know you're there. And I won't think of you at all."

# CE 40

Pete and I had dinner that evening in a private garden, alone but for the children.

They laughed and played all across the garden, Revan pulling peals of giggles from little Owen, toddling along behind her as fast as his chubby legs would carry him.

Pete watched them, a faint, unconscious smile on his face.

"It can't last," I said.

Pete frowned. I knew what he was thinking. We'd only touched on the subject, but it didn't need to be said that Revan's place in our lives was complicated.

"It would be hard for her here," Pete said. I nodded. I didn't want to think of how the palace children would treat her, or what the public would say if this unclass child was even near the line of succession, no matter what the official stance was.

I sighed. "Yes."

Owen, at least, we knew would be better off with us. Safer in every way. Any number of problems could come from letting any other noble family adopt or even foster him. And, in reality, he had nothing. Blaine's assets and titles had been forfeit to the crown. Pete had granted them all to me, though we both knew that they would all be returned to Owen once he was of age.

Still, it was odd, and made me feel more than a little guilty that I had decided to raise the child who was not mine and send away the one who was—no matter how good the reasons. My life had always been complicated, that wasn't ever going to change.

"We don't have to make any decisions now," Pete said.

"Except one."

Pete raised a curious eyebrow.

"Maybe we should have that talk with Dr. Heinriksen now."

Pete beamed.

And, so long as I could make him happy like that, my life would be just fine.